A Travelling Tale

Jim McEwan

A Travelling Tale

This book is a work of fiction, names, characters, places, incidents or phrases are either the product of the author's imagination or are used fictitiously and any resemblance to actual persons living or dead, events or locales is entirely coincidental.

tellwell

Tellwell Talent
www.tellwell.ca

ISBN
978-0-2288-0924-1 (Hardcover)
978-0-2288-0923-4 (Paperback)
978-0-2288-0925-8 (eBook)

Dedication

To my family and friends, thank you for travelling with me on the journey of life.

Some of you, sadly, I have lost along the way, but all will return and we will meet again, as if for the first time.

To see the world in a grain of sand
And a heaven in a wild flower
Hold infinity in the palm of your hand
And eternity in an hour

William Blake

Table of Contents

Chapter 1

The Journey Begins

I suppose the real reason Paul wanted to begin this journey had nothing to do with wanting adventure, but more to do with avoiding the tedium of regular life. Climbing another mountain was no longer his idea of fun, nor would he consider it a challenge anymore; it would simply add a new, 'been there, done that' to his list of achievements.

And Paul had done it all: ballooning, skydiving, white-water rafting, scuba diving in the coral reefs off the coast of Australia and the Philippines, watching polar bears on the ice flows of upper Manitoba on their annual journey north—all these things were fun and had left a photograph or two in a corner of his memory ... yet he could not find a subject or challenge to replace the living dream of his lost love, Jessica. His relatively short engagement and even shorter marriage to Jessica had given him more precious moments than all his adventurous experiences put together. Why did she have to die? He still loved her. He wasn't ready for her to go.

He could hardly believe that five years had passed since the day she died, five years in which he'd challenged himself with extreme pursuits, all of which he nicely documented, properly researched and presented to the world, earning himself an occasional touch of passing fame and a little money to boot. Spectacular photographs he took of rare animals captured Time magazine's prestigious first prize for amateur photography. A near death experience due to 'a faulty parachute' on a 30,000-foot skydiving trip over the plains of Montana brought him into the attention of the world. Everyone loves a survivor!

But still he pined for his lost love.

It was a short note from his perennially-travelling father—who was visiting Lhasa, a traditional part of Tibet—that suddenly brought him out of his remenising about her. In his youth, his dad had taken him to Nepal for a prolonged stay ... and upon receiving the note inviting him to meet his parents in Kathmandu, he felt an urge to return to his childhood haunts. It was bound to knock him out of this emotional slump.

Since he'd stopped all his crazy adventures, he'd enjoyed a year or so of being quite settled, and he and his sister Naomi ran a water filtration business in Minneapolis, Minnesota called Keanon Filtration Company. The business was quite successful and had a staff of 14 people; 16 counting him and Naomi—Paul Keanon, Chief Executive Officer and Naomi Keanon, Chief Financial Analyst.

He thought he was happy and settled ... but upon receiving his father's note, he realized he was restless.

Paul was not a university graduate or an engineer, a standard designation in this industry; instead, he was an enthusiastic hard worker who inherited his father's passion for trying to improve the planet by minimizing pollution caused by waste products in water around the globe. It was a safe and decent job.

The business did well because of its green focus and great employees. This allowed Paul to have a large house and nice cars. But while he was fortunate to have luxuries, he knew he didn't really need them to be happy; he preferred freedom and solitude, things most highflying businessmen forgot to enjoy. He also understood that it was important to stop, breathe and take in the scenery in order to stay grounded.

At work, his staff respected his ability to put the important things in life first, because it made him a better manager. Ultimately, his kind and caring management style produced success in his business that other companies often spent millions to achieve—not to mention staff who were loyal to a fault. Because his company was successful, he was too: he made good money, worked reasonable hours and was able to take long holidays and rely on his trusted colleagues and employees to keep things running smoothly when he was away. Bill Gates he would never be, but he didn't care. That level of wealth was only fun if you had the time to spend it. Paul chose time over money and both flowed in his direction.

As he stared at the little piece of paper—a hand-written note from his father, he realized suddenly that maybe it was time for a change. He had a choice to make: he could stay in his nice, comfortable, suburban existence and continue to grow his company, or he could step away from his comfortable life into the unknown, joining his adventurous father on the type of wild and crazy adventure his old man was known for.

Jack Keanon, Paul's father, had always been an inspiration to him. At 65 years young, he was healthy, strong of mind and body and enjoying his retirement. Jack took on life with a teenager's vigor. He seemed to have no need to relax—he always joked that relaxing was what he did while he slept—but he also knew when to enjoy peace and when to get on the fast track of change ... after all, no matter how much a person enjoys introspection, change is exciting. In turn, Paul's own approach to life very much followed in his father's footsteps. Like his dad, he was prone to laughing in the face of challenges; like his dad, he enjoyed tempting fate.

His father's message had taken three weeks to arrive. It was one page, written in his father's concise, graceful hand, in the old-school script that schools have long since neglected to teach. At first glance its content seemed rather innocent, if somewhat obscure; however, Paul knew his father thrived on adventure, so despite not really understanding the note, his interest was piqued. And suddenly he found himself thinking of going to Nepal.

The note read:

Dear Paul,

I've found something very unusual, not yet discovered by the world's prying eyes and I really want to share it with you! That's why I've written instead of sending an email. I'd really like you to come and meet me.

I'll be staying at a spa with your Mum in the centre of Kathmandu (the usual place) and then I'll move back home in the next few days.

I know this message might seem a little strange, but I can't divulge any more details until you arrive.

Don't tell anyone other than Naomi that you are leaving for Nepal. She will help make travel arrangements. You must see what I've found.

I'm looking forward to seeing you soon!

Love, Dad

Whatever is the old man up to? Paul wondered. It was a strange letter, but it was so like his dad to want him to take part in whatever he'd got himself involved in. The man loved adventure! *So much for my skiing trip in the Alps*, thought Paul. *All that training! Now all I'll be doing is trekking over a few hills*. But Paul knew his father well enough to know that what he was really saying was, 'Come! Now'! *Why is he being so insistent and what is he planning?*

As Paul pondered his dad's strange note, Naomi, who'd moved in after Jessica died, stood near him, reviewing the collection of books lining his study. Paul was an avid book collector; he researched everything that caught his interest to the point where lately, when not at work, he'd become a bit of a recluse.

"Is dad trying to get you out on an adventure?" asked Naomi.

Paul nodded, still pondering the note.

"You need a break and some exercise, you've got to get rid of that little 'podge' you've been cultivating through the summer," teased Naomi.

"I'd be giving up a skiing trip to meet them in Nepal," Paul said.

"Skiing is overrated," she said. "Too much snow."

Paul just shot her a look that said, 'what's wrong with you?' He knew she loved to ski.

"Oh, come on, Paul. Since Jessica passed you've been flying solo. I think you'd probably enjoy some time with mum and dad. Besides, maybe there's a cute lady in Nepal just dying to meet you."

This caught Paul off guard. Naomi didn't usually speak so openly to him. "Hey sis, are you trying to fix me up?" Paul smiled, happy that she cared.

"No, but time's ticking and if you don't do something about your lack of a social life, there'll be nobody to share your memories with."

"You should talk," Paul said. "Besides, I'm happy as I am and ..." Paul was going to tell her it was none of her business, but the phone rang, interrupting him.

Naomi picked it up. "Hello?" she asked. It was an operator asking if she would take a collect call from Kathmandu. She immediately accepted. "Dad, what a pleasant surprise!" she said when the call was put through. "Both of us are here, how's mum? Here, I'll put you on speakerphone."

"It's remarkable, she is walking the legs off me!" Paul heard his father say. "It must be the clean mountain air or something!"

Both Paul and Naomi were relieved to hear that news. Their mum had not been too well recently; she had angina problems and neither of her offspring had been happy about their parents' decision to trek around Tibet on a strenuous journey.

"We just wish you and Paul had come along," Jack continued. "It would be nice if we were all together. Did Paul tell you about the letter, Naomi?"

Naomi was aware of some urgency in her father's voice. He really was excited about something.

"Yes, he did," she said. "It's a bit weird and obscure, but I'm sure you have your reasons. Are you going to share?"

Paul was looking through the patio doors into the garden as he listened to Naomi talking to Jack. He secretly hoped his father was going to tell her it was no longer necessary for him to come to Nepal, so he could carry on with his skiing plans.

"Sorry about the vagueness," Jack said. "I have to be careful what I say. Paul, you'll understand when you get here!"

Paul resigned himself to the inevitable. "Dad, would it be possible for me to stick to my plans for skiing in Austria and *then* carry on to Kathmandu? Or do you expect me to drop everything and come right away?"

"Not possible to delay, dear chap," Jack said.

Paul now knew something *really* important was up; his father only called him 'dear chap' when he there was something extraordinary going on.

"You'll have plenty of time to pursue such adventures when you return from our adventure ... if you return!" his father said enigmatically, as if trying to tempt him.

"This better be good, dad," Paul retorted. "You enticed me into skydiving and look what happened!" It had taken Paul months to recover from his parachute crash. He was lucky to be alive.

"This is much more exciting and hopefully less dangerous, don't you worry. Did Naomi book the flight for you? You're hopeless at that stuff. Are you going to leave tomorrow? That's what I want you to do."

"What do you mean, 'hopefully less dangerous'?" asked Paul.

His father chuckled. "You'll find out when you get here," he said.

Paul was in a corner. Saying 'no' to his father was pointless; Jack only insisted Paul fall in line when it was important to their family or to their business. The rest of the time, he left his grown children to live their own lives. He'd never pushed for regular Sunday lunches or holiday get-togethers; there'd been no insistence on grand-kids ... Jack knew that whatever it was that his dad was up to was important and that he had to go. There was no getting out of it. *I only wish I knew why,* he thought.

"Yes," he heard Naomi say. "I booked the flight. And I talked to Jack about the list of stuff you gave me when you called me last week. I've prepared all the equipment you asked for. Hopefully the airline won't charge Paul for extra baggage!"

"You can afford it, son," Jack said to Paul. "After all, it's only money. I look forward to seeing you ... oh, and before you leave, could you please give Ian, my lawyer, a call and tell him I asked you to bring some papers for me? He'll know what I mean."

Papers? Paul was intrigued.

"Okay, will do," he said. Then they said their good-byes and hung up.

Naomi poured them each a glass of wine and she and Paul sat on the back deck. There was a chill in the early evening air, but it was mild and refreshing. A silence settled between them, the type of silence that exists only between siblings and close friends; the type of silence that allows you to be alone in your own thoughts. They both knew something was about to happen, but what it was, they did not know.

"Naomi, you remember Ian Sutherland, Dad's lawyer friend, don't you?" Paul asked as he tried to gather his thoughts.

"Yes, I always enjoyed his visits—and walking in the mountains with him, back home," she said. Both Naomi and Paul regarded the Lake District of northwest England as one of their many homes. "Why do you ask?"

"Well, you heard what Dad said to me ... he asked me to collect some papers from him during my stop-over in London. I wonder what they are? Surely not his will or something like that!"

"Hey, maybe he's going to retire in Kathmandu after all! He always said he would," Naomi half-joked in an attempt to lighten the conversation.

Paul laughed a little. Then abruptly he said, "Let's go eat at Tony's. I could do with a good steak."

Before another word was spoken they had switched out the lights, locked the doors and were soon walking the short half-mile to their favorite Italian restaurant.

Tony's Steakhouse consistently served amazing Italian food as well as an excellent steak and had been doing so for almost 30 years. When Paul and Naomi were seated, they each ordered a glass of wine then looked at the menu as the television in the kitchen, relayed the results the latest European 'football' game. Paul knew that Tony's attention would be on the Italian league as he prepared the evening meals and he, like all Tony's patrons, had learned not to complain if their food was a little overloaded with garlic when a game was on.

Tony and Paul had grown close as Paul and Jessica often stayed until after closing to share a bottle or two of Barolo with the man. Tonight was no exception; it was 3:00 a.m. when he, Naomi and Tony said good night and brother and sister walked the longer, slightly more winding road back home.

The next morning, as Paul poured a third cup of coffee down his dry throat to try to counteract the effects of the previous night's wine consumption, he wondered why he did that to himself. It was Saturday and he had a lot to get done before he left for Nepal. *You'd think I'd know better by now,* he thought. It didn't help that Naomi showed no ill effects from the night's debauchery.

As he printed his flight tickets for a late evening flight to London, he called in to work to notify his operations manager that he would be away and ask him to ensure that all relevant business situations were covered in his absence. He had his secretary cancel all meetings and he arranged for his communications manager to look after his customers in his absence. His head was pounding by the time these chores were done.

One thing he didn't do was *pack*. Naomi, efficient as ever, organized his suitcase of clothes for him and also arranged for the equipment their father had requested to be FedExed to Nepal, saving Paul the hassle of carrying extra baggage. Then she packed his briefcase with his laptop, passport and a large amount of American money, which she discreetly stashed in a small pocket in the lining. They both knew that in some areas of the world, American dollars were more than just currency; sometimes hard, cold cash meant survival.

Within a few hours, Paul was on a plane headed for London. He immediately fell asleep, awakening only for the meal that was served. For the first time in his life, he was happy to be hungover. It made the flight go faster.

Paul disembarked at Heathrow and took a taxi straight to Ian Sutherland's house, an old, turn-of-the-century, stately house just outside London, where he planned to stay the night. He climbed the steps and rang the doorbell. The door opened almost immediately and there stood Ian.

"Paul, it's so nice to see you, come in," said Ian's familiar voice as soon as Paul arrived. The men hugged it out.

"I'm starved," Paul said, and so Ian called to his housekeeper. "April? I have a guest. Can you prepare a light meal for Paul to help him adjust to the local time?"

A woman's voice called from the kitchen, "Of course. I'll leave it in the kitchen for you; I've got to change the sheets on the guest bed for Paul."

It had been a nine-hour flight and a two-hour taxi ride from Heathrow and Paul should have been tired, but seeing Ian instantly recharged his energy. Soon the two friends settled down to a long evening of exchanging news and views, along with general reminiscing.

"Your home definitely suits your 'established and successful lawyer' status, Ian," Paul observed with admiration. Ian had an instinctive talent for style, he noted appreciatively; not pretentious, just comfortable. "It's almost as if you acquired Joan's creative ability," he added, referring to Ian's dead wife. "Her happiness is captured throughout."

"Thank you, but I've not changed a thing since I lost her, it wouldn't seem right, especially when we were so happy here," Ian replied, a touch of sadness appearing around his eyes.

When Paul was done eating, Ian ushered him into his study. There, Paul took in the books that covered the walls—mostly legal tomes. However, Paul noted that Ian was not without imagination; he clearly loved to venture into the supernatural, and some old Dennis Wheatley classics, such as *The Devil Rides Out* were mixed in with the more scholarly offerings.

Paul also noticed that his host seemed to be interested in various faiths, particularly Buddhism. This didn't surprise him; Paul had known Ian a long time and knew Ian had spent time with Paul's father Jack in Nepal when he was young; it was his understanding Ian had been a Buddhist since then. He looked at Ian's unlined face and noted that he gave off a feeling of calmness. *It's the Buddhism*, Paul thought. Then he found himself wishing *he* could find such contentment.

Ian went over to the corner of the study and Paul was surprised to realize he was opening a safe. From it, he retrieved a large, brown, paper-wrapped package.

"Is that the papers dad wants?" he asked Ian. Then, with the warm rush of brandy heating his senses, he asked, "Where do you think the old boy is leading me now? I'm a courier, apparently."

Ian smiled and trusted the moment to silence.

"Do you think he's finally lost it?" Paul continued. "What can be so important that he wanted me to stop over in London? Don't get me wrong, it's really nice being here with you ... but I can't help wondering at this rather clandestine journey my father insists I make."

Ian smiled. "Your guess is as good as mine," he said as he passed a brown-paper wrapped package to Paul. "I never understood the message he left with this. I've had this package since before you moved to the States. It's at least 50 years old."

Ian reluctantly let go of it, the first time all evening Paul had seen a troubled emotion pass over his face. He wondered why. Did Ian felt as if the package belonged to him?

But Ian did nothing but smile as Paul received it ... completely letting go as he said, "When I took possession of this package all those years ago, your father swore me to total secrecy. And I remember him being *insistent* on the message that accompanies it. It's strange wording if you ask me ..."

Paul looked down at the package in his hands, which was marked 'Do not open in the event of my death'. It certainly *was* strange wording. He picked up the package and weighed it in both hands, trying to guess its contents.

"Am I supposed to open it, or give it to him unopened?" he asked Ian.

"You're to give it to him unopened," Ian replied with a hint of revulsion, as if the package was dangerous, and he wanted the whole transaction over with immediately.

"I agree, it's a strange message," Paul said, pondering the object he held in his hands, "'Do not open in the event of my death'... it's normally the reverse message received when someone dies!"

The crackle of dried timber popping in Ian's fireplace interrupted their conversation. Outside, the wind howled; it was a typical, British, winter evening and they were glad of the fire's warmth.

"There was nothing special about dad's research in Grasmere, was there?" asked Paul, assuming the contents originated from the English Lakes. "Do you think the package has anything to do with that?"

"Nothing I can specifically remember," Ian answered. "All Jack ever worked on was a basic filtration system—better than most, but basic nonetheless."

Paul thought Ian looked as if he was holding something back. However, he decided not to push it. Instead, he lightened the mood by asking, "Are you sure he isn't just playing a game to get me to sneak some pot into Nepal for him?"

Ian laughed; both knew his father liked the occasional smoke. "I'm sure he could get enough in India if he so wished," Ian said. "Besides, if it was pot in that package, I'm sure it would be in a sorry state by now!"

Ian indicated some markings on the front of the package and Paul looked to where he pointed.

"It looks like some form of stamp, but it could be anything. I assume it's a date of some kind," he told Paul.

Paul squinted, trying to make out what the faded ink said. "It looks like a year, 1941—and here … this part looks like the number 'ten'… possibly for the month of October." He squinted harder and brought the package closer to his face. "And the last digit, which looks like a 'four' could easily be the day," he added, feeling less sure than his comments belied.

"You've been in the U.S. too long; I'd say it's actually the tenth of April 1951," Ian remarked, correcting the order of day, then month, in the British manner.

"That's my father's birthday!" Paul exclaimed, realizing that since the package had remained closed, his father did not know the parcel's contents either. "Do you think this was sealed before his birth?" Paul asked Ian.

"I have no idea; I'm just the messenger," Ian replied. "When he gave me the package, your father swore me to secrecy and requested I not be too inquisitive. I did as he asked. I stored it in my safe and, to be honest, I'd forgotten all about it until Jack called me a few days ago."

Paul was intrigued. Why would his father create so much mystery around a package that had remained unopened for at the better part of a century? *He* must know its contents—or else he would not have gone to such extremes to protect it by leaving it in Ian's safe hands. And whose death did the message refer to? He assumed it was his father's own death, since it was dated with his father's birth date … but maybe that was just a coincidence? Did his dad create the package or receive it from someone else? If from another, then did the contents of the package even originate in England? Paul's thoughts exploded with so many questions.

Just then, there was a timid knock on the door. It opened and April, the housekeeper, asked if the 'gentlemen' would require anything else before she went to bed.

"No thanks, April," Ian said kindly. Then he wished her a pleasant night's sleep.

"In this wind, I hope so," April responded. "You know how much I hate the trees rattling … it always sounds like we're being invaded by an army of long-nailed animals!" Paul could tell April genuinely feared the wind.

When she left the room, Ian said, "April always hated the wind, and with the amount of it we get here, I've often wondered why she has stayed so long with us—with me—in this old house. But I couldn't do without her," he added.

The door clicked, and Paul understood that April's departure had been perfectly timed so that she could hear Ian's praise.

Ian continued, unaware. "Since Joan died, she's been a close friend. It's quite sad really, her devotion. She should find herself a husband and get a life of her own, but she hasn't. It must be my charisma," he said, attempting a joke. But he sounded sad.

Paul felt certain there was more than friendship between them, but he knew that for Ian, keeping up appearances was a virtue. He decided not to rock the boat with uncomfortable questions. *Five years … who would have thought we could carry on after our losses?* Paul thought. In a way, he and Ian shared the same thing. Both had lost their spouses in violent, unnecessary ways on the same, fateful night. Both were lonely and sad.

"They say time is a great healer," Ian said, gazing into the roaring fire that continued to crackle and pop in the cozy study.

Paul nodded. Suddenly he was very tired and as warmth and silence filled the room, he began to feel the effects of his long journey and soon he fell asleep in the comfortable lounge chair.

Ian threw a few more logs on the fire to keep the room warm on this cold English winter night and left his friend quietly sleeping. He knew Paul would make his way to bed, should he feel the need.

Chapter 2

A Meeting of Friends

Paul was wide awake and wandering around the kitchen at 6:00 a.m. This was early for him—he liked his bed and normally enjoyed a relaxing lie-in—but the time difference had really messed up his interior clock.

Looking out the window in the early dawn hours, he wondered why he didn't take advantage of this quiet time more often. It was peaceful listening to the birds and watching the world awake.

As Paul enjoyed his first sip of coffee, he studied the markings on the package which lay on the table in the lounge. He puzzled it over again and again, almost as if expecting something to jump off the paper and reveal both the contents and origin of the mysterious bundle. Unsurprisingly, this didn't happen.

The phone rang, startling him from his thoughts. Since Ian was still sleeping he let the answering machine pick up.

"Hi Ian, I met with your friend last night, she really is a charmer, kept me up 'til four this morning. Before your mind goes racing, we were just enjoying each other's company, purely platonic ... honest. She did give me the information you needed. I'll give it to you when you arrive."

Paul left the package where it was on the table and tried to distract himself by opening the Sunday Times newspaper that had been delivered earlier. He was about to help himself to another cup of coffee when April the housekeeper arrived.

"Good morning, April," Paul said cheerily, admiring her morning loveliness and how her makeup-free face glowed with natural beauty. April appeared to be no more than 30 years of age, but Paul was sure she must be closer to 35—his own age—since she had been with Ian and Joan for almost 15 years.

"Good morning, sir. You should have wakened me and I would have fixed your breakfast," April said. Her dark eyes took him in with interest as she smiled kindly.

Paul surveyed her right back. She was slim and strong, extremely fit, with smooth skin and a tanned complexion, and she carried herself with confidence. Paul suddenly felt envious of Ian for having the company of this girl on a regular basis. He hid it, though, saying, "Not at all ... I woke early due to the time difference and have been enjoying this cup of coffee. I don't have slow mornings at home. As soon as I'm up, I'm out."

He reflected that he would have to change his routine when he returned to the United States ... *if I ever do*, came an unbidden thought.

"Isn't it a lovely morning?" April asked. "There's hardly a cloud in the sky. It's a nice day for a walk in the park. Ian and I always make a point of a brisk walk every Sunday morning to clear the cobwebs. It helps dispose of the week's stress. Perhaps you'll join us?"

"Sure," agreed Paul. "I'd love to. I've plenty of time today as my flight is not until later this evening. I'd enjoy some fresh air; it'll help me recover from overdoing the brandy last night. I forgot how much Ian likes the good things in life."

April laughed. "That he does," she agreed.

"April, why don't you relax and we'll all go out for breakfast when Ian is up," Paul suggested. "It'll be on me."

At that moment, there was a knock on the door. April walked down the hallway to answer. "Mr. Sutherland is not available now," Paul overheard her say firmly and he was struck by the discomfort in her voice.

He instinctively got up and joined her at the door. "May I help?" he asked before even seeing who he was speaking to. "I'm a friend of the family."

He didn't need to see who was there to sense a threat. He could see April using force to stop someone from pushing the door open. Upon Paul's arrival, she let go a little and the door opened to reveal a slouching, nondescript man in his 60s. The man immediately stepped inside, only to be stopped by Paul's bulk in front of him. He glanced coolly at Paul, and Paul felt uncomfortable as their eyes connected. It was as if the stranger was trying to peer into his mind. He was on guard immediately.

"Good morning, sir." The stranger's voice was syrupy; he was clearly attempting to appear friendly. "I, too, am an old friend of Ian ... and I've been trying to reach him for the past few weeks. He's a difficult chap to catch."

Paul didn't warm to the man's false politeness. "Yes, I agree. Ian is a busy man. May I ask your name and give him a message?" he asked politely. "I will make sure he contacts you when he returns from his early morning jog. You know how he is about fitness!" Paul knew Ian didn't jog, but he wanted to see if the stranger did. The man didn't bite.

"Don't worry, I'll catch him soon enough," the stranger said. Then he turned and slipped out the door swiftly, calling back over his shoulder, "I'm sure we'll meet again. Good-bye."

The man entered a waiting taxi, leaving Paul to puzzle over the fact that this seemingly older, slouching man had quickly and energetically turned on his heel and practically bounded down the stairs. This struck him as strange ... and the man's prompt escape left him feeling uneasy.

Paul looked at April, whose expression had changed from calm beauty to drained fear. She said nothing, but just walked into the lounge to look through the bay window, almost as if she was making sure the stranger had left.

"Is there a problem, April?" Paul asked, concerned.

"No ... I, uh ... I'm going to go and get dressed and wake Ian for that breakfast you promised us."

April moved quickly upstairs, leaving Paul confused. He thought it strange that she hadn't commented on his lie about Ian jogging. Clearly, she was intimidated by that strange man. Did she know him? Did Ian know him? Did *he* know him? As he ran the incident over in his mind, the stranger's face seemed somehow familiar. What did the man see when they exchanged glances and why had it made Paul so uncomfortable? He couldn't put his finger on it, but it made him uneasy. Paul shivered as if someone had just walked over his grave.

When Ian was up and dressed, the three of them hailed a cab to go to the promised breakfast ... at the Ritz.

"The Ritz is a place everyone must visit at some point in their life," said Ian as they were shown to a table by the window. Paul suspected Ian had visited the Ritz far more than his fair share in *this* lifetime; the waiters all knew him, and the table seemed to be his regular spot.

It was a beautiful setting and it was clear they would be treated like royalty ... but despite the ambience and the joy of being with his close friends, Paul was still reeling from the stranger's visit, which—peculiarly—Ian had not yet mentioned. It was only after the formalities of ordering were complete and a glass of water was in front of him that Ian began to discuss the incident.

"Did our friend leave you a name this morning?" Ian asked, knowing Paul's answer before he spoke.

"No, he didn't," Paul replied. Then he looked his friend in the eye and asked, "Ian, buddy, you got money problems or something? That guy was weird ... no name, strange eyes, and a terrible liar, saying that he was an old friend and all that crap. What's going on?"

"I wish I knew, Paul," Ian said solemnly. "Would you believe I have no idea who he is? However, I suspect it's the same person who's been leaving messages on my answering machine. I don't have a clue what he wants. And this is the first time he's turned up at my house."

"What kind of messages?"

"Someone has been calling and babbling on about meeting up with me to discuss a deal that will set me up for life. Whoever it is sounds just like a jumped-up life insurance salesman, building his hopes around mutual funds. You know the kind I mean, 'latter day money men' they call them. They come on strong and think they will be the saviors of your financial world."

The cynical tone in Ian's voice is very unlike him, thought Paul, *not to mention a complete contrast to the relaxed, confident gentleman of last night.* Obviously, this stranger on his doorstep and the phone calls he'd been receiving was bothering him a lot.

Paul looked at April, whose eyes indicated her thoughts were far from the room. The dark-brown, almost-black pupils seemed to be hiding a forest of fear.

The waiter arrived with breakfast on a silver platter, a large pot of Earl Grey tea and a surplus of toast. The timing was good; it broke the hypnotic silence that had settled on the small group and as they began to eat, the conversation became more casual. There was no further mention of the stranger's visit.

The morning sun shone brightly into the breakfast room, its warmth filling the three diners with fresh energy. Inspired, Ian talked of walking in the Lakes, bubbling with stories that brought laughter back to the table. Soon they were comfortable with each other once again.

"I'm looking forward to seeing my father," Paul shared, "though I had to cancel a skiing trip for this crazy journey."

Ian paused, his teacup half-way to his mouth. He appeared to be considering something. Then he said, "Okay, Paul here's the deal. My law practice can run itself for a few months. I've decided my partners owe me a break, so I'm coming with you to Nepal. Your father and I haven't seen each other for a few years and I need a vacation. I'd like some adventure and there seems to be enough intrigue relating to your trip and the package you're taking to him for both of us."

Paul was surprised. "You, making a spontaneous decision?" he questioned. "Are you sure you're feeling all right? When did you come to this decision, my friend, and why? Do you think you're going to miss out on something, or are you just bored?"

Ian smiled, pleased at the idea of getting away from it all. He didn't find his job particularly stressful—there wasn't stress doing private property deals—but he hadn't taken any kind of vacation since his wife had died five years ago. It was time.

His life had changed dramatically when Joan died. First, he'd understood just how painful it is to lose a spouse. And second, he'd lost his social network. All his friends still had their wives and he didn't like being a third wheel. He didn't fit any more because he was no longer part of a couple, and while April was always there to help him around the house—a companion of sorts, and a close one—both Ian and April lived as if Joan were still part of their lives and were uncomfortable trying to close the gap.

Yes, Ian thought, *one day things may change* ... but he wasn't about to spoil a good relationship by starting a romance that might not work.

Little did he realize April's thoughts were similar and that the lady sitting at his left was very unhappy at the thought of being alone for a few months in his house without him in it. "If you think you're leaving me behind to dust your books, you can find yourself another skivvy!" she exclaimed heatedly. Ian smiled as April's Irish brogue sang through in the excitement of making her point.

Paul grasped the moment. "A threesome it is!" he said, then he blushed at the terminology.

"Just a minute ... this is not a holiday in the south of France we're talking about, April," Ian said, pondering the situation. "I'm sure there's more than a little danger in this expedition!"

"You don't understand, Ian," April responded. "I'm not asking your approval, I've made the decision!" April's Irish accent was even more prevalent now.

Paul loved their bantering; he enjoyed April's sassy spirit and relished the fact that such a beautiful companion and independent soul would brighten the journey. Suddenly he was now looking forward to the trip.

"One thing," Ian said, lifting his index finger, anticipating a dispute, "Paul and I are making a slight detour tonight ... and before you start complaining, Paul, the tickets are already arranged. I phoned Naomi early this morning and she took care of it. Yes, while you thought I was lazing in bed, I was busy re-scheduling your international travel. We depart—with a first-class upgrade, may I add—on Tuesday night. Naomi has emailed you father and he's already aware of our change of plans ... in fact it was his suggestion!"

"Oh my God ... you of all people should know not to let my father make suggestions," Paul said with a laugh. "First, he had me stop off in London, next will be a 'short trip' to who-knows-where! Now you'll be telling me that we are not flying directly to Kathmandu but stopping off in Kyrgyzstan or some such out-of-the-way place!"

Paul noticed the glint in Ian's eye. "My God, I'm right, we *are* going to Kyrgyzstan!"

"Not quite, my friend—but a short stopover on our journey will keep the trip interesting."

"Ian, please stop playing games, where, when and why?" asked Paul.

Ian rearranged himself in his seat, sitting back comfortably to soak in Paul's torment, then with a teasing smile said, "Not to worry, Paul. It's just an overnight stop in the Lakes District. You'll enjoy seeing your old stomping grounds, I'm sure."

April smiled to herself as Ian divulged this, then immediately began planning a few days of shopping. *She* wasn't going to stomp around in those muddy hills!

Relaxed and happy about their impending trip, none of them noticed a man at the corner table, sitting within earshot just a few feet away. He was not particularly noticeable; he was dressed to blend in with the 'old money' that regularly frequented the Ritz and was almost chameleon-like in the way he melted into the expensive, richly-decorated room.

If they *had* glanced at him, neither Paul, Ian nor April would have guessed he was listening to them; to look at his face and eyes, one would believe he was totally engrossed in his copy of the Times. But he hadn't read one single word—instead he was committing the trio's words to memory ... and while his memory was good, the recorder in his pocket was even more efficient.

However, the man's 'listening luck' was about to run out; Ian didn't respond to Paul's question of 'where, when and why'. Instead the waiter arrived, the bill was settled, and the trio got to their feet and moved toward the door.

That's when Ian's senses started to tingle and as he led his companions outside through the restaurant's revolving glass doors, he asked them to move quickly; he may not have noticed the man *listening*, but he'd noticed the man at the table get agitated as they rose to leave, his expression changing from nonchalance to panic.

"What's the rush?" asked April, surprised at Ian's sudden change of attitude.

"I noticed a fellow at a table near us as I signed the bill ... I think he might have been watching us. As soon as you two stood up, there he was packing up his paper like he realized he was just about to miss a train—which I thought peculiar since he didn't even glance at his watch."

Paul thought he was joking. He patted Ian on the back and said, "Yeah, buddy you're right. You do need a break. You're imagining things ... that's a bad sign, I'd say."

But Ian paid him no mind. "Look, there he is now," he said, indicating the man by tilting his head in his direction. "Paul, do me a favor. Walk to the corner, hail a cab and follow him. April and I will get in a different cab and go directly home. I suspect he'll follow us, but maybe not. In any case, let's meet back at home in an hour or so."

Five minutes later, Ian and April jumped in a cab and a few minutes after that, Paul was in a hackney watching the stranger as he ran to a black, sporty BMW with a private number plate, AB 12, jumped in and followed them. It just was as Ian said.

"Follow that car," he told the taxi driver, thinking he sounded like a TV show. The cabbie complied and as they drove on, Paul wondered if it was all a joke ... *Ian's playing a game again*, he thought. But as the taxi wound its way toward Ian's house, he realized it was not. Paul's was only about four or five vehicles behind Ian and the BMW stayed right in between them, never losing sight of Ian's cab.

The cars finally arrived in Ian's neighborhood and Paul suggested his cab driver carry on past Ian's house. He did and soon the cab passed the BMW, now parked a few hundred yards from Ian's driveway. When he was sure the BMW's occupant couldn't see him, Paul jumped out, paid the cabbie, then went around into the back lane. Then he climbed a few fences and scrambled through one or two back gardens—unnoticed on this sleepy Sunday morning—to arrive at Ian's back door.

•

"I assume you know he's parked just around the corner?" asked Paul as he took off his muddy shoes. "I'm phoning the police. I've got his number plate number and I want some information about this fellow."

"Hold on a minute Paul," cut in Ian. "If you start this detective work you'll only bring in investigators who will ask lots of questions and we'll never make it to the Lakes!"

"I'm not sure I want to go up to the Lakes with funny people snooping around, especially if April changes her mind about coming. We can't leave her alone to fend off intruders like our spooky friend who showed up this morning."

When Ian didn't respond to that, Paul looked over at him. He registered worry on his face—but Paul suspected it wasn't to do with April's safety.

"Ian, what's the game? Are you into something over your head?" he asked, glancing between Ian and April.

"Let's not get back into that discussion," Ian said curtly. "I'm packed, and you never really *unpacked* ... so we can get on our way immediately. April, you can throw some clothes into a case and join us, of course. We settled that at breakfast, did we not?"

April nodded and scuttled off to pack some things. She looked frightened, noted Paul.

"We'll not be taking the Manchester shuttle," continued Ian. "I've got a friend who can take us in his private jet. It's parked nearby." As Paul looked at him, incredulous, he added, "Yeah, I know ... but he's one of the privileged few, born into old money, private school, Eton—the whole nine yards. There's a landing strip nearby and some hangars. That's where he keeps his plane."

Paul just looked at him. Then he said, "And this gentleman would drop everything at a moment's notice to help us ... because?

"He owes me," said Ian. "Basically, he's a normal chap, but he's half-pissed most of the time. He likes his wine and it gets him into trouble sometimes. And I happen to be a lawyer ... tit for tat and all that, old boy."

Paul didn't believe the speed of the change of plans. *He's done this before, it seems!*

Ian made a call and within 15 minutes a man and woman, both in their mid-forties, arrived at the back door, suitcases in hand.

"Meet Ed and Germaine, our nearest neighbors. They fancy a few days in Spain—and since my car should be going to Heathrow in five minutes, it seems sensible for them to keep our nosy BMW friend out there busy."

Paul shook their hands and exchanged courteous comments, then Ian handed his car keys over to Ed and Germaine so that, right on schedule, Ian's car rolled down the driveway, turned right and disappeared down the road. Paul and Ian peered discreetly out the window to make sure the BMW followed, which it did. Then, satisfied that the bait had been taken, the trio loaded their luggage into April's Volkswagen and drove directly to a private airfield which, as Ian had said, was only 15 minutes from his home.

When they arrived, a large, burly man in his 40s welcomed Ian as a long-lost friend. Then he crushed Paul's hand with a firm handshake and within minutes they were sitting comfortably in a sleek Lear jet, wine glasses in hand, 20,000 feet in the air.

"We'll land near Windermere," said their burly pilot. "I know the local air traffic guy there and he'll not make any fuss when he hears it's me. We can park the plane in a private hanger with nobody the wiser. I'll radio ahead for a car, so don't get too soused ... I'm only the pilot, not the chauffeur. By the way what's the deal? Can you let me in on the fun?"

"Martin, I told you, it's just a little treat for my American friend, here. He's not seen the Lakes for a few years now and he hasn't got much time. We couldn't be bothered waiting on scheduled flights—you know how British Airways are with their delays—and we didn't want the hassle of driving from Manchester to Grasmere. So that's really what the 'fun' is ... and if you *like* the fun, there'll be a nice game of serious bridge tonight now that we've got a foursome," Ian explained.

"You're just a bum, Ian," huffed the pilot. "I know a sortie when I see one. But if you won't tell me, I'll settle for a nice bottle of '82 Rioja when I get there. And stuff the bridge. I know a good pub; you can join me if you want."

Paul liked this man. He did not put on airs, but instead was sincere and given to creating camaraderie. Paul decided he was a good person to have on side—especially considering his size ... Paul's hand still ached from Martin's handshake.

When they arrived at their hotel they checked into two suites, April in one and Paul and Ian in another. Martin made his own arrangements and remained on standby for their return.

The Queens Head was still a busy pub and hotel and it had hardly changed since the last time Paul had seen it. It was as warm and welcoming as ever. The centres of attraction were the two log fires at either end of the main lounge along with the 'four poster bed' bar that served all types of English ales and a few European beers as well.

They ate dinner in the upstairs section—which had been converted into a stylish restaurant, paneled in dark, rich wood—that served amazing fish and chips. All three of them ordered the house specialty and enjoyed it They all retired early to their respective rooms. Tomorrow Paul and Ian would go hiking. And then Paul hoped he would find out what Ian had *really* brought him here for.

The next morning, Ian and Paul left early, on foot, for their hike in the Lakes.

"I think a good half-hour's brisk walk through a few fields and back roads will prepare us for a good breakfast," said Ian.

"Back at the hotel?" Paul asked.

Ian laughed. "Of course," he said.

When they got back to the Queen's Head, instead of going into the restaurant, they went into the pub. The log fire was lit, and smoke lay heavily in the air. The pub was old, beginning its days in the mid-seventeenth century as a pit-stop for horse-drawn coaches. Along with the dual fireplaces, it featured the low, heavy, oak-beamed ceiling and the short doorways of the time, which created a feeling of timeless comfort, the feeling that one was safe from the cold winter weather.

Jenny, the barmaid (and chambermaid), offered them tea or coffee—or something stronger—when they came in. Both ordered coffee and then sat close to the fire. Ian lit a small cigar and settled back as if he expected a long wait.

"Who are we waiting for?" Paul asked as he glanced over yesterday's paper.

"An old friend," said Ian.

Paul settled for that and started reading. About 15 minutes later, Alan, the owner of the Queen's Head, appeared.

Paul recognized him and jumped up to greet him right away.

"Alan, old chap! How good to see you!" he said. Alan was smiling but he looked tired. "I was wondering if you'd grace us with your presence!" Paul said.

Ian gave Alan a great hug but thought, *he seems to have aged greatly since I saw him a few years ago.*

More coffee was ordered and the three sat around the warmth of the morning fire. Since they'd come inside from their walk, the weather had changed. It had been relatively mild while they were walking, but now the wind was howling outside, making the fire's flames flicker from the draft. It should have given comfort, but somehow Paul found that while he enjoyed being in a familiar place with old friends, something was not quite right about the whole situation. He couldn't put his finger on it and wondered if it was because of the chill wind howling outside or the constant sense being watched. He looked out the window at dark clouds ominously gathering and a shiver ran down his spine. Then he shook it off and started listening to what Alan and Ian were discussing.

"As you know, Paul's father's asked that we bring the package to him. After all these years, I'd almost forgotten about it," said Ian.

Alan looked into Ian's eyes. "Did you bring it?" he asked, clearly concerned.

"It's safely hidden in London, at a locker at Heathrow," Ian said.

Paul looked at Ian, surprised. "That's an unusual action," he said. "Why didn't you consult with me? After all, my father asked *me* to deliver it."

"I'm sorry, Paul, but in all the rush, and with the unexpected, last-minute changes we had to make to our travel plans after breakfast yesterday, I forgot to mention that I had a friend pick up the package and deliver it to a safety deposit box at Heathrow," he said. Ian held up a small key as if to reassure Paul everything was under control. "He had the key delivered here. We'll pick it up on our way through the airport tomorrow night."

"Thanks for letting me know," Paul said. Then he turned to Alan. "From the way you're both speaking, I gather you're joining us, Alan?" Paul asked, resigned to the obvious.

"Of course, did you think I would miss this?" replied Alan.

"Miss what?" Paul asked, now a little annoyed. "Do you guys know something I don't? Do you know why we're going to visit my father?"

"Not exactly," Ian said, "But we do have an advantage ... we know how your father came by the package and who gave it to him; the rest is speculation."

"Okay, bring me up to date," Paul demanded.

"Not so quick ... we're going to have a spot of late breakfast—I believe you call it brunch over in the big, old U.S. of A.!"

Just then, in walked Jenny with a large tray of bacon, sausages, egg, beans, tomatoes, fried bread and a side order of black pudding. *A wonderful, but not so healthy breakfast,* thought Paul. While they ate, the wind continued to blast against the pub's front windows. The bleak gray clouds reminded Paul of one of the reasons he enjoyed living in the United States—the weather was not so dreary.

It was around eleven o'clock and the pub had not yet opened for business, so when a knock came at the door, all were surprised. Jenny opened the door to reveal a short, middle-aged man in a grey overcoat. Paul noted that she seemed to know the man's face but nevertheless, she glanced at Alan to gain approval to allow the visitor in.

The stranger, dripping wet from the downpour outside, stepped into the pub. Immediately he stuck out his hand and shook Paul's own with a firm, but cold, grip. He said. "You'll be Paul." Then he shook Ian's hand and said, "Ian, it's nice to see you again. I hope you're looking after this young man. He really has grown up to look like his father, good looks and all!"

Paul was trying to place him. He was obviously an old acquaintance of his father's, but he could not recognize him. Jack and he must have known each other many years ago.

The man noticed Paul's assessing gaze. "No, you won't know me, Paul," he said, "but your two friends can vouch for my character. I was a very close friend of your father's during his early days in the Lakes. Those were good days ... we worked hard but had a lot of fun along the way."

Paul studied the man's face, still trying to place him in his father's past. Only three close companions were regularly mentioned by Jack: Ian, of course; Alan, who was his right-hand man in the business; and, Anthony the engineer who helped develop the innovative filtering systems that made their business so successful. Basically, without this team, Paul's own thriving company would not exist.

"Let me guess, you must be Anthony Cohen, my dad's engineer?"

"Spot on, young man! It's nice to meet you after all these years. How's the old man? Is he still traveling as much?"

"Well, you might say that ... he's in Kathmandu. In fact, we're all going to ..."

"I know, I'm just leading you on," said Anthony, patting Paul on the back as if Paul was a long-lost buddy.

"Don't tell me you're coming as well?" asked Paul.

"This guy's intelligent as *well* as good-looking—watch out, ladies!" Anthony teased, making everyone laugh. Then he said, "Well Jenny, it's now past eleven, time for a well-earned pint. The weather's turning nasty out there and we'll not miss a few hours in good company."

Anthony quickly glanced around the table, looking to see if his colleagues would order as well and when no one else indicated interest, he raised four fingers. Jenny smiled and was already pouring the beer before anyone could get a word of refusal in.

It had been so long since Paul had been in England that he'd forgotten how much he enjoyed that favorite British pastime, the pub. He managed to finish his gigantic brunch and now was about to have his first drink of the day ... and he had a distinct feeling it wouldn't be his last. Outside, the wind continued to buffet the doors and, now that the pub was actually open for business, the early lunchtime crowd had started to drift in, dripping wet and happy to be in the comforting atmosphere of the Queen's Head.

As beer got consumed, the buzz in the pub grew louder. The warm glow from the open fires contributed to the happy atmosphere. Passing tales were sewn into the fabric of this country pub; some good and hearty and others fearsome, matching the mood of the weather outside. Paul felt satisfied. It was a style of living that could not be re-created in America.

The four friends had the best seat in the house, close by the fire, within shouting distance from the bar and just out of the way of the regular traffic to and from the 'loo'. When the first round was done, they ordered another ... then started to get down to business.

"Your dad and I still work on the odd project together, as you know, Paul," said Anthony. "However, last year, when he told me he wanted to wrap things up, I knew he wanted to travel again. But I didn't realize *why* until Ian called me a few weeks ago to tell me you were coming over."

"Ian called you a few weeks ago? *I* didn't even know I was coming here until last week!" exclaimed Paul. "This trip has been nothing but surprises, changes of plans, unwelcome intrusions from strangers—present company accepted, of course—and car chases round London. I'm telling you, I'm beginning to feel like a mixture of 007 and Indiana Jones! Next you'll be telling me we've found the lost Ark of the Covenant or something!"

The companions looked at each other and, after a moment of unsteady silence, laughed at the thought of anything so extraordinary. But it was laughter tinged with something dangerous that Paul couldn't identify ... and for a moment Paul once again silently wished he were back in Minneapolis, planning a short trip to Phoenix to go golfing (as the thin air always allowed his average drive to look professional), or to Austria for his long-awaited skiing trip. Suddenly this adventure his father had steered him on seemed to be taking a mysterious and dangerous turn.

"It's not the Ark—at least we don't think so," said Alan. "But we have something interesting here. Something that had to be hidden during World War II as no one could imagine it being in the hand of the Germans."

"That's why the stamp looked strange," added Ian, speaking to Paul. "It was a German stamp. It was smuggled out of Germany."

"Believe me, Paul. It's worth it to stick with us," the usually quiet Alan chimed in, his face aglow from either the fire or an early beer rush. "This is a once-in-a-lifetime experience you're going to have. Your dad is on to something. The fact that so many people are now showing an interest just proves it. The visitors you had in London are nothing compared to the creepy crews who've been looking up Anthony and me, all claiming to be long lost friends of your dad!"

"I'm glad you all took the private jet," said Anthony, "but I'm sure that's only bought us a day or so ...hopefully that's enough!"

"Enough for what?" asked Paul, thoroughly confused now.

"Okay, Paul, here's the scoop, as you Americans put it ..." said Anthony, but he was cut off by Ian.

"Hold on Anthony, it's my round," Ian said, already on his feet before Paul could let out the moan of frustration building in his chest. He felt as though he was never going to find out any why he was here; certainly, he wouldn't find out before this lot got drunk, with him in tow.

Chapter 3

The Truth Unfolds

As the friends continued to visit with each other in the pub, their conversation got more animated.

"Adventures begin beyond your doorstep," intoned a semi-drunk Anthony, "Taking that first step toward adventure opens a new world!"

Paul thought he was right ... *as a group of friends we've all taken on our separate forms of challenges,* he thought.

Anthony continued, "Paul here doesn't shirk from some fun—climbing mountains, parachuting and so on," he said. "And you, Alan my friend, have done your fair share of mountaineering with Jack ... in Austria, wasn't it?"

Alan nodded.

"And let's not forget what an adventurous business person you've been," said Anthony. "Business success made you independently wealthy, though your journey was not without quicksand. You were down and fought your way back from the depression of the early eighties and when you saw the early nineties going downhill, you quite rightly pulled your resources, bought this historic pub, converted it into a small private hotel and made it a great success!"

"Guilty as charged!" Alan smiled at the praise. Drunkenly delivered or not, it was heartfelt.

Anthony wasn't done. "Ian, my 'trusted lawyer'... now those words don't usually combine well, but in your case, I have personal experience that you are the exception," he said. Ian laughed.

"Do you remember when our landlord tried to drain the business dry by increasing rent on the factory by 200 percent? Jack and I knew that if we tried to fight that on our own—just when our filtration business was getting going—we would go under. But you saved us. Your research and support saved us."

Ian remembered it well. His research into the unjust increase resulted in him uncovering a rather large commission that was finding its way from the estate agent to their landlord. Revealing this to the authorities forced the sale of the land on which Jack and Anthony's small factory was standing. It was purchased by a local hotelier—Alan.

"We cooked up a deal that got us the land at cost and Alan donated the nearby, disused mill to our business, deed and all, for ten percent of the business. Thank you, Alan," concluded Anthony.

"Ah yes, I know this part," Paul butted in. "The building needed some refurbishing, but local grants took care of the majority of the costs—that and good, old blood sweat and tears!"

There was laughter all around. "I couldn't have said it better, my boy," said Anthony. Then he added, "I understand the same fellow—Lambhowe was his name if I recall—tried his scam on someone else and this time he was caught red-handed by a local lawyer. I think they got him, along with the estate agent, on two or three counts of fraud and evading taxes. Lambhowe lost his land, at least two or three hundred acres, worth a fortune. What a shame! Most of the land went to the Her Majesty's National Trust."

The friends were relaxed and beginning to forget the reason for their meeting. Anthony would have carried on reminiscing had Paul not taken the short break in the story as an opportunity to get them back on track.

"Anthony, I remember dad talking about you. He mentioned your 'gift of the gab' which was true to every word, may I say. But please let me hear the story about why we're *really* here before we're all lying on our back, pissed out of our brains. Please talk about the parcel ... what do you know about it and where did it come from?" Paul put his hands together in a gesture of prayer, partly asking forgiveness at disturbing the flow of Anthony's tale, but also showing he was begging for an end to the mystery.

"Okay," Anthony acquiesced. "Ian? I suggest you begin."

Ian nodded solemnly. First, he told the others about the recent events in London and the guy in the BMW who had followed him, Paul and April ... but then he quickly turned to five years before ... a night both he and Paul wanted to forget ... the night both of their wives had died.

"We were together in Keswick, eating at a small Spanish restaurant in a hotel just outside the town—me and my wife, Paul's parents and Paul and his wife. We had a wonderful meal and copious amounts of exceedingly good wine."

Everyone nodded. They understood this type of dinner.

"It was a cold November night and a brief, freak snowfall had covered the land, but we didn't care. We were sitting by the fireplace in the restaurant and my father's house was just a short walk away. We were all guests at his house that night. It was a quiet evening for a Saturday, but I guess it was because of the time of year and the miserable weather. The brandy was beginning to flow along with the conversation. There was even the possibility of sing-song, though none of us were likely capable of hitting a note in tune!"

"Paul's father—Jack—was certainly on form; jokes were flying, laughter abounded, we didn't talk business at all! It was as perfect an evening in today's stressful world as one could hope for ...until we heard gunshots.

There was a quick intake of breath around the table.

"This was not a simple revolver discharge; the shots came from an automatic weapon. We heard repeated loud cracks and explosions. Everyone was terrified and no one in the restaurant moved. We were frozen to the spot, silent in fear. It felt as if time had stopped. I'm sure everyone in the room remembers that ghastly moment well."

Paul certainly did. He nodded in solemn reply.

"A minute or so passed without any sound. Fear was thick in the air. Everyone held their breath. Suddenly the door burst open, scattering splinters of wood around the room. Four men stormed in, machine guns held high in front of them. They began issuing orders to all of us, speaking with accents that sounded east European. One stood by the doorway, another stood beside our group and another two moved around the tables looking for someone. They stopped by an older gentleman who was sitting alone. He didn't even look up; instead he calmly and slowly wiped his mouth with a napkin, backed his chair away from the table and stood. One of the gunmen ushered him out the door into the hallway. We thought for sure he was going to be executed."

Paul remembered the incident well. He gulped slightly as the memory of that day flooded his mind.

Ian continued, "At that point a young waiter, who had been hiding behind the bar, suddenly stood up and fired at the leader, hitting him right between the eyes and killing him instantly. It caused mayhem; glass and bullets sprayed all around the room and everyone tried to crouch for cover. Screams pierced the air ..." Ian shuddered. The pain of his memories made him sweat and clouded his eyes.

"Paul, you know the rest," he said sadly. "Our wives were taken to hospital with multiple bullet wounds and both died that evening. Paul's mother, bless her, somehow was uninjured. It was a miracle, really, because the three women happened to be closest to the young man who killed the gunman and when the other three assailants turned to shoot at him ..." The words could not come from Ian's mouth, but everyone visualized the bullets pounding into the helpless women.

Ian composed himself and carried on. "The man they were after, the man they took away, was tall, slim and well-dressed with a sad face and dark, sunken eyes ... and as they led him out of the restaurant, your father recognized him. When he was escorted out, he stood straight, fastened his jacket, looked the nearest gunman straight in the eye, and discreetly dropped the package on the floor. The gunman never noticed, but our friend caught your father's gaze as he was marched out and he indicated toward the floor under the table he'd been seated at. As soon as he was gone, Jack managed to retrieve it and he hid it under his hiking jacket."

"Who was the fellow who dropped the package and what happened to him?" asked Alan.

"Dan Flynn, who Jack recognized from his university days, was never heard of again," said Ian. Ian looked at Paul wondering if he should continue and Paul gave a subtle nod of his head.

"Jack just sort of forgot about the package over the next few days. We were all in mourning for our loved ones. It was a terrible, terrible time," Ian said with a catch in his voice. "Then after the funerals we simply lost our direction. The fact that such a major explosion of violence had entered our lives, especially at a time when everything was going so well, was unbearably shocking."

"Ian, you've kept these details about the package from me all these years ... why?" Paul asked.

"Your father will explain the reason when we get to Kathmandu, Paul," Ian reassured him.

Paul wasn't happy with that answer; all the fast travel plans and mysterious individuals appearing out of nowhere had disturbed his sense of ordered life; he used to feel in control and now he felt like everything was slipping from his grasp. And he still had no idea what was in the package.

Anthony could almost sense what Paul was thinking. He said, "Patience is a virtue that has never been part of your makeup, Paul." Then he smiled an elfish, Irish smile.

Paul wouldn't be dissuaded from pushing. "I need you to add a few details, please. Let's start with this Dan Flynn ... who is he? Why did he happen to be in that restaurant at the same time as us?" Paul asked Ian.

"Dan studied astronomy with your father at university," Ian said. "They kept in close contact for a few years after graduation, but Jack's business didn't let them pursue their star-watching hobby together as often as they would have liked. Eventually, Dan took a job working for NASA, based in Peru. He helped plan and design the Hubble telescope and rose to the top of his profession. Occasionally Jack heard from him when Dan visited the Jodrell Bank Observatory at the University of Manchester; other than that, their communication was limited to a few phone calls and letters each year."

"And why was he in the restaurant that night?"

"That I can't answer, Paul," said Ian. "You will have to ask your father. It's seems a coincidence, but I don't know for sure."

"It is not clear is how the package got into *Dan's* hands in the first place," said Paul.

"He may have had the thing for years. Possibly the note on the package is his and not your father's. Unfortunately, I don't know much else about Dan; your father is your best source of information there."

Paul pondered this. "'Do not open in the event of my death'," he muttered to himself. What was the significance of the mystical package? Whatever was in there, it seemed a good bet that Dan was aware of the contents—and the people who had shot up the restaurant probably were as well.

Was Dan dead? No one had heard from him after that fateful night. And how were they to know what to do next if the note on the package was left by Dan? Could they find out if he was still alive, and if so, where he was?

The beer was affecting Paul's power of concentration and he found he could not string together logical questions anymore. He stopped pondering the mystery of the package and let his mind drift to happier times when he and his wife sat by the fire in this very hotel on a cold winter night and drank wine. He remembered trying to smoke a cigar he'd purchased from the bar, but it had dried out so much it split in half before he could light it. The bar provided some cello-tape to hold it together. Jessica had laughed about his broken cigar and then worried about him smoking the cello tape. He never made it that far; he'd had to put it out for choking on the terrible thing.

"That will teach you," Jessica said. "Putting that stinky thing in your mouth!" They had both laughed, drank more wine, and then later they fell into each other's arms, giggling all the while. How he missed her!

While Paul sank into his own thoughts, activity at the opposite end of the room started attracting attention. Three men, less discreet after a few drinks, were getting rowdy and arguing. Paul's little group did not pay much attention until a particularly loud shout brought Paul out of his reverie and he suddenly recognized one of the individuals as the slouching stranger he'd met at Ian's door just yesterday. He quickly touched Ian on the shoulder and quietly asked Ian if he recognized the man.

"I recognize his face, but I can't place where I've met him," Ian whispered back, and Paul promptly informed him who it was he was looking at.

Ian was shocked. How could that be? Could this man have tracked them here or was it just a coincidence? Whatever the case, it was clear they had to discreetly leave ... but how? After quietly presenting the problem to the group, Alan acted and had a few of his strongman bartenders oust the trio. But the group realized that this only delayed the inevitable; how was the team going to get past their stalkers once outside?

Anthony peeked out the window and noted the strangers had packed into a Range Rover and were driving off into the rain and wind of this typical, gloomy northern England winter afternoon, wheels spinning on the wet concrete as they roared away. Two cars swerved violently to avoid a collision with the vehicle as it sped off in the direction of Grasmere.

"Well, they're gone, mates," Anthony said. All of them wondered just how much of their conversation had been overheard.

Ian was immediately on his cell to Martin. "Keep an eye out for them," he told Martin. "They must know how we got here. They must be staying somewhere near you in Grasmere."

"Sure, Ian ... I'll keep a look-out for them. But you've no idea where they're staying, or even *if* they're staying here, is that right?"

"Well, do your best," said Ian. "We've decided to hang on here for a short while, but this changes things. Call me back in half an hour. We're going to decide on the next step."

"It's a bit of luck that Martin stayed in Grasmere, isn't it?" Paul reflected, more to himself than the others. Then, as Ian hung up the phone, Paul noticed a bag just under one of the chairs where the men had been sitting.

"Clear the bar," he immediately shouted, "Get out! Now! Bomb!"

His friends wasted no time moving toward the door, pushing any patrons within reach ahead of them. Once outside they herded as many people as quickly as they could as far away from the building as possible. Unfortunately, not everyone got out; however, as it was a Monday, there were not too many customers at the Queens Head. Nevertheless, when the blast shook the small building, it was clear there would be fatalities.

The blast destroyed the whole back section of the room, killing five people in all. The group of Paul, Ian, Alan and Anthony were, thankfully, fine. Later, it was discovered that those at the back of the room nearest the explosion didn't make it; while the blast was relatively small by bomb standards, it was powerful.

As they stood in shock in the parking lot, the group quickly decided that Paul, Ian and Anthony shouldn't hang around waiting for the authorities to arrive. Alan hurried them into their cars and stayed behind to deal with the inevitable investigation.

Meanwhile Martin was parked on the main street in Grasmere, waiting for a Range Rover to drive by. He was surprised and pleased when it pulled up in front of the hotel across the street and parked.

A bit of luck, he thought, then realized luck had nothing to do with it. *They must have known where Paul's group was staying all along,* he realized. *How many moves ahead are these strangers? Do they know I'm due to fly them back to London tomorrow morning?*

Within moments, Anthony drove up with Paul and Ian. Martin quickly told them, "They're in the hotel next door. You have to assume they know your next moves."

"Maybe we should fly back to London tonight," suggested Paul.

"I agree. We've got each other's backs, we're partially ready to get to Nepal—though Alan now has the bother of dealing with his destroyed pub—but basically we're ready to get out of here," said Ian. Then he produced a note from his pocket that appeared to have directions on it. "But first we must stop pick up another package," he told Paul solemnly. "We can collect it in Keswick, my old stomping ground."

By this point, Paul was too shocked by the explosion to question things. Immediately, Anthony and Ian left for Keswick while Paul and Martin stayed behind to contact Alan and urge him to leave as soon as possible.

"I'm almost done here," Alan said when they called him. "I'm arranging the insurance and letting my head bartender handle the rest. He's a good chap. I trust him to take over while I'm away."

April, who was on her way back from shopping in Windermere, heard the news about the bombing over the radio and was immediately terrified for Ian and Paul. *A bomb at the Queen's Head?* She tried to phone the pub but got no response; cell phones never worked properly in the mountains.

Panic set in; she was at least 30 minutes from the hotel. She pressed hard on the gas pedal, which she knew was not a good idea on the wet, winding roads of this region—but care and reasoning had been replaced by worry. As she accelerated, she glanced in her mirror and noticed a small sports car very close behind her, possibly some crank wanting to race ... but somehow, she felt otherwise.

What should I do? There was no chance of outrunning the vehicle and on these roads, not a lot of opportunity to let it to pass. She determinedly set her jaw and decided to play the odds: she concentrated on the road and accelerated. She drove fast but remained in control; she knew these roads and felt safe. She'd show that sports car how to drive!

As she whipped along, she thought about the events that had brought her to this moment. She was loyal to Ian and had been very supportive of him since that terrible day when his wife had died. Things had been fine for a while as he recovered from his grief, but in the last six months, Ian's life had gone from quiet, lawyerly order revolving around the slow pace of property law to life in the fast lane. He'd worked on a deal to sell some London wasteland to eastern Europeans and since then he'd had strangers calling and turning up at his doorstep—such as the guy who'd arrived when Paul was visiting—all acting vaguely threatening.

April had been grateful when Paul had taken charge at the door, but not so grateful that she felt comfortable telling him of the problems Ian was having. But she'd wanted to. As much as she cared for Ian, she found Paul interesting and attractive and there was something about him that felt *capable*. She trusted him. She wanted his opinion. But if she discussed Ian's business dealings with Paul—who she barely knew—it seemed disloyal. But she was worried about Ian, and Paul was clearly someone he trusted, so she decided to talk with Paul at the next chance ... if there was one, given the bombing today.

She gripped the steering wheel in fear, her hands tightening as she swerved quickly to avoid an oncoming vehicle. She gasped as she realized that her daydreaming at high speed almost caused an accident. The oncoming driver saluted her with an ungentlemanly gesture.

Snapping back to full consciousness, she paled as she realized that the sports car had pulled out to pass. It quickly overtook her and braked suddenly, forcing her to come to a squealing stop. Immediately two men jumped out, guns waving, and forced her from her car.

April screamed but was silenced in short order by the butt of a gun, which knocked her unconscious. Then the men bundled her into the trunk of their sports car and pushed April's car off the road down the steep, grassy verge. The car gathered speed as it rolled down the slope then dropped over a riverbank and plunged into the icy, cold water below. It momentarily popped to the surface, floated for a short while and then sank out of sight.

While Paul and Martin kept an eye on the Range Rover and waited for their friends to return, Ian and Anthony traveled at high speed through weather that did not let up; the rain was relentless against their windshield and the wind created turbulence that made it difficult to see the road ahead.

Thankfully, they reached their destination—their meeting point—safely. In short order they were inside the small lobby of the Spanish restaurant where Joan and Jessica had met their untimely deaths. Ian had not been back to the place since that night and felt very uncomfortable, but their host met them with a warm embrace and led them into a private room behind the reception area.

"Ian, I knew you'd have to come back sometime and I'm glad it's not too late," said James, the restaurant owner. Then he said, "Anthony, my dear friend ... you look tired, sit down and relax."

"We've had an interesting morning," Anthony said. "You're probably aware of the Queen's Head bombing ... they're getting too close. Has April arrived yet?"

"Not yet, but she may be delayed by the weather. I'm sure she'll be here soon. Can I fix you a drink while we wait?" asked James.

"Coffee will be fine," Ian said worriedly, clearly concerned about April. "She should have been here over an hour ago."

"I'm sure April will be along soon," said Anthony. "In the meantime, let's get down to business. We've not much time. "There was a key Jack left with you for safekeeping, James," Anthony continued. "I know it's been a long time, but would you please get it for us? We're on our way to visit Jack and he asked us to obtain the contents of our lock box."

"Of course," said James.

Ian was still thinking about April when suddenly the front door blew open, startling them all. It was only the wind, but it brought to the fore how on edge they all were. Time was working against them and their pursuers seemed one step ahead of them. Ian hoped their private jet remained a secret. But unless they rendezvoused soon, their stalkers would find out about it.

The phone rang and James turned to answer it. Wide-eyed, he started waving at Ian to pick up an extension.

Ian did, and heard Paul say on the other end, "... and there is no trace of her car." Ian couldn't believe what he was hearing; April had been dumped unconscious just outside the hotel where Paul waited with Martin and had just been revived by the local doctor.

"Ian, if they can play games with us and are so cocksure of themselves that they don't consider hostage-taking and bombing a pub as important, then whoever it is who wants this package is someone to fear! What are we getting into?" he demanded.

When Ian didn't answer, he said, "April can't remember anything about who took her; she only remembers a sports car chasing her, overtaking her and blocking the road ... and then just pain as she passed out. Thank God she's okay!"

Paul was truly worried. Though he didn't know her well, he had a strange attraction to the girl. That she should come so close to death over a mysterious package seemed beyond pointless.

"Where are you now?" asked Ian, relieved that April was alive, if shaken.

"We convinced the doctor to release April into our care and we're at the airfield. Martin is standing by, ready to fly. Will you be here soon?"

"Yes, soonest," promised Ian.

James produced the lock box. A seal on the box proved it had not been opened since Jack had closed it many years ago. Jack's instruction to Ian was to read it then give it to Paul. He took the key James gave him and opened the box. Inside was a letter addressed to Jack Keanon. It was postmarked a few months after the fateful night Joan and Jessica died. It read:

I'm sorry your lady friends were caught in the crossfire and I'm indebted to you for the rest of my life for taking my package without question.

Trust me when I say the world will become a much worse place if the gunmen, who I won't name for your own safety, get a hold of my—sorry your 'present'.

I entrust the security of this important package and everything associated with it to you, my good and trusted friend. Thank you for taking ownership.

I am leaving England, under the direction of my captors. Please keep the package unopened, it is safer for all concerned that it is never opened.

I will not be able to contact you again after you receive this letter.

Ian stared at the paper blankly, trying to process the recent events all caused by this package. What was this ... this *burden*, that they were to deliver? What havoc it had caused! April was alive ... but it was overwhelming to think her being kidnapped and of his friend's pub being bombed.

He also wondered why Jack had seen fit to keep Paul so innocent and he felt guilty that April was trapped in this vicious chain of events as well. They had no idea where the enemy would appear next—or who the enemy even was and now time was against them as well! All he could do was to try and stay calm ... and maybe it was time to tell Paul a little more about what was going on. However, he was starting to doubt the depth of his own knowledge and beginning to question whether there were details Jack had kept from *him*.

At the airfield, as Paul and Martin waited for Ian and Anthony to arrive, Paul tried to help April recover from her traumatic experience. She was quite shaken up. He wrapped her in a warm blanket around her and gave her a hug.

"Are you sure you're okay?" he asked.

She nodded.

He was worried about her, but even more worried that he was not equipped for whatever this crazy adventure his father had gotten him into. He wondered if his father had anticipated the problems and dangers facing him and the others in the group. He supposed that if his father was aware of the extent of the danger to which he was exposing his own son, this must be a very important mission.

Just then, Ian and Anthony arrived at the airfield. "I'm glad you got here safe," Paul said as Ian gave April a warm embrace. Paul felt a surprising burst of jealousy at that. Was he falling in love with April? He didn't know what to think.

"Listen," said Ian hurriedly. "I can see you are a logical thinker. It's probably not lost on you that not all of our group can go on this trip ..."

"I have thought about that," said Paul.

"Have you also thought about who might be best to remain here? We will need decoys when we leave here," Ian said.

"Obviously it's necessary for me to go," Paul said. "My father specifically asked for me. But I think you also need to go. It's clear you know more about this than you divulge."

He looked at April, who'd shaken off her blanket and stood, proud, strong and fierce in the rain. She was solid despite today's ordeal. He wondered if this determined Irish lady should come and decided her strength would be an asset. But he wondered also if he would feel the need to watch over her while they traveled. Would that be a problem? Would she welcome it? Would it make him weak? *What are April's feeling for me?* he wondered. It didn't matter. Ian needed her ... and he wanted her.

"April should also come," he said firmly, "And Anthony is close to my father and a trusted friend, so he should come too. That makes four."

But what about James? While Paul could apply reason to selecting Ian, Anthony and April, he knew nothing about James or his character. Nevertheless, something told him that James was also a close friend of his dad's. He could only rely on instinct when it came to James and instinct dictated that he should come as well.

At that moment, Paul's phone rang. Coincidentally, it was James, asking what the plan was.

"You're coming with us. Get to the airport as soon as possible, please," Paul said.

Ian smiled as Paul took decisive action. He had selected the exact team that Ian wanted. It was reassuring to know they were on the same page.

It was agreed that Martin and Alan would stay in the UK. Alan would round up enough people to give the impression of a larger group and then take the private jet to Manchester to act as a decoy. Hopefully this would buy Paul and his team some time to get out of the country and safely on their way to Nepal.

This new plan required them to wait for Martin and Anthony to arrive with decoy people to put on the plane to Manchester, which they did. Then James discreetly bundled the team into his mini-van and they started off on the five-hour drive to London.

As they drove, Paul sat silent, somehow, he could sense dark forces gathering. He could not know that the unknowable enemy enjoyed this game and was confident that the moment was near when it could obtain the prize Paul and his group were guarding. He didn't understand that it relished the feeling of power it got by releasing April instead of killing her ... it successfully warned Paul and the others that it was the one who was in control.

The enemy had watchers everywhere and it knew that soon the future would be its own. The decoys arranged by Ian and Paul were humorous—and pointless—to the enemy. It knew the small, insignificant team of Paul and Ian and their cronies was no match for its own worldwide enterprise, an enterprise that had been working quietly toward world domination for many centuries. It had unimaginable power at every level of business and government; in fact, government reported to it without even knowing of its involvement! The Masons and other secret societies were mere puppets to its whim; such brotherhoods were only useful for collecting power-hungry people together and their collective greed fed the enemy and made it stronger.

Yet no one truly knew who the enemy really was ... it had many names, names that drifted through myths and legends of the past. History books were unclear in accounts of its true past; when it came to things and people it had manipulated, it left no trace. Many famous and righteous people were destroyed by evil lies and stories it, and the groups who worshipped it, planted in the corridors of power—believers could not allow their plans to be changed by those governed by fine moral standards. They were masters at manipulating the press; newspapers and social media were used to great effect to create illusion. Even religion had no power to resist them; using dogma to set one nation against another, one denomination against another, was a favourite tool it used to keep humans infighting.

Its orchestrators of chaos were scattered about the world and the flock's membership counted in the millions. Yet only a handful of the faithful knew who pulled the strings. This evil had been dormant for a while ... but now it was gaining strength.

The pendulum was swinging in its direction once again.

Chapter 4

The Court of the Crimson King

All was quiet on the journey south, though the rain drizzling on the motorway and glistening off the windscreen made the driver's job tiring. However, James was used to these conditions; he had driven the equivalent miles of the earth's circumference at least two dozen times—a total of almost 600,000 miles—during many trips he'd taken, both for work and pleasure. He quite enjoyed driving; it allowed him to think without continuous distraction.

The radio was low, his friends in the back were dozing and so his mind wandered over the events that had led to this journey. Two years ago, he had been married to Janis, his devoted partner for 35 years. His family included three children, now all happily married with families of their own. He and Janis were set to enjoy their golden years ... and then Janis died and his life changed forever. He missed her very much, although running his small hotel provided distraction and at type of solace since then. Cancer is a terrible thing.

Born in Scotland of Irish parents, James had the strength and passion of a true Celt. He was a strong, independent type of guy, but fiercely loyal to family. When he was a child, his parents had run a small hotel in the Windermere area of the English lakes and that time of his life provided fond memories for him. The whole family used to vacation together in the off season at that hotel, enjoying the freedom and space of a ten-bedroom house. In this way, James came by his hotelier status honestly; he'd followed in his parents' footsteps and, using money he inherited from them, bought his small, Spanish-style hotel ... which, unfortunately, was the site of the disastrous event that left Paul's and Ian's wives dead. After that night, he'd wanted to sell, but both Paul and Ian convinced him not to. They'd advised him well; since then he'd worked to create happier events and memories there.

He was proud of his hotel; the garden surrounding it was regarded locally as the best in the Lake District. The long, winding driveway enclosed by leafy trees gave the effect of a royal entrance and colors abounded in the south-facing property during all seasons. The driveway opened out to a circular courtyard that featured a splendid fountain as the main centerpiece and, while the building was not visible from the road, its glorious grandeur emerged as one approached the main entrance. James had spent many an evening walking alone or with guests in the carefully-tended gardens. Although he was not a gardener himself, he knew all the plants, flowers and shrubbery that surrounded the walkways. He'd had no option but to learn about plants, as visitors—the majority of whom were amateur 'expert gardeners'—routinely asked him questions.

James loved the quiet, summer evenings at his hotel. On those nights, when all guests were either walking or visiting local restaurants or pubs, he would sit on his favourite secluded bench, just out of sight of the front entrance, look over the valley toward the mountains, drink a few glasses of his favorite wine, smoke an occasional cigar and drift away. Yes, those nights were the strongest medicine to help him get over Janis; no money could buy the solace he felt sitting in the fresh, chill air, admiring the view.

When pondering his wife's death, in his more philosophical moments, he wondered if life gave us the cards we received or if we chose our own suit. He found it hard to believe that life was random. But he also didn't know what choices to make next. Now that he was alone, he sometimes thought about selling the hotel, buying a boat and sailing the world. Maybe he would meet someone else. Being on his own was something he only enjoyed part of the time, but he didn't want to be alone forever. He enjoyed female company; he'd missed it these past two years.

He looked in the rearview mirror at his sleeping companions in the back of the van and wondered at the events that had brought him to this moment, on this adventure of uncertain destiny. He'd traveled the world and felt Mediterranean sand under his feet, the cold mountain waters of Bavarian lakes, the sticky temperatures of Asia and the cool, clean air of the Himalayas and never felt apprehensive during any of his adventures ... until now. He knew there was something special but extremely dangerous ahead—but how or why this trip caused such uncertainty he could not yet understand.

Time moved quickly, and traffic was mercifully light. They arrived at Heathrow with a few hours to spare.

As James parked the vehicle, his companions woke and quickly sprang into action. Ian had already arranged for one of his assistants who lived locally to collect the package and meet them at the gate. However, he did not want to take chances by carrying the package any further, as he was uncertain if their decoy had worked. They still might be being followed. Unbeknownst to the rest of the group, this package was a replica ... the original was by now in Paul's father's hands in

Kathmandu. Ian knew the real danger was to have the package in their hands if they were caught by their shadowy followers.

Ian's man met them at the gate as planned and handed over a parcel wrapped to look exactly like the original. Along with the parcel, Ian received a note bearing information from Jack. Jack relayed the information to Ian's man in the guise of a request for a woman's phone number, but, using a code known only to the two of them, Ian immediately understood that Jack was telling him there would be somebody trustworthy on the flight with them. He also managed to transmit that this person would not reveal his or her identity unless trouble flared up during the flight. Ian read the note, committed it to memory, and then disposed of it.

Upon boarding the plane, the refreshed group enjoyed first class service. Only two other passengers were with them in this part of the aircraft and there was nothing suspicious about them. As the journey got underway, Ian and April began a conversation with them. Meanwhile Anthony, Paul and James played cribbage while quietly discussing their theories about the contents of the package, enjoying their first real opportunity to share their thoughts without distraction. Questions they had included: What made it so important that it had attracted such serious attention? Who were the aggressors who had been pursuing them? Why did ownership of this package seem to haunt the Keanon family? How did the enemy manage to keep one step ahead of them, especially when they had made changes at such short notice? Why had it taken five years for their mysterious enemies to come after this package?

Meanwhile, the elderly couple sitting by April and Ian began confided that they were on a fiftieth anniversary trip to Nepal, a place they'd dreamed of visiting all their lives. Ian excused himself at this point and asked Paul if he could spare a few moments to chat. Paul nodded assent and they moved over to a vacant seat to converse in low whispers.

"There are some things you need to know, Paul," began Ian.

"I'll say," said Paul.

"I'm sorry to have been so secretive," Ian said, "it's just that your father and I agreed that it was important that you not be too concerned about what you're getting into. We need you, and we didn't want you to turn us down. But now that we're on the final stage of the journey, it's only fair to tell you all I know."

Paul sighed with frustration. Part of him resented the secrecy, but he trusted Ian and was certain there was good reason for it.

"Remember the old man in Keswick, the one who dropped the parcel?" asked Ian.

"Yes, you said his name was Dan Flynn ... an astronomer or something."

"That's right," Ian said. "Dan was a friend of your father's ... and it's no coincidence he was in the restaurant the night of the shooting. He was there to deliver the package to Jack. As you know, circumstances simply changed the method of delivery."

Paul waited for him to go on. Ian sipped a glass of water. "The strange thing was that your father had not heard from Dan for 30 years. 'Why so long?' is the question on your lips, I would imagine," Ian said, watching Paul's face for confirmation.

"Well you said he moved to Peru to be an astronomer and that he was working for NASA," said Paul. "I imagine working for an outfit as secretive as NASA would be enough to make friendships sparse."

"That's not quite true," said Ian. "The truth is Dan became a man of solitude, a monk ... at least that's the nearest description I can provide. He studied and practices some of the great spiritual traditions, including the ways of lamas in the Tibetan tradition; the ways of First Nations shamans, which we do not hear too much about nowadays; the teachings of both Buddha and Christ ... His spiritual awakening was the reason he departed from the daily routine of what he called 'making money to die'."

"Well that is truly noble," said Paul. "But what does it have to do with the package?"

"I'm not quite sure," said Ian, "though I have an idea. The work he does is very controversial. He has focused a great deal of energy on trying to reconcile Muslim and Christian differences. His efforts are mainly behind the scenes—partly because he would never be seen in the limelight but also due to the dangers of the forces working against him."

Paul nodded his understanding. This was a concept he could wrap his head around.

"It's not self-preservation he's worried about, let me make that clear," Ian added. "It's more that he would not be able to properly continue his work without interference if people knew what he did. He can't even trust the leaders of some of the spiritual traditions to aid him, as everyone has their own agenda. So, he must work alone and with only a few trusted souls at his side. After all, evil prevails when good men do nothing!"

Paul wondered if Ian was caught up in a cult and should go on an extended holiday ... preferably in a tight jacket! This was *way* out of his comfort zone.

Ian could sense his discomfort. "I realize this may be a little off-base for your liking, Paul, but a new kind of reality is going to be your friend in the future. Not the reality of your past and present that you know and understand, but something much deeper and more relevant. There is much for you to learn about where we are going, but if we'd tried to tell you about it earlier, your father and I were pretty sure you would have decided he'd lost his marbles."

Paul wasn't so sure they hadn't lost their marbles, but he decided to suspend his disbelief for the moment.

"So, who *is* Dan Flynn, if not an old friend of my father's, from university?" he asked. "And where did he get that package and why did he pass it to my father? More importantly, why is it so valuable to some that they would kill for it?" Paul was confounded.

"Let me try to explain," said Ian, aware of his distress. "First, you have to consider where we are going as a race … and when I say 'we' I mean the *human race*. Look at us … After millennia we are still fighting, mostly because of politics and religion, institutions that have been created *by* man to *control* man. Even the haven of family is being destroyed. Fear has become the norm."

Paul nodded. He had thought many of the same thoughts over the years.

Ian continued, "We are taught that change is good and that we should accept and make it work for us—a positive philosophy indeed—but change also creates openings for controversial ideas that good sense and intelligence would otherwise discard. For some, it is easy to join the 'sheep' of change. It is much harder to stand solid with your beliefs and find faith in the mist of confusion."

"What do you mean by that, Ian?" asked Paul. "I'm not following."

"I guess what I'm trying to tell you is that there are many people out there who have risen above the need to belong. They think independently—and the resulting independence is creating a new generation of 'free radicals', so to speak."

Paul pondered this. "What an interesting idea … 'free radicals'." He chuckled.

"Yes, such people will not be constrained by the limitations of the previous generation. A brave new world indeed!"

Paul still found himself a bit lost. His only interest was to get this package delivered safely to his father in Nepal and after that he planned to have a bit of a vacation in Tibet. Then he hoped to get back to normal ... back to his house, his sister and running his small business. What was Ian babbling about?

"Ian, I'm not sure what that has to do with delivering this package, but if you're trying to tell me that there are people with super powers out there, I think it's probably simpler than that," replied Paul with confidence, feeling better now that Ian had stopped rambling. "I suspect Dad had a friend who had a secret which various parties are now trying to obtain. It's probably details on how to build a better rocket ship or something. Dad has always had very scientific friends. We have something they want ... and maybe we should just give it to them. I'm not sure I want to get killed over this. But I won't do a damn thing until my dad tells me a little more about that secret package."

Ian looked pained at Paul's glib response.

Paul laughed. "Are you sure you're all right, Ian? Has all this espionage stuff had a little bit of an effect on the old brain? Come on let's have a drink and enjoy the journey!"

"What else would I expect from a foreigner?" asked Ian with a cynical smile. Paul hated it when Ian referred him as a foreigner; his upbringing was British, even if he *had* been born in America and he considered himself to be anything but foreign.

"I'll still have a pint with you though," Ian jostled Paul boisterously, making Paul smile. He immediately forgave him.

As they ordered beer from the stewardess, a disturbance broke out in the back of the plane. At first, they were unaware of it, but a frightened stewardess came into the first-class section where they were and told them, "A passenger has decided he wants to visit the pilot and a gun is his way of negotiating the deal. Please do as he says." Then she turned around and they all heard an excited man yelling for her to get her ass out there.

Ian undertood what was needed, took control and briefed the team with a plan.

"Follow my instructions, no questions," he commanded. Everyone nodded and prepared themselves for dealing with the threat that would soon come through their section of the plane. They didn't wait long. In minutes, a long-haired, tall gentleman brushed through the curtain separating the cabins. They all prepared to jump him, but Ian gave a hand signal for them to stand down. The man sat quietly next to Ian and Paul knew immediately that this was Dan Flynn, the package carrier. Somehow, he didn't look as old as he'd looked the day of the shooting, that fateful day when he'd delivered the package to Jack all those years ago.

Seconds after Dan's entrance, the gunman arrived, making his way through the cabin holding a gun to the stewardess's back as he forced her to escort him to the cockpit. Beyond the first-class curtains, Paul could hear the economy class passengers in turmoil. Children were crying, and the feeling of panic was so strong it choked the air.

However, there was little time to consider Dan's sudden reappearance as at this point the gunman was in the cabin and the plane suddenly descended as he threatened the pilot. People were falling forward in their seats, screaming with fear—yet when Dan stood up, he walked to the front as if unaffected by gravity, everyone was frozen in time and space. Paul noticed he and the rest of the passengers were paralysed ... yet Dan was able to move normally. Paul watched in awe as Dan walked into the cockpit, grabbed the terrorist and pulled him back into the first class section and then quickly and effortlessly disarmed him. Dan held the moment as if he controlled time while everyone else sat like statues. Then, after sitting the stewardess comfortably down in one of the seats, he proceeded to restrain the terrorist by tying him up.

The whole thing appeared effortless and seemed to take no time at all; as suddenly as it started, it was over, everyone was able to move again ... and Paul realized his mouth was hanging open. He was bewildered; what had just happened?

As the captain took control of the plane once again and it began to level off, Ian began to interrogate the terrorist. Paul looked at Dan as he did so and realized that, whereas Dan had seemed old on the day of the shootings, he now looked like a man in his thirties ... but it was definitely Dan. Then he looked at his father's good friend Ian and strangely, Ian *also* seemed younger than he had just hours ago! Paul blinked rapidly, trying to process this. The whole thing was too much for him to understand, yet he was acutely aware that something significant had just happened.

It was too much. The events Paul had witnessed events had broken all the rules, and he suddenly understood that life would never be the same. He wasn't sure how he felt about it, but it was as if a portal to a new dimension had opened in his soul. For the first time in his life he felt as if he was really, truly *aware*. It seemed, suddenly, that he'd been simply observing his life, no matter what wonderful adventures he'd created for himself. This, however, was something new and was the beginning of a *real* adventure ... an adventure into mystery and awe. His emotions exploded and tears sprang to his eyes as he understood that he had seen something divine.

April looked across the aisle at him. "Are you all right?" she asked.

Paul, embarrassed, replied that he had something in his eye. She knew he was lying and moved over to sit next to him ... and if he had been connected to a heart monitor, it would have shown off the chart. In his already heightened state of awareness, Paul realized just how much he was attracted to this dream lady. She held his hand, the warmth of her soft palms sending tingles up his fingers, and Paul melted under her disarming gaze. It had been many years since he'd experienced such a meeting of souls ... if ever.

"What just happened?" asked April excitedly. He knew she was talking about the miracle that Dan had just created. He shrugged his shoulders in silent response, as confused as she was. Alterations in time and space had taken place before their eyes, yet the scenery had remained the same. Paul wondered if he was in a dream ... maybe he had fallen asleep. But the warmth of April's hand brought him back to the present and he knew he was fully awake and there was no reasonable explanation for what he'd just observed.

How is it possible for the same person to appear old and young moments apart? He could not answer this.

Meanwhile, James was busy in the cockpit, talking to the pilot who was an old air force buddy. He assured him that the terrorist had been apprehended. At his request, one of the stewardesses brought him a passenger list so the team could identify the terrorist by his seat number. James went over the list with Ian. The seat allocated to the man bore the name Reid, but there was no way of determining if that was his real name. They checked the identity papers he carried. They identified him as a marketing manager for an international communications agency in Germany. They decided to check out his details when they arrived at Kathmandu.

Anthony had slept through the whole event but now Ian woke him up and brought him up to date about their captive terrorist. "I'm getting nothing out of him," said Ian. "How about if I play the bad guy lawyer and you play the innocent engineer?" Ian agreed, and they got to it.

'Reid' proved to be a tough customer. "Reid is the name you used to get on this flight ... but who is the real man behind the false papers?" Ian asked Reid. "We know they're false, a terrorist or saboteur would never travel under his own name!"

"First of all, I'm not a terrorist or a saboteur," Reid replied calmly. "Second, I'm trying to stop you from killing yourselves. You're flying into chaos. Do you really understand what waits for you in Kathmandu? Do you know what you are chasing?"

"Maybe you're going to enlighten us?" Ian pursued, giving Reid a cynical stare. Reid remained stone-faced and non-responsive.

"You can be sure we'll find out who you really are and why you're here," Ian said sternly. Behind him, Anthony nodded.

Reid decided to speak. "Do you realize that only a handful of individuals control our future? Do you understand how sad it is that most of the Earth's population are merely puppets, bowing to false gods presented by politicians, religion and 'get rich quick' schemes?" he asked.

"This is not so surprising," Ian countered.

"We're overworked, underpaid, lotto-chasing dreamers. We've lost touch with our souls. Certain religions don't accept that we even *have* souls ... unless it's in line with what they're preaching. The old, standard religions are having trouble translating their spiritually good intentions into language their disappearing flocks can understand," Reid said, "and so people are turning to other, less wholesome belief systems."

"So what?" asked Ian, "Is that a reason to try to take over a plane?"

Reid acted like he hadn't heard the question. "In comes the competition, in whatever guise they're wearing today, and their marketing ploy is first class," he said wryly. All they have to do to get converts is to tell them that all they ever need will be taken care of. People believe them. They don't feel a need to work on their soul because the attitude is, 'who needs a soul, when we die—we die?'"

"Hey, we've got a preacher, not a saboteur," Paul commented. "I wonder who's more dangerous?"

"Just let him finish," interrupted James, which surprised Paul since James usually listened without comment. In different circumstances, the group would have found this funny.

"We're flying into chaos," Reid continued, "That's the only way I can describe it. I know what I'm saying seems out of context with your daily lives, I know I sound like a preacher and you have every reason to doubt me—especially considering my gun-toting tactics—but I assure you I am trying to help!"

Ian thought of the message from Jack. He'd told him in code that someone would be on the plane and would make himself known in the event of danger. Now he had a dilemma, was Dan the secret weapon … or was the preacher?

"I assume your lecture will lead somewhere?" Ian asked drily, a little frustration creeping in. "We listen to clowns like you on street corners telling us the end is nigh, but few of us accept or believe the message. I know you're trying to underline our lack of respect for the truth, but why should we accept your version of it? Loonies leading cults abound, complete with their naïve followers. You're probably one of them."

"I'm not the enemy," said Reid. "I may be misguided, but I am not evil. Sometimes a person just wants to do good for others. Tell me, have you ever had one of those moments when your soul lets you know of its presence? A moment when you see colors more brightly and feel free and exhilarated? Let's face it; we all witnessed an extraordinary event in just the last few moments. I know that Paul and April noticed a change in both Dan's and Ian's appearances. Paul, I saw your eyes; I saw that your soul smiled … yet you don't know why."

"How do you know our names?" gulped Paul.

Reid knew he now had their attention. "We're approaching a serious crossroads in the history of man," Reid said. "As a group, you have to make the decision to fight. You can't laze around and pretend the cavalry is going to arrive, wave a magic wand and let you go back to your comfortable existence. If you think your group's misadventures of the past few days are exciting, you're only at the warm-up stage! The problem is, this game doesn't have rules—at least not earth-bound rules. And we're not playing for simple stakes, like money or prestige ... we are at the edge of the chasm," Reid proclaimed.

"What chasm?" asked Paul.

Reid ignored him and instead said, "It's too late to turn your back on humanity now; we're all part of this fight. But the battle will not be waged with crude weapons like guns and swords—though they may be necessary at some stage of this venture. Instead, you will be using forces much greater than that."

"From a preacher to a riddler in a few moments!" Paul exclaimed.

"What I am is not important," Reid said. "What *you* are and what you have to fight with is *much* more significant. Yet, you fear the unknown more than the known, a western dilemma. And so now we have to plan."

"Not so fast," said Ian. "Where have you come from, whose side are you on and what's in it for you?" he asked.

But no sooner were the words out of his mouth when the plane abruptly nose-dived, throwing everyone who was not seat-belted in onto the floor. Loose articles catapulted around the cabin and chaos reigned ... but only for an instant. Just as quickly, the plane pulled out of the dive and within moments, apart from a few cuts and bruises, normality returned.

Reid smiled mysteriously at the team's shock and horror ... and then he positively grinned as, before anyone could catch their startled breath, broken glasses were returned to their tables unbroken with their spilled contents refilled! They all looked at him in wonder and, with a gesture of open hands and an elfish grin, Reid convinced the group that he was behind this strange event. He further confirmed this by standing up without anyone untying him and bowing to his audience as if he expected applause.

"Andrew Reid is my name and I am your host for this moment in time. I will be with you in your time of need—and since Jack said you would be a bunch of doubting Thomases, I'm here to tell you it's time to believe and to trust in the world you cannot see."

At that, Andrew waved his hand and suddenly Paul realized he was frozen while everyone else was aware and moving. "Don't worry, he's not in pain and will not come to any harm," Andrew said. "I've simply suspended his movement and adjusted his awareness."

Then, with a snap of Andrew's fingers, Paul came out of his trance-like state, a little bemused yet aware of his participation in this show.

"This demonstration of tricks does not convince me you're with us," said Ian, staring sternly into Andrew's eyes.

"My dear Ian, if I was against you this plane would have crashed long ago and all they'd find of it would be the black box recording that would say electrical problems were the cause. A lawsuit would follow and ease all the survivor's grief a bit, I suppose. Money always makes the hurt better, doesn't it?" The elfish smile returned, but the comfort level of the audience did not. Reid added, "Further, April would not have survived her captors and the package would have never reached Jack!"

He smiled impishly at Ian, who, as the only one who knew that Jack already *had* the package, was thankful no one else noticed the comment.

The group was convinced. Respect and disbelief hung in the air and it was clear that there was no longer a need to interrogate the man. Besides, what was the point? He could untie himself and manipulate space and matter if he so chose.

Ian and Reid quickly became locked in conversation and Paul could tell Ian didn't like him yet.

Paul looked down at his hand and realized it was still squeezing April's. He smiled. There was nothing he could do about Reid, but there was something he could do about April.

"Who are you?" he asked quietly as the rest of their team settled into the new reality of having Andrew Reid in their midst.

"I'm April," she said, teasing. And then she told him of her life.

"I've had many dangerous people in my life," she began. "Some were friends fighting for the side of justice—but they were dangerous all the same." As her story came out, Paul learned that she had left Ireland when both her mother and father were killed in an IRA bomb attack. She'd moved to England and kept the horrors of her past to herself, settling into life in the Sutherland house as a maid, plain and simple.

"I know it's no coincidence that I'm here for this ... it's my destiny," she confided to Paul. "But I'm a long way from home."

April grew up in a cottage on Rathlin Island, off the north coast of Ireland. With a population of fewer than 90 people, it was a tight community and her early years among the farmers and fishermen of her youth were happy, though that happiness was coloured by the fight for Irish independence from Britain.

She remembered watching the British Navy operating controlled explosions just off the harbor where the IRA had hidden explosives in an old, underwater sea-wreck. At every explosion the water would cascade hundreds of feet in the air, which provided much-needed entertainment for her and her young friends. Life on the island may have been peaceful but it wasn't exactly overflowing with entertainment options.

She told him she knew more than most about the package, as it was she who had kept it secure in Ian's safe ... but she had no knowledge of its contents—at least, not yet.

Paul listened with fascination to her stories, until he was nearly lulled to sleep, comforted by her presence and her lovely, warm hand, which still held his.

Chapter 5

Reunion

From the moment we begin earthbound existence until the arrival of awareness, we sleep in the darkness of our mothers' wombs, our souls silent observers of our efforts to awaken. The soul waits patiently for us to come to awareness in life. Then, once we do, it watches our ego drive us around like marionettes. Driven by our egos, we enjoy the free will that is God's grace ... until the day we finally come to our senses and innocence returns.

Paul was thinking about how much the 'awakening' imposed on him by Reid was impacting him and he understood for the first time that his innocence had been lost. Before this day, he'd never understood that there were such powers in the world. He'd thought God was unattainable. Yet he'd just seen something God-like and it had shaken his beliefs. Suddenly he truly understood that in faith, an easy and fruitful life, safe from evil, was possible. Having seen both Dan and Reid display God-like power, he now understood the grace of such prophets as Buddha and Christ. Emotion welled up inside him and he gulped back tears. Those prophetic leaders did more than save souls, he realized ... they protected mankind from danger and for millennia the faithful had inherited their love, giving and receiving without judging.

Overwhelmed, he wondered, *what do the aware* do *with such awareness?*

During the brief hypnosis imposed by Reid, Paul's thoughts had continued despite how the man had manipulated the surroundings. Under Reid's spell, it had felt like he was asleep, though he'd known something was happening. Ultimately, the best way to describe how he felt was that he was experiencing a peaceful meditation, and it was this that had given him sudden clarity about life. Deep inside his soul, he'd become aware of something more, something deeper, and his newfound understanding affected his reasoning, though it felt strangely familiar, as if he'd met an old friend. What was happening to him? How could he feel his own ego sitting side-by-side with his soul?

He could see his life like a movie now, picturing times from his youth in lucid clarity. He could tap any moment of his life and watch his actions and surroundings as if they were happening in the present. He wasn't sure if he was dreaming or if he was actually *there*. Who was controlling his thoughts? His awareness grew, and, in his mind, he was at his childhood home, present in a happy time that brought with it the warmth of family and friends. He looked around at their comfortable living space in Lhasa and saw his parents sitting by the fireside, conversing with two men who were unfamiliar to him. He smelled the rancid smell of burning butter lamps and heard his sister playing in the room next door. Looking down at his hands, he saw a small, toy car, a replica of a diecast Corgi car he'd been given on this day, his seventh birthday.

Paul was confounded. How could he be here on this plane and there, in Lhasa—in his childhood, no less—at the same time? Because he wasn't merely dreaming; he was certain he was in two places at once. His senses were in his old house, his emotions were those of a seven-year-old ... but his knowledge and experience were part of his adult being.

His parents were laughing and talking with their friends and he started to tune into the conversation. They were talking about a discovery, something one of the men had brought to their house, but he could not see the item. Was it there, on the table? His eyes scanned the room, but he could not make this younger body move over to the table to look. He heard his father talk about the importance of secrecy and how this item might change the future and destroy the past.

Paul now recognized one of the men as Dan—younger, but not that different—and the other man clearly was Ian! The shock of recognition made the young Paul drop his toy. Instinctively he moved to pick it up as it landed by the table and, as he retrieved it, he noticed something lying near the edge of the table. The object was a strange shape and his young eyes had never seen such a thing before ... but his adult eyes had no doubt about its familiarity ...

Suddenly, Paul woke from the trance Reid had placed upon him. He was confused, and while to the rest of the team he'd been hypnotized only a minute, to him it seemed as if he'd been in his old, child's body for several hours. Now, jolted back to the present, he was aware of a flash of a memory of his coveted Corgi toy. *Curious* he thought to himself.

He caught Andrew's eye; Andrew smiled knowingly. No one else knew what Paul had seen but Andrew. Paul could tell by looking at him that he knew the story and saw what Paul's young eyes had seen.

"Now, where were we?" Andrew exclaimed when he was sure Paul was back in the present. "Ah, we were talking about the state of humanity! Yes, we have a chance of saving this excuse of a race. Wars keep coming, drugs are everywhere, greed is now a new religion, lying has been minimized to being 'fake news' and the loss of family values has passed without even a fleeting tear. Ten million children became orphans in Africa due to their parents contracting AIDS ... and pandemics are the 'new normal'... It's a rather sad state, don't you agree?"

"Mr. Reid, you're preaching again," chastised Ian. "Your list of sad realities does not clarify who you are or what we're expected to do. What expectations do you have for our ability to fight the good fight? That's what I'd like to know. We don't even know who, or what, we are fighting!"

"Yes, this is true, and probably now, it's just as well. I can tell you this, though—the power of our enemy is in their ability to escalate fear. They have used this power to control nations. Further, their power is rooted in evil, in the type of energy that runs through the back streets of society. They win converts to their evil ways in the same way many so-called religions do ... by filtering out all the difficult rules and making it easy to follow the leader."

Paul didn't understand what Andrew Reid was getting at. He looked around the cabin and, by the looks on their faces, he was sure his friends weren't quite in tune either. *Where is this rambling going? What does it have to do with our visit to Kathmandu? Who is this guy, anyway?*

Finally, he'd had enough. "Andrew!" Paul exclaimed. "You seem to want us to understand your ramblings and grasp your statements of enlightenment ... but you still haven't given a real explanation of who you are or why you're here—or how you've managed to create illusions of reality. What are you? A nomad of awareness?"

"Paul, you understand more than you think," answered Andrew. "And 'nomads of awareness' is an insightful comment that shows appreciation of the new age in which you now live! However, awareness—by its nature—must be nomadic to grow!"

Oh dear, was all Paul could think. If he'd been confused before, he now felt neither insightful *nor* aware!

"I think this idea of awareness is where we should concentrate our thoughts for a moment," Reid said. Paul could see the rest of the group had resigned themselves to listening. It was obvious Reid was pulling the strings, good or bad.

"We are born with pure spiritual awareness, which is knocked out of us in the first seven years on earth, an innocence great gurus and prophets strive a lifetime to regain. What happens in those first seven years is that we develop an ego, and it becomes our focus and drives our actions. Before the development of the ego, we were more in touch with our souls. After the development of the ego, our soul becomes a watcher."

The group nodded. This, they could understand.

"If you consider that we are born with free will, and driven by our ego, clearly that indicates that our souls are not being recognized and nurtured. They get pushed aside as the ego, driven by our free will, runs amok. Free will is a devilish trick, don't you think?"

There were nods of approval. "Go on," said Paul.

"We have a duality born into us," Andrew continued. "Our souls are part of God, but our egos are part of this world. Who gets to drive? That is the eternal question. Good or bad, right or wrong, fate or divine plan ... these are outside dualities that we experience. But inside, it's the soul versus the ego."

When the audience made no effort to comment or question, he continued.

"The earth is falling apart, and people need to get back to their soul states if we are to save ourselves. Religion supports the fact that we need to strive toward that which we have lost. History, recorded in works such as the Bible, Bhagavad Gita and the Koran, drive the idea that we must work our way back to God ... yet we have used those same teachings to excuse the atrocities of war—in the name of religion, of course—for profit and ego-driven gain."

"That's all well and good," cut in Ian, "but you're not really saying anything that's not obvious. Get to the point." It was clear that he still didn't trust Andrew.

Andrew ignored him and carried on. "We are controlled from within by our ego and are boxed into jobs where we are over-worked and underpaid as we pursue the almighty dollar. We need so much less than we strive to have. We have lost the will to be spiritual in the true sense of the word."

"And by delivering this package, we can help the world regain its spirituality?" guessed Paul.

Ian looked at Paul gratefully. He seemed to be searching for a way to tie Andrew's lectures to their assigned task.

Suddenly April piped up. "There was a time in Ireland when elves and leprechauns were an accepted part of everyday living—like gods. They are in most Irish folklore, yet there is no substantiating evidence they exist. But ask any levelheaded Irishman and he will swear they do!"

Everyone laughed, mainly because they were happy for a brief respite from the seriousness of the conversation.

"True they are, as sure as we sit here!" confirmed Anthony with a glint in his eye!

"Come with me," stated Andrew. "I have something to show you!"

The group exchanged quizzical glances then stood up as requested. Andrew made his way from the first-class section of the plane into the economy section and they followed. What the group saw made them stop in their tracks. Every passenger was sitting motionless in the same mesmerized state in which Paul had earlier been placed. This time, however, it was not for a fleeting moment ... it was as if time was standing still.

"Someone arranged for our fellow passengers to have a break from their busy lives and the tedium of travel," said Andrew. "They will not be harmed and won't remember this break in their lives."

"Who did this?" demanded James, "Was it you?"

Andrew didn't answer. He just said, "It's time to look at one or two of our friends on board."

"No way! That's not appropriate!" exclaimed James indignantly, positioning himself between Reid and the passengers.

"Don't worry, we're not going to abuse their privacy in any way. I just want you all to look at their faces and let me know if any appear familiar."

With that reassurance, James stepped aside—but he kept a close eye on Reid just the same. The team moved down the aisle, studiously examining each face. Paul, Ian and April recognized one man as the man who had turned up at Ian's house a few days ago. There was no mistaking the eyes; they were cold and empty. April could not hide her fear and she backed away. Paul immediately picked up her vibes. Ian took a closer look.

"April, that's the same reaction you had to this man when he arrived at Ian's door a few days ago and you avoided my questions about him. But you can tell me now. Who is he and why do you break out into a sweat each time you see him?"

"I can answer that," reported Ian. "This man has been sniffing around my house for a few months and I've reported his persistent stalking habits to the police. Unfortunately, they said they can't do anything unless he shows signs of aggression or interferes with us in any way. But until he came to the door that morning he hadn't talked to either of us ... he was just watching us. At first, I thought he was an undercover investigator—or maybe someone who had a crush on April. To be safe, I took a few photos using my zoom lens and had them checked by Interpol ... and the search came up blank!"

As they continued looking around the cabin, Ian and Paul also recognized the man who had followed them from the Ritz the previous Sunday morning and it quickly became was obvious to the team that their efforts to avoid being pursued had not worked. Here were at least two individuals known to be involved in the chase. How many others were on board?

"I suppose you won't tell us how this suspended state of animation has been achieved?" Ian asked drily.

"For the moment that's not important," answered Andrew. Our real problem is how we can get to Paul's father without these dangerous people on our tail. How can we avoid the ones on this plane, or the ones who will be at the airport when we arrive, or even the ones who will inevitably show up at Jack's house in Kathmandu?"

Andrew looked into the eyes of each of his companions as he delivered his questions, looking for understanding about the seriousness of the situation. He wanted to be sure the message was getting through.

"It would help if we knew why we're on this adventure and what the item we're protecting is," Paul fumed.

"First, let's try to minimize the risk to our fellow passengers by identifying the other players on board," Andrew said. "The two we've recognized will stay in the present state, unharmed, until we can find a suitable way of securing them. Please help make them comfortable, as we've a few hours before we land."

Andrew looked to James for assistance. James still doubted Andrew's motives but chose to accommodate his wishes for the moment. While James positioned the two men as if they were merely sleeping, the others searched the plane for other familiar faces. Paul and Ian worked together in the business cabin while April, Anthony and Dan searched economy section. Neither team recognized anyone else.

Andrew, too, kept searching ... but he seemed to be looking deep into each person's mind instead of at their faces as he walked through the aircraft. He didn't seem to be paying much attention to the work of the others. He stopped at one individual, a rather attractive woman with raven hair. She seemed to be in her mid-30s and of Asian origin; a stunning beauty. He didn't know the woman, but instinctively felt something was unusual about her. Although he had special talents, he could not see into a person's mind if that individual was trained to protect their thoughts. This was the case with the Asian lady—and it made Andrew suspicious. He asked Ian to look more closely at the woman and really try to remember if he had recently come across anyone of her description. Ian drew a blank.

To be on the safe side, Andrew decided it would be sensible to have this woman also remain in her sleeping state. Ian made her comfortable and the group returned to their seat in preparation for the rest of the passengers being re-awakened. When they awoke, Paul could not help noticing how their faces had a relaxed, pleasant demeanor ... but only for a moment. Once they reoriented themselves to the world, their guards were back up and their expressions became harder.

The group reassembled in the first-class cabin. Paul noticed the old couple who were seated with them in first class had been left sleeping.

"My friends, now that we are back together," Andrew said, gesturing broadly to the group, "I would like to help you understand who and what we are dealing with. I do not expect you to grasp the whole picture—that will become clear when we meet with Jack—but I am responsible for helping you prepare for the challenges ahead."

"Let's start with who our enemy is, and why," said April.

"No," interrupted Paul, "let's start with who *you* are and how you have these extraordinary powers. Once we understand that, we may be more inclined to listen to the rest."

"You are your father's son!" exclaimed Andrew. "Jack mentioned I'd have to prove myself before you would buy into the plan! He knows you well and maintained you'd be a good judge of character, especially when someone with my expertise came around. I'm only too pleased to help allay your misgivings

... but I do urge that we move on quickly, as there is a lot to prepare for. I'll start by saying that you *know* who I am ... yet you've all forgotten—after all, it has been some time since we last met. I'd venture it's been almost a million years of Earth time!"

He looked around at the baffled faces, then smiled mischievously. "Well, I guess being reunited calls for a celebration, don't you think?"

The others could only gasp as a pitcher of beer appeared in Andrew's hand.

Chapter 6

In the Beginning

"We should always start at the beginning," said Andrew with a mischievous smile. His audience doubted his sincerity and his sanity. The claims he was making were beyond any level of belief and comprehension, and his tricks were becoming distinctly unnerving and possibly dangerous. The group of individuals assembled before him all lived in the real world and, while they had belief systems, most weren't devout about anything. They *did* believe in science and had seen it's evidential developments. How were they to believe such statements as Andrew was making?

"Doubting Thomases, without exception!" he quipped affectionately as he viewed their confused faces.

"What do you expect?" Paul asked, eying Andrew with suspicion. "Do you seriously think we are going to sit back and believe your outrageous bedtime stories? The tricks you've played are weird enough. But I can't imagine we've known you for a million years. I say prove it!"

Andrew sighed and tried to encourage them. "If you look within, or should I say *feel* within, you will know this to be true!" Then, after a moment of reflection, he added, "I am in no way playing with words or your minds; I am simply more aware than you are, my close friends. But you will wake up soon."

"Now you're acting superior. Is that supposed to endear you to us?" Paul's face was red with indignation. "I can hardly remember the details of my childhood, never mind a million years ago ..."

"But you did recall what was on the table at your home, when you were seven," Andrew pointed out. Paul stopped talking. He suddenly felt uncomfortable; it was troubling that Andrew knew of his 'dream' during the suspended state he'd been in.

"I'm not trying to pry Paul—that's not my goal," said Andrew. "I simply wanted to show you that only a short while ago you slept for less than a few seconds—at least, that's what your colleagues in the group observed—but you were engaged with yourself in a different period of your life, and that lasted much longer."

"Is this true, Paul?" asked April.

Paul nodded. Ian looked bemused.

"I not only saw my parents, and you, Ian ... but I saw Dan. And I felt the air, smelled the smells ... it was real. And I was there—and for much longer than I was lying in a trance on this plane. It was like time was moving at a different rate and I was at two places at once. I moved with my younger body but did not control it."

"Your mind was in the present and your body was in the past," added Andrew, "although time as we perceive it didn't move in either direction."

Probably for the first time in my life, Paul thought to himself in awe. Paul wanted to believe the things he was hearing, seeing and experiencing, but his rational mind kept getting in the way. It was shocking, and he could not gather his composure. On the one hand, he was excited by it, but on the other hand, he wanted to run a mile in the other direction.

As he tried to process what was happening, his emotions raced from fear to anger and back again, while his legs shook with anticipation in the 'fight or flight' response. His brain almost imploded. He felt he was be spiraling down a black hole … it was a panic attack and it was unnerving and uncomfortable. His breath quickened, and, aware that all eyes were on him, for the first time in his life he passed out.

"Ian, please help your friend," Andrew said nonchalantly." But Ian was already checking Paul's heart rate and examining his eyes.

"He's passed out, you bastard! Did you do this?" Ian demanded. "What gives you the right to harm one of us? James, get this guy in chains and gag him!" he shouted. James jumped into action, but he was surprised Ian had demanded this; after all,, they knew full well that restraints couldn't hold Andrew. He'd already simply slipped out of the first restraints he'd been in. Then, as James tightened the restraints April yelled out angrily, "Put a blindfold on him as well!" She surprised herself more than the others with this demand, spoken with fear in her voice. Then she broke down in tears.

Just then Dan, who had remained in the economy section of the airplane for the last hour or so, came back. Being an observant fellow, he sensed the tension. Instead of getting involved, he sat down quietly and said nothing, pondering the emotions of his colleagues. He saw the group remained strong as a team, but he noticed the frailty of their mental condition. What was causing their sudden emotional weakness? Why was Paul so affected by simple rhetoric that otherwise would have stimulated him into a deep conversation? From what Jack had told him of Paul, the boy normally loved this kind of conversation. And Ian—solid, calm Ian—was never without patience, even for the most antagonistic person. So why did he command such constraints on Andrew, especially when everyone knew that physical bonds would have no effect on this stranger? It was odd to see him fearful and angry. Just as it was odd that poor April, sweet April who had so much love to give, had attacked Andrew without provocation too! Normally she would retreat into the background and allow others to drive. What made her shout out like that ... it seemed a primal fear now filled the room, overpowering people's good intentions.

Andrew's powers were strong, and Dan knew what the 'million years' statement meant; nevertheless, Dan was concerned about Andrew's intentions and so, while he was restrained and blindfolded, he made sure Andrew's special powers were also restricted. The others were unaware that he was able to do this, and he did not enlighten them; he did not want to confuse his friends by displaying a few exceptional powers of his own—they were better off remaining ignorant of his role in this plan, at least for the time being.

However, Dan found it strange that Andrew seemed unaware of what a threat to him Dan might be; Andrew had not picked up on Dan's power. This was a concern, a gap that made him feel uncertain. Those of like abilities usually recognize one another.

Under Dan's gentle influence, Andrew began to feel tired and within a few moments the 'saboteur' drifted into a deep sleep. Dan now had time to plan the next step, but he was not sure how much time he had, as he was unsure of Andrew's full ability and how effective his own powers had been on the man.

All of this happened in a few seconds. The group were largely unaware of Dan's influence on Andrew. They saw he went to sleep after he was restrained, but they didn't know why. However, Dan's presence seemed to bring some light into their darkness and the group seemed happy to see him.

"Hi Dan," said Ian. "Too bad you missed Andrew's show."

"I was busy watching our evil friends out there," Dan said, indicating the economy section. "I wanted to ensure they didn't wake up.

Dan didn't want them to know he'd been 'traveling' and that he'd gone to tell Jack about the evil men who had followed them onto the plane. It was best that the others think he'd just been sitting and guarding their sleeping captives. It was important to maintain a strong team and to keep them focused. They would need all their energy for the challenge ahead.

He settled in with the others, listening to them chat. They were speeding at 500 miles per hour toward a destiny unknown and only one person had any idea of what they were chasing. The knowledge weighed heavily on Dan and the possibility of a break in the strength of their enemy was small. Yet they must carry on; mankind had come a long way toward its second chance at a glorious destiny. He was going to make sure they got there. The past was the past, but it was intertwined with the present. Despite his powers, he left the future to chance and made no attempt to influence its direction. He knew better. Instead, the trick was to fight in the *now.*

He reflected about how sad it was that mankind had no idea of the journey they were on—nor of the journey they had previously failed to complete. Sheepishly, they followed the past, building their future based on what their forefathers laid out for them, completely unaware of how free they could be.

What next, Dan thought? Was a free, happy future reliant on this small band's action? Would this team be able to sustain each leg of this journey or would it be too hard for them to endure? How many years would the world have to go on in ignorance of the devilish forces disguised as gods that were manipulating them? Money, oil, technology, power ... all led nowhere. It was time to find a different future. Leaders, good and bad, had perished without even glimpsing the possibilities, frightened of the unknown, their eyes had seen only what they wanted to see. They had not opened their hearts to the unknown and so they weren't aware of what wonder awaited them.

"Are you with us, old friend?" asked Ian.

"We need to get in touch with Jack," Dan said calmly. "He had the foresight to keep us together and at least maintain the team's innocence long enough to give us a chance to bypass the enemy nets. Yes, they have us in their sights ... but I feel they may yet have underestimated our ability, a bit like David and Goliath!" he chuckled.

"I have no idea who we are fighting or why they are trying so hard to stop us meeting in Kathmandu. I don't know what is in the package, but I trust Jack and I trust you. I have found it difficult to drag Paul and our friends into this foray. I feel we have brought them into something beyond our reckoning, but I have followed all of Jack's instructions, without question. I know the package is safe in his hands but what is so important about it? Why are we risking our lives for an unknown object that sat in my safe in London without anyone giving it even a passing thought for over five years?" Ian asked in frustration.

Dan studied Ian, willing primordial awareness to return to his consciousness. He smiled when he saw Ian's mind shift and understanding arrive. *Closeness to wisdom is a glimpse of the divine*, he thought.

In the hypnotic state inspired by Dan, Ian felt warmth fill the cabin; he felt no fear, no uncertainty and no distraction and he was completely comfortable in his surroundings. Boundaries were removed, and Ian's perception shifted; he suddenly clearly understood that they were on a predestined path. He also understood that it felt familiar, though he did not know why.

In his trance, he could see Jack in his hotel in Kathmandu. He could see there was peace in that room. Ian felt he could reach out and touch his friend, yet he was aware that he was not actually there with him. This experience was not uncomfortable, but it was strange. He was in two places at one time, physically on one plane (on an airplane) but spiritually in Jack's room. He felt the power of the plane's engine in his physical body, but his attention was a thousand miles away in Kathmandu. Looking around Jack's room he felt something was wrong—yet visually the scene seemed far removed from danger.

Jack was reading while his wife Harriet slept peacefully on the couch, the slumber of the aged. Curtains blew softly at the open patio door as a warm breeze drifted in. Jack's eyes grew heavy in the early afternoon; he appeared to need a nap. Outside, the sound of children playing in the street added a hypnotic quality to the moment. Jack drifted into the silent bliss of sleep as the book he'd been reading dropped gently onto his lap.

Ian's intuition told him the presence of danger was subtle, but powerful. What was the threat and how could he warn Jack when he had no physical way to contact him?

He looked around the room for clues to the source of the unnerving feeling. Everything looked normal. Ian's consciousness drifted outside, experiencing the heat of the mid-afternoon sun. The children in the street began to drift away and the birds became silent ... in fact, there was suddenly no sound; no movement other than the invisible drift of the warm air as it softly played in the eerie presence of danger and Ian's fear. Then the curtains stopped moving and time stood still—Ian's awareness seemed to be the only moving entity. Yet his presence seemed essential to the moment. He drifted back inside to view his sleeping friend, feeling powerless that he could not wake and warn him.

Bewildered, he wondered what had moved his senses from back into the room. He knew it was not a dream. What made him feel the fear? Who?

Out of nothingness appeared a shape, seemingly human, yet different ... almost benevolent but at the same time sinister. Ian did not want to look at it, yet he could not pull away; the shape magnetized his attention. Something familiar was becoming visible. He did not want to come face to face with this being, whatever it was. Yet when it manifested he was intoxicated by its presence. It shimmered with gold streaks and appeared to have hundreds of arms. It was strangely beautiful.

He attempted to run, and he tried to hide his feelings of primal fear, but this ghostly shape stopped him with its evil, sticky mist. He wanted to scream out and wake Jack, but his lips were frozen. Slowly the devilish form manifested fully in front of Jack. Ian kept trying to shout to Jack and he tried to leave ... but he was not in control of his thoughts. How could he awaken him? He was very worried for his friend.

Just then Jack stirred and opened his eyes. Immediately he started at the sight of the evil energy in front of him. Ian could see him gag. He could sense a smell, rancid and sickening, in his nostrils and he was sure if he could smell it, then it must be a hundred times worse for Jack.

He was right. Jack recoiled at the smell and the evil taste in the back of his throat that the creature left behind. Immediately he was vomiting on the floor from the putrid effects of its odor. Ian watched, powerless to come to his aid. But Jack's gaze moved in Ian's direction, as if sensing someone was there. He was confused that he could not see what he felt, so his attention reverted to the creature. Trapped in silence, Ian was helpless to come to Jack's aid.

The presence spoke, but Ian couldn't hear what it said. He felt Dan pushing him closer to Jack and suddenly he could see through Jack's eyes and hear through Jack's senses! Now Ian was watching what was happening from Jack's perspective. He felt his nausea and he also felt his anger. Was this a nightmare? Was it real? He knew he wasn't physically in Jack's room, but he could feel all of Jack's emotions! He felt like a puppet; he was not sure who or what was pulling the strings, though. Was it his imagination going wild, or was he really here? How could he see so clearly and feel so acutely?

The beast leaned over Jack, uncomfortably close, and Ian could hear this devilish being say, "You feel the fear, you puny excuse for a being! Ha! Humans were never much of a challenge."

As Jack recoiled from its stench, it asked, "Where is the Scion? Do you really think you can hide it from me? I've been with you for millennia and yet you still will not recognize me. Why do you waste my time?"

Ian suddenly realized he *knew* this thing; if he reached deep inside his past he could find a distant memory of it, but the memory was oblique and unclear. His psyche struggled with his will to identify it. It was as if the memory had been erased and was now struggling to find its way to his consciousness again.

Jack stood tall in a deliberate action of defiance and Ian's awareness as observer took over once again. He wished he could help his friend because, in one sharp thrust the animal sliced at Jack, making Ian cringe.

But just as its limbs were about to gouge Jack's flesh, instead they passed right through him, leaving the monster bewildered.

Ian saw Jack smile as he said, "Do you think we've learned nothing Moloch? Do you feel that humanity just traveled down the merry road of time, bowing to your every whim? Some of us are still mesmerized by your game of life, but not all have been in your trance!"

The creature snarled.

"Do you think the trials and tribulations of our wars and religious strife mean we're sitting helpless in the swamp we've created with our so-called free will, waiting for you to save us from our mistakes? Some of us escaped that falsehood. Some of us have recaptured true freedom. It was a struggle, but eons of time are nothing when we have eternity. *You*, on the other hand, only control the ignorant ... and those who are not ignorant have learned much while you were playing in the dark corridors of the universe!"

The beast, enraged by Jack's words, erupted in a furious display of strength and anger. In a few seconds of rampage everything was tossed around and destroyed, leaving the room like a bombsite—except for Harriet, who remained peacefully sleeping, as if in a trance of her own. And in a few seconds of restoration, Jack reversed the damage with a simple wave of his hand.

"You'll need to do better than that," he smiled. And at that, the form began to dissolve. Within moments, all signs of its presence had vanished.

Immediately Ian was back in the airplane's cabin with all memory intact, staring at Dan. He blinked and withdrew his gaze, wondering how he could have experienced all of this yet have remained in the plane!

"I'm confused," he said to Dan. "I could see and feel the emotions as if I was in the room, but it was thousands of miles away. I was in Jack's body and smelt the stench and witnessed the destruction ... yet all the time I was an observer in the scene. What was that thing in Jack's room, and for that matter, where was the real Jack?"

"Moloch?" Dan asked. "He is a presence older than time and he only used a ghostly form to test Jack's level of development since they last met."

"You talk as if that thing was an old acquaintance!" Ian reproached. "It was evil personified. What's so friendly about that?"

"Ian, good and evil sit in the same camp; they're a swinging pendulum and right now I can't tell which way it's about to swing. You're beginning to understand the dilemma we're facing. There's a small team of us about to take on a force that's been threatening man's darkest hours since he first became aware."

"Dan," said Ian, some frustration setting in, "Let me enlighten you. I'm just a man, not a super being who plays around with the physical state of matter … like you seem to be …"

"No Ian, you've just forgotten who you really are," replied Dan. Then he reached over and shook Andrew's shoulder. It was time to wake him.

The others had been silent while Ian had been on his mental 'journey' and now that he was back, they looked in awe at Dan. He smiled at their curiosity.

"There are stranger things than you know," he said by way of explanation. Then he said, "April, will you help me while we talk with our preachy companion?" He indicated the sleeping prisoner. April nodded, no longer afraid of the man.

Ian replayed the past few moments in his mind; he felt nervous about how easy it had been for Dan to take control of him, as if he were a child's toy. He realized that he was afraid for the first time since he'd been a child. Then, it was the darkness of his room when his mother put out the light. But now he was struggling with the realization that this experience was not as strange as it should have been. Somehow, he knew he had the capability to control his awareness … and that Moloch was a part of his past. But the psychological barriers within him were tightly closed and at the moment could not be penetrated; try as he might, he could not draw his memories forward.

He let it go; instead, turned his attention to the awakening Andrew. Andrew looked somewhat bemused as he stretched his untied limbs. The others didn't know his thoughts, but he was pondering the fact that his unexpected drowsiness was not caused by overexertion. *What, then?* He stood up and ran his fingers through his hair. "Must have drifted off, did I miss anything?"

Ian looked at the person in front of him, the way he smiled so mischievously, the way he moved and talked and shook his head and … all of a sudden, he realized that Andrew was a past companion! Suddenly, for Ian, Andrew's presence filled his senses just like a taste or a smell from childhood; a sharp rush of memory from times gone by. The memory was too deep to fully uncover, but his instinct told him the truth. Andrew was family, of a sort, at least.

Andrew, fully awake now, smiled at the people around him—which belied his thoughts, which were ... *another person on this plane has developed similar abilities to mine* ... but he didn't know whom.

He continued to wonder about who had induced his slumber when a voice entered his head, more telepathy than audible sound. "It's nice to see you again, my old friend. It has been some time ... sorry about the nap, but I needed to deal with a distraction and could not handle you being so overbearing in your efforts to impress our friends. I'm glad you could make it and happy to see your powers are improving, but I thought by now you'd have advanced a little further?"

Andrew smiled and immediately recognized his old teacher, but he still did not know which individual had communicated with him; *metamorphosis talents sometimes work against us*, he thought.

"Okay my friend. You know I'm here and we have much work to do. Can you please let me see which of this motley crew is you?" he said telepathically.

Andrew quickly realized why there was no reply. Dan stood in the passageway, just inside the first-class cabin, quietly observing the rest of the group as they drifted out into the economy section of the plane to check on the sleeping agents who had followed them onto the aircraft. One by one they walked by Dan, but their gaze didn't even acknowledge him for a moment. It was as if they were being controlled by him ... which they were.

Andrew smiled. He was glad he was not alone.

Chapter 7

Mechta - The Dream

'Lunik 1', the first Soviet-launched spacecraft to reach the vicinity of earth's moon, went into space in 1959. The Russians hoped to place the craft in orbit around the moon. Unfortunately, it missed the target, so the Russians renamed the craft 'Mechta', or 'dream', and proceeded to keep trying.

Dan thought that was a great metaphor for life. *Sometimes, when we test ourselves to the limit of our knowledge, we catch glimpses of the impossible*, he thought. Unfortunately, our minds pull us back from our dreams. We create our reality on this little blue planet ... the result is restriction of our free will.

He wondered about the few geniuses who escape—such as Einstein or DaVinci. Were they truly free? Were they happy?

Chaos, Dan had decided, was a stream of unexpected happenings with disaster as a crescendo. *Is there a way to break free? Will this group I am shepherding be able to stop the chaos that is now overtaking the world?*

As he contemplated teaching this group, which he was sure was his destiny, he remembered what his own wise teacher had told him:

> *When we dream we see a collection of unusual scenes, which, under waking hours could not stand together in one set. A chaotic observation of circumstances transpires, but the mind in a dream state does not panic, it just observes. We fly without wings or effort; we see the deepest blue sea ... but a dark cloudy sky hangs above. We meet people who are dead, but we don't find it strange. We wind up in recurring events that either make us comfortable or frightened. We can awaken from a dream and feel the warmest attachment to a total stranger; we travel across oceans and continents within a fraction of a second and the lengthiest experience can happen in an instant. A dream in our childhood can be remembered as if it happened only yesterday. Yet we don't think, at least during the dream, that anything will harm us—we simply observe. Chaos reigns in this region of our consciousness. Nightmares are different altogether.*

Dan had been amazed by his insight he'd also told him:

The process of thought is a powerful tool that can bring about amazing changes. When powerful beings such as us focus our thoughts, those changes happen at the speed of thought. It's a bit like the old phrase from the Bible, 'In the beginning there was the word and the word was made flesh' ... before the word was the thought of creation and we would not be here if God had thought anything else but 'let there be light'. That thought was the start; billions of years later humanity emerged. Of course, the process seems slow but it's a blink of an eye to a God ... if that's how you chose to see it. But how else can you see it? Science is all well and good ... I believe the Big Bang happened, Dan. However, there is a sentience to the galaxy, to the universe ... to life. It wasn't random, my boy. It happened by will and the power of thought in a force of energy too large for any human to understand.

Meanwhile, Andrew was lost in thought himself. He was reliving his recent venture into chaos and how it had brought him to the current day ... as well as what it's connection to the package was. Andrew's travel was not in his dreams; he had literally been travelling for longer than he cared to remember ...*but I certainly was not exaggerating that the last time the group was together was a million years ago, give or take a few thousand years in earth time,* he mused.

He wondered how long it would take to 'awaken' his friends—the misfit group consisting of Paul, Ian, April and the others— who had also travelled through many life times, not all human, to arrive at this crucial point in humanity's history. He was certainly glad to see this team, as journeys without companions can be tiresome and not particularly fruitful. He chuckled to himself as he thought about how it would feel to learn to ski and, upon making it down the first black diamond on your own, to have no one believe your story. *Ah, well*, he thought, *they may or may not believe, but the experience is true nonetheless.*

As he continued to ponder over the many lifetimes in his journey, Andrew contemplated what a tragedy it was that so few of us have the awareness to remember past lives ... and even *fewer* recognize that who they were before this life holds no station on who they are today ... with one important exception—we reap what we sow. Karmic rules dictate that time will bring all souls to that supreme level, whether it takes a thousand trials or more.

Andrew's experiences and memories included lifetimes of trouble, adventure and love, mostly lived without a care, for this was his fortune, or karma, in this life. The energy and unique knowledge he'd gained during successive lives for him had culminated in extraordinary powers … a truly advanced soul, he was able to harness the very air to be his sword or shield.

He thought to himself, *if only we knew that we all have these capabilities …* But most humans had forgotten their divine natures. And like any muscle neglected, they'd become weak. *Should we learn our possibilities, we would truly be gods and goddesses, just like the characters in Egyptian, Greek and Roman mythologies.*

Andrew was grateful for the wondrous powers he possessed. They were gifts from the divine and he would use them well. The evil forces that were combining to threaten the Earth would require more than manual weapons to stop them; his powers would be needed. He realized that he was incarnated now for a special purpose … to help save the world in the upcoming battle between good and evil.

At least Dan is not living in a dream state, thought Andrews. Clearly, he was excellent at mesmerizing people, such as the passengers. He would be a strong ally and teacher.

Andrew's knew his duty was to prepare the assembled team for the challenges ahead. But first he had to gain their trust; only then could he get them ready for action. But he had to do it because he knew they all had a battle to fight, probably the most important battle in the history of the Earth.

Andrew wasn't scared of the upcoming battle; instead, what scared him was the state of the human beings in the world. The way they were living was sucking their souls dry. In some countries, it was famine, drought or war that caused unbearable living conditions. In more wealthy countries, during the past 50 years they'd had to keep pace with technological advances that only a few generations before would have been considered impossible.

Today our children hunger for the latest iPhone or Android as if their life depends on it ... and 'Apple' would tell them the same. Office-bound individuals cope with hundreds of emails a day when only 20 years ago handling five to ten letters would have been a stretch. Computers which collate data often misinform us because the origin of data is human, and frailty resides within ... thought Andrew. "All you have to do is think about the most recent US election and the manipulation of the results," he said out loud.

But it was the changes in the souls of man that worried him most. Wars come, go and remain. *Man can evolve beyond that type of behavior ...* he thought. However, the evil that had been unleashed on the world, and the war they would have to fight to stop it, was of a totally different caliber. This was the type of war that ate souls. It turned children on their parents, husbands on their wives, brothers and sisters on each other. It was Sodom and Gomorrah times a billion. People would no longer have respect for themselves or one another if this evil won.

He sighed. Most of humanity was unaware of their damaged condition and would not believe him if he alerted them to the danger of their immanent extinction. That was one of the biggest challenges the team would face as they prepared for battle. He wished he could share what he knew, share the path that had made him the man he was ... it could save so many souls. Long ago, he'd turned to Eastern traditions. He'd learned to meditate under his guru and started having the most amazing experiences as he learned how to access higher planes of realization and enlightenment. He wished he could share the secrets with more people. Even someone who doesn't care to learn the secrets of conquering time could benefit from meditation: it brings peace to the angry, lowers blood pressure in seconds, and calms the stressed. *It makes us aware that we are aware.*

Andrew was certain the mass practice of meditation would bring peace faster than heads of government battling over egoistic ambitions ever could. However, he knew how most of the world would either not make the time to meditate or would just laugh and continue, deeper and deeper into ignorance. *We survive as puppets on a string of egoism,* he thought.

Andrew had a theory about personal depth. There is the watcher the 'soul', the manipulator the 'ego' and finally, that third occupant of the human—which had long stood dormant and was about to be awakened in the people he had assembled to help him—'a connection to the divine'.

"Lost?" questioned Dan, startling Andrew from his reverie.

"Just deep in thought," responded the daydreaming Andrew.

"The passengers are now awake, with a few exceptions. I can see you're now with us also, after your blackout!"

"Glad you brought that up, Dan. I don't think that was a blackout; it felt much more like hypnosis, and I'm guessing you're the organ grinder?"

Dan laughed.

"You don't remember me, Dan, but I know you. And I can see you have developed skills of your own since we last met. I'm guessing our sleepy passengers were you're doing ... am I right?"

Dan wasn't sure whether he should own up. He was powerful, but he suspected Andrew might be even more so.

Andrew understood his hesitation right away. "Don't worry, my friend, we'll cover this later ... for the moment, did you see the tall, skinny, individual with sunken eyes? He was a little hunched and darker-skinned than most. He looked as if he'd spent a summer in the Mediterranean.

Dan's eyes sharpened, and he indicated that he knew who Andrew was talking about.

"His aura reeked of darkness," Andrew said. "Did you feel it too?"

"Yes, he didn't drift off as easy as the others," Dan said thoughtfully. "It took more effort ... but he finally succumbed. I'm not sure of his background, but you're right about where he's been living. His passport shows he's been in Malta and Greece recently. Apparently, he's English by birth ... but I know little else and his mind is very hard to read."

"You mean you can't read his thoughts?" Andrew asked, smiling. Dan was beginning to realize there was more to Andrew than he thought. Something told him their past was eons old.

As Andrew and Ian worked out their differences, Paul carried on looking through the economy section as he and the others had been asked to do. April, James, Anthony and Ian didn't accompany him; they were relaxing back in first class. The airplane was now only an hour away from landing and they hadn't slept or relaxed for a minute as yet.

As he checked on the sleeping passengers—most of whom were sleeping naturally and had *not* been induced—the recent things he'd learned caused him concern. He tried to interpret the meaning of a 'million years of companionship'. What did that mean and how was it possible?

Since the seat beside the sleeping Asian lady was unoccupied, he decided to relax next to her and idly browse through some books she appeared to have been reading. He needed to get his mind off things.

Interesting selection, he thought ... a few love stories, some technical astronomical volumes, but most peculiarly a book from a yogi known in the 60s, Mehar Baba. This Indian guru displayed extraordinary insight into the origin of humanity, espousing how awareness evolved over millions of years, from an inanimate stone state up through vegetable then fish, birds, animals and ultimately to human ... 'an evolution process' driven by the soul. This was not exactly how Darwin presented his theory of natural selection, but it wasn't that different either; Mehar Baba brought awareness to how the soul evolved through multiple levels. He proclaimed that our respective life journeys generally went in a one-way direction and that eventually we humans evolve through a realization process into a God state; we return home, as it were. Souls who arrived at higher levels of being can sometimes return to human form and acquire capabilities that seem miraculous. *Like Jesus*, he thought and then wondered if he was being blasphemous. *But Jesus himself stated 'anything that I have done, you can do and even greater things'.*

It wasn't all fun and games, though. Should a soul with such power abuse his or her gifts, or 'super human abilities', upon death they would have to start their cycle all over again ... in essence, they'd have to go straight back to being a rock, without any knowledge of higher existence.

Paul pondered the Maher Baba book; he remembered reading it many years ago in his father's library. He began to look at the extraordinary happenings he'd recently witnessed in the context of Maher Baba's teachings. Somehow, they didn't seem so weird any more. It was something he was familiar with.

The owner of the book had used her seat ticket as a bookmark and as Paul thumbed through the book, he found out that Kathmandu was her final destination ... and written on the ticket was the name of the same hotel his father was staying at!

This is not likely a coincidence, thought Paul. Gently he put the woman's books back in the same order in which he'd found them. Then he went back to first class to rejoin the rest of the team.

Meanwhile, in Kathmandu Jack was eagerly awaiting the incoming flight and preparing for everyone's arrival. He had some idea of the inflight activities since he had mind connections with both Andrew and Dan. He knew there had been some of the enemy spotted on board, but he was hopeful his strong group of allies were more than capable of handling any situation presented by the dark forces.

He and Harriet had decided to leave the hotel to return to the home they owned outside the city. He'd called ahead to his help staff and preparations were underway at his residence to create a comfortable, safe meeting place for the group. His home was a secure setting away from the city and that's what the group needed. Further preparations included having a highly trained security team stationed at the airport to bring the friends quietly into the country without too much scrutiny.

The extensive grounds of Jack's home were enclosed by high stone walls on all sides and protected by every type of modern security device. The property was gated and had only one entrance and exit, which were monitored 24 hours a day, every day of the year. More than 20 guards demonstrated a powerful presence.

The locals were unaware of the true nature of the imposing property; gossip-mongers declared the place was simply a large castle owned by an eccentric Englishman, who'd made his money back in England and now wanted to enjoy the solitude of a quiet environment. Little did they know that the family regarded as 'the owners' were simply trusted friends of Jack who were keeping the house active. This pretense allowed Jack and Harriet to come and go with without drawing attention.

Inside the gated estate were reserves of food, provisions enough to last for up to five years; a deep and protected water well, drilled strategically inside under the house; solar-powered generators; and, a vault stocked with a variety of currencies in amounts that would finance an army for many decades.

There was an underground labyrinth of shelters as well as an armory with enough ammunition and weaponry to defend a small country. Though outside, this imposing residence resembled a fair-sized castle, few knew of the extent of the reserves held underneath it; it just appeared, inside and out, to be a luxurious home.

Jack was proud of this amazing estate he'd built. It had taken 20 years of careful planning and blood, sweat and tears. But it was what he had envisioned for the coming battle and he was more than pleased that it functioned also as a wonderful home. Very few had an inkling of its true purpose as a secure fortress.

Harriet interrupted his thoughts. "We better make our way home quickly," she said as she started packing their small suitcases. "Paul's plane was due to land shortly."

Jack met with his drivers for a last briefing before they left to pick up his friends and family from the airport. The plan was that Jack would drive with Harriet to the residence to ensure everyone's comfort had been provided for by the staff. Jack wanted all guests to feel welcome and at home ... and Harriet, the ultimate hostess, planned to focus on the menus for the coming weeks.

Harriet, lost in her world of medical troubles, had always known there was something different and powerful about her husband, but she didn't care to know more. She focused on her own life and so was oblivious to her husband's involvement in the intrigues that shaped him. To her, it was a testament to her husband's most endearing feature, his love for his wife and family and his desire to protect her from all troubles were what motivated him, and that was enough for her.

Their residence was over an hour's drive away, but considering it was late in the afternoon, and they were driving against the flow, the journey was lighter than they expected, and they could make it to their home in the country within 45 minutes. It helped that they were riding in Jack's sleek Aston

Martin DB5, which he owned because he always liked the association with Bond.

However, Jack did not take the normal, direct route home ... that would have left him open to the power that pursued him, and he was careful to be aware of watchful eyes and not take unnecessary chances.

It didn't help, though. Just as Jack was warming up to the rugged, but graceful, maneuvering of his 1962 car, he sensed he was being followed. He didn't immediately adjust speed or direction, but his awareness became more tuned in as he noticed a white SUV maintaining the same speed and distance behind him.

He thought it was careless of his pursuer to bring such an obvious vehicle on a chase during the clear light of day; however, he knew the enemy feared no-one. Their arrogance made them all-the-more dangerous. Human life was meaningless and that included their own lives too. They would die for their cause and others would replace them. There were so many in their flock that even losing a few thousand would not make a dent in their force.

As Jack planned his next move, he noticed a fallen tree across the winding roadway. Now he had a chance to use some of the tools he had available to him in his 'Bond DB5'! After all, it wasn't a dumb replica, as people thought ... he had it fitted with *many* toys. Before acting, however, with a wave of his hand he induced Harriet to sleep. Then he checked her seatbelt, which had been upgraded to the highest level of safety when he'd had fitted the car with the new safety technology he needed.

When he was sure Harriet was safe, he flipped a switch on the dash that instantly released a small, front-loaded missile he had stashed under the car's front hood. It launched quickly and hit its target cleanly, managing to clear a path through the tree. At the same time, it discharged an array of small, barbed nails onto the roadway behind them. When the SUV hit the nails, it blew out all fours tires. It was over in a few seconds, ending when the SUV tumbled down a steep cliff and exploded in a ball of fire.

Jack simply smiled and then returned to enjoying a quiet drive. It was too quiet; he waved his hand and his darling Harriet woke, surprised to have dozed off on this short ride home. She apologized for being rude and said, "I don't understand why I drifted off, darling. I had such a nice, relaxing few days of being pampered at the hotel with massages and visits to the spa each day ... I don't know how I could possibly be so tired!"

Jack smiled and took her hand as they drove on. "Don't worry, my lady, you're just catching up with your old man. You need your naps now that you're over 50!"

At this, Harriet gave a playful slap to Jack's knee and they both laughed, enjoying the warmth of each other company, of which neither of them had grown tired. The remaining journey was uneventful.

As Jack approached the gate of their stately home, Paul called and announced the plane had landed safely. "I have some stories to tell," he said, "and one or two new guests will be joining us, if you don't mind."

"I'm going to assume you met Andrew," Jack said, "And I'm sure you're happy to have met your new Asian friend, a lovely lady and long-term associate of mine. She will be introduced properly when you all get here and have freshened up."

"Oh my God, I knew there was something about her ..." Paul laughed, knowing his father was once again in charge. Jack was a capable leader and would bring sense and security to the situation.

"Take care ... and rest assured my guys will look after your safe passage through customs," Jack said to his son. Then he added, "Follow their instruction as you are transported from the airport."

At that, the phone clicked into silence. Paul looked around to make sure all the team members were accounted for and, satisfied they were safe in the hands of his father's trusted security team, they proceeded through the airport. Already two of the security men were attending to the troublemakers who had accompanied them on the plane. Those were ushered into a private room with Customs officers following behind.

At last, Paul felt he could relax. They were in safe hands and had been loaded into three military-style 'punishers', the Russian version of a Humvee and were now speeding away from the airport in close formation.

What Paul didn't know was that they were much safer than he thought; drones had monitored them, courtesy Jack. They'd been unnoticed by the team, but they brought comfort to him and they followed the convoy as extra security. They were capable of engaging any threat and were the 'eyes' looking in all directions to keep his newly assembled team safe.

Chapter 8

A Gathering of Clans

Dark matter, the glue holding the universe together, is the subject of much speculation. Scientists agree it exists but have yet to define what it consists of. However, it is generally accepted that dark matter has an interactive connection with all matter, anti-matter, time and space. From Jack's perspective, dark matter was as essential gravity. He firmly believed that, if not for its influence in the cosmos, we would not exist.

The individuals colluding to disrupt the movements of Jack's team seemed to understand dark matter better than Jack and to be able to use it to their advantage; after all, their very existence had to do with the darkness that was growing in the collective mind of humankind. *The link between 'dark matter' and these 'dark forces' is not so far apart and they are equally powerful,* thought Jack.

Throughout time, this dark enemy travelled the corridors of power, influencing the decisions of leaders, causing wars in the name of nations; removing whole generations of people through genocide until finally arriving at this point in time ... for a final push toward chaos. It was up to Jack and his team to stop them.

History records shadow and light, and each disaster the world has faced has, for the most part, included facets of both yin and yang. For example, the atrocities inflicted on the Jews during World War II had the positive effect of lessening discrimination. The horrific battles between Muslims and Christians during the crusades. The message quietly arising from conversations about faith ultimately must revolve not around religious differences, but the nature of good and evil.

However, thought Jack, *the evil that faces us now seems to have no end and will go in only one direction. I can't let that happen.* Therein lay the dilemma confronting him and his peacemaking team: since the evil force that was growing fed on evil from the minds of humankind, what was the best strategy for he and his team fight it? He needed to tap into a another power source.

Dan was having similar thoughts as he travelled with the group to the safety of Jack's fortress and he was keen to get to Jack's and start working with the team to help them prepare for the worst kind of war ... one which could cost them their home—Earth—and remove humans from existence.

He looked over at Ian, who was also deep in thought. While Dan and Jack had some idea what was in the package, Ian did not. And now that things were getting so strange with their journey, the words written on the package were starting to really make him curious. 'Do not open in the event of my death' ... He wondered, *whose death does this refer to?*

Initially, he'd thought the statement was Jack's ... but now he felt it was someone else who'd created that instruction and that Jack had simply passed it on. *The message is so puzzling,* he thought to himself, *like a riddle. I wish I knew who wrote it.* If the author of this instruction was dead, then it would never get opened and no one would know the contents of the package. So why would anyone care? But the individuals chasing them across the globe clearly care, and probably knew what it was. It seemed they wanted to obtain the package and use its contents for an evil purpose. He wished Jack would tell them more, but he trusted that in time he would understand.

Ian had never flat-out asked Dan or Jack if they knew what the contents of the package were. He was aware that whatever was in there, none of the team could know because they could not protect their minds and hide the knowledge from their evil pursuers. As he sat there thinking about it, Dan said, "The knowledge will arrive when you need it, and not before."

"Were you reading my mind?" asked Ian. Dan just smiled.

Ian knew Jack and Dan were lifetime friends; he also respected and admired Dan and knew him to be of good character and a loyal companion to Jack. But he didn't know when, how and why Dan got mixed up in the situation they were facing. Was Dan the cause? Or the effect? Chicken or egg? Dan's friendly demeanor and humble attitude to life indicated that he was more of a follower ... but was it possible that he was the leader of it all? Was it possible he was the author of that strange directive?

I have too many questions, thought Ian.

He was still hoping for answers when they arrived at Jack and Harriet's fortress, a reunion with his good friend he was looking forward to. He nudged Paul awake. Paul had slept most of the way to his parents' place and was quietly snoring when Ian woke him. As he woke, he enjoyed noticing that April was fast asleep with her head unwittingly on his shoulder.

This had not gone unnoticed by Ian, but he didn't mind too much. They were both two 'innocents' and it was amusing to watch them connect. He looked forward to bringing the subject up, when appropriate, sometime over the next few days.

In the second vehicle, Anthony, James, Andrew and the Asian lady—who Jack had insisted they bring with them, and who was still drifting in and out of the slumber imposed on her in the plane—rode together. A tail vehicle contained four of Jack's security team, and it kept the group in a convoy formation like that used for heads of state.

Andrew was attempting to identify what was familiar about the beautiful Asian lady. He felt he'd seen her somewhere before and wondered whether she was Chinese or Korean. She didn't look Thai or Cambodian. As he stared at her, she startled awake.

"So, you're trying to figure me out ... it's rude to stare, you know," she stated. Then she smiled a dreamy smile that made Andrew turn a bright red. "I'm Elena and you must be Andrew. I sensed you probing my mind earlier on the plane."

"How did you manage to block me? I've never had any trouble seeing or feeling another's thoughts," said Andrew.

"My dear friend, you talked of millions of years of travelling, but I guess you're getting too old to remember me," said Elena, intriguingly.

Andrew shifted a little uneasily in his seat but understood what she was saying. Then suddenly he remembered her, and he said, "It's been a few millennia and generations of incarnations, but we continue to find each other, don't we! I think the most recent incarnation with you was not on this world, though. But I'm sure we were together for a lifetime ... and we were happy."

Elena was pleased that he remembered her. "Yes, we were on one of three companion planets circling binary stars," she said. "It was a wonderful solar system. Each planet was close enough to travel to within a few months. Do you remember?"

"I do!" exclaimed Andrew. "It was perfect. All beings had evolved beyond wars and enjoyed the transition between birth and death because they looked forward to adventures in their coming lives! It was a place of such peace!"

Andrew suddenly felt love in the pit of his stomach, as if he was on a first date with a cherished woman. He knew he had loved Elena before and for many lifetimes. Emotion overtook him, and tears flowed down his cheeks as he reached out to her.

She had been lost in his human memory until this moment but now, with no words spoken, their spirits had found each other after millennia. Their silent embrace remained throughout the journey.

Anthony and James, unaware of the nature of Andrew and Elena's reunion, were deep in conversation about roles and expectations for the team. After witnessing the strange events on the plane, both were surprised at their friends' fantastic abilities. This made them wonder how *they* would contribute to Jack's plan, but they both knew Jack well enough to realize they must be here for a good reason. If nothing else, their human skills would be useful. Anthony was an accomplished engineer and pilot and James a rally driver with cooking skills. It might not be much when surrounded by super beings, but at least it was something.

Finally, they drove up to Jack's security gate and were guided safely into the courtyard where welcoming family, friends and house attendants awaited. Paul felt as if he'd been transported back to Elizabethan England and was coming home to the family manor, with servants waiting to attend to their every whim. *What a transition*, he thought, *from the fast and commercial world of America*. Not to mention, from the beautiful but chilly mountains of the Lakes District where he'd most recently been.

His parents' home featured every comfort a person could desire. His dad had first started building it in 1960, using stone quarried at England's Lakes District and shipped to Nepal. It had taken him decades to finish and Paul had lived there as much of the work was going on. As soon as he saw the building, Paul felt the memories of his childhood flooding back into his soul. The sound of crushed pebbles underfoot also reminded Paul of his youth. He had spent many years riding his bike on long summer afternoons on the gravel driveway.

It was dark, but his father had some high visibility lights installed that showed off the English garden his mother had created to remind her of home. She had also cultivated many south Asian plants and trees and he knew that every detail had been overseen by her. It was all so wonderful. For a moment he wished he had never left home and wanted, at least in this instant, to never leave again.

As soon as she saw him, she called out, "Saul!" He smiled at his nickname, which only his mother used—a reference to the story of Saul, who lost his sight for three days while on the road to Damascus. In Paul's case it was a bang to the head after falling from his bicycle that made him see stars. But Paul loved the reference; it made him feel regal and helped create a special relationship with his mother.

"Mum!" he called to her as she ran toward him and held him in the tightest embrace; the kind that only a mother offers a son.

"You look tired, let's get you settled in," she said. "Then she turned to April, who had been standing right behind Paul and kissed her fondly.

"April, so good to see you and Ian again," she said. "I hope you are well. If it's possible to describe someone as radiantly tired, that's what you are! And you are as beautiful as ever!"

At that, Harriet guided the team toward a welcoming doorway. Jack stood in the entrance, with open arms, smiling broadly. He was delighted to bring his family and close friends under his protection once again. "Come, you must all be exhausted. We have a warm house filled with comfortable beds where you can all relax and sleep until the drain of the past few days is removed from your mind and body," he said. "And then we will enjoy our days ahead while planning the future of humanity!" He stated this light-heartedly and so no one knew that he really meant it.

Ian was delighted to now be able to pass the responsibility of the team on to Jack who welcomed him with a strong, manly embrace, as if he was recharging Ian's energy in reward for bringing them all safely to his castle. Ian was delighted to pass the responsibility of the team on to Jack.

Jack said, "Anthony, Dan, James, Andrew ... and finally, Elena, welcome to you all! Now let's get inside before the night brings the chilly mountain air of the evening inside!"

As the group moved happily into the security of this well-guarded fortress, Jack greeted Elena with a special fatherly hug and whispered in her ear, "I'm especially happy to see you, young lady, welcome! And I'm sure you had time to meet your Andrew again." At that, he smiled and ushered her in to follow the rest.

Elena had never been here before, but it instantly felt like she was at home, that this was a place she possibly had been in a past life. There was a feeling that warmed her from the inside and brought a silent, happy tear.

Jack's household employees busily attended to the distribution of luggage and had ensured that a light snack awaited the hungry guests in the dining room. They made sure everyone was comfortable—which wasn't too difficult given their luxurious surroundings and accommodation. The rooms in the castle would bring shame to the best penthouse suites money could buy!

The group was tired, but after quickly freshening up and changing their clothes, they were delighted to partake in some tasty finger food. The servants had laid out everything from sausage rolls, to beans on toast, accompanied by Earl Grey tea and scones, in the best of British traditions. Everything was deliciously fresh, yet not too filling, leaving room for those who wished to wash the snacks down with light wine or beer. Some softened their resistance to sleep with a nice, glowing cognac—but all, in the end, quietly drifted off to bed. It was so peaceful it seemed that even the house settled into a warm, silent slumber. The only people still alert were the ever-aware security team, whose professionalism enabled all the guests to forget the purpose for their trip and enjoy a relaxing sleep.

Jack's home featured 25 bedrooms, each with its own bathroom; an elaborate and well-stocked wine cellar; an oak-paneled library of thousands of books; a private study; a conference room; an auditorium; a snooker and games room; several luxurious lounges with castle-style open fireplaces; a gourmet kitchen that any five-star restaurant would be proud of; an indoor swimming pool; a gym and sauna; and, finally, servants' quarters. It also had the underground bunkers, though all the team except for Dan remained unaware of that for the moment.

This extensive basement contained the most important aspects of this fortress, as it was the home of the substantial armory and defense system, that the team might need for the upcoming battle. Whether or not it was needed would be determined in the next few days.

As night fell around the castle, the guests remained safely tucked in bed while the security 'knights' kept constant watch throughout the extensive grounds, guarding every door. A second security team was in the basement, monitoring an advanced video system that extended well beyond the castle walls and into virtually every corner of the nearby village.

But watch as they might, they could not see that in a chasm deep beneath the surface of the earth, not far from Jack's fortress, a malevolent force was gathering. Without form it stirred in darkness. Shapeless and nameless, neither eyes nor ears could detect its existence—let alone security systems—but still it was there, waiting, like a thought. The earth had never felt such a presence before and every element of Gaia's awareness told her something terrible, old but unborn, lingered. No being existing on earth or in its waters was able to feel the change that was about to come except Gaia herself. Something strange and dangerous was about to exist in this part of the universe for the very first time.

Jack and Dan were the only two souls who understood what this force was. They had encountered it millions of years ago and billions of light years away. But they were now becoming aware that it was so very close to them. Very few had an inkling that such an entity existed; it had never been documented and was nowhere in man's history, not even in mythology. Jack and Dan were right to fear it; they knew its power and that it was sentient. They knew it was motivated. They knew it could quite easily wipe out humanity.

As the rest of the group slumbered, only Jack and Dan remained awake. These two had retired to the library with perfectly warmed brandies. They sat, comfortable in Elizabethan lounge chairs, ready to discuss recent events and plan the days ahead.

"I'm relieved you all made it here safely and that, at least for a few days, we will be unhindered by the men who are chasing us. My contacts have had them followed and I regret to inform you that there are quite a few of them ... but no one really knows what they're chasing, or why," Jack whispered, as if he concerned the air itself could hear him.

Then Dan told Jack of Andrew's actions on the plane and how he had induced the passengers into silent sleep, avoiding any trouble posed by certain individuals. "There was a tall, middle-aged man who had been following us since London," Dan said. "I'm not certain of his motivation, but with the help of your security teams we lost him at the airport when we arrived. Other than that, our new lady friend, Elena, has reunited with Andrew and I'm sure they're playing catch-up in one of your rooms," said Dan with a smile.

"Paul and the others will have a chance to understand their mission better over the next few days when I open their memory to hidden past experiences," Dan continued. "At least they've had a chance to enjoy a normal human life without any burden of who they really are and why we're together at this place and time. Not so for us Jack, my old friend," said Dan, raising his glass in salute.

"By 'old friend' I'm sure you mean 'old soul'," remarked Jack. "You and I are certainly that. Our journey has been so interesting ... we've travelled so far. It's restricting to now be embodied in human form and limited to earth-bound activities ... I'm so grateful for the extraordinary abilities we've gained over these millions of years. It will help us in this upcoming war."

Dan said, "Yes, and we live longer than the average human ... but as you know, the Old Testament has recorded many characters who lived for hundreds of years. So, we're not alone. I don't know about you, but I've enjoyed this visit to this temporal plane and have found myself feeling quite close to our human companions."

"We should retire now and enjoy a few hours of sleep in the safety of this fortress," Jack suggested. "We don't have to worry because it's not only guarded by the 'knights' of my security team, but by advanced artificial intelligence. I have eyes and ears throughout the region."

They embraced before heading off to sleep.

As the night progressed, from a distant galaxy, a being from the earliest universe set sail for Earth. No one person or thing had the ability to detect its arrival; not Jack, not Dan and not Andrew. It would simply appear at will whenever it desired.

Chapter 9

Awakening

The real meaning of being human is lost in time, hidden in the eons, thought Dan as he pondered how to approach helping his friends recover their memories of their past selves and true natures. *Being human has blinded us to our true nature. We live in these body-vessels but forget that we are* not *our bodies and thoughts; we are the one who says 'I am'...*

He looked around the walls of his bedroom. He had so much to tell them.

Our ego says, 'I am ... mortal', thereby defining our destiny because of our mortal free will. However, soon humankind will remember ... and they will recognize that the soul-state is our true being ... that we are immortal. He would start today to teach that to the team.

The aroma of fresh coffee sent its inviting smell throughout the house, attracting the well-rested travelers into the salubrious dining room. Inside the room, they were greeted by the sight of a well-stocked table featuring a breakfast of sausage, egg, bacon, black pudding, beans, toast, yogurt, fruit and cereal.

Lighthearted banter filled the room as the friends ate their breakfast. Laughter and stories created a feeling of comfort.

Even though only a few of them could remember their past lives, everyone sensed that the camaraderie they were experiencing went beyond this time and space.

Paul's whole family was there; the surprise of the early morning arrival of Paul's sister Naomi, looking a little travel weary, but bright and smiling as usual, was a good one.

As the morning progressed, some of Jack's guests took a pleasant walk around the sun-dappled grounds and along the riverside to help relieve their overfilled bellies. After a few hours, the guests drifted back to the castle to meet with Jack and Dan in the relaxed surroundings of the massive living room. They sat on comfortable couches and helped themselves to pots of coffee and tea laid out for them.

"I hope everyone is now relaxed and your bellies are filled with our home-made English breakfast," said Jack. The people in the room responded with groans indicating that they all had over-filled bellies. "Thanks to Naomi for flying in this morning to complete our group," he said, acknowledging his tired daughter.

Everyone turned to look at her and greetings were exchanged.

"You may wonder why we're gathered, but all will be revealed soon. Dan, if you would be so kind, please help me by telling this group our purpose and why we are gathered," said Jack, inviting Dan to begin his presentation.

"Some of you will find what I'm about to say preposterous and a little unnerving, but as the morning rolls on, you'll understand more," smiled Dan as he engaged all with direct eye contact. "First, a small display," he said, nodding in Andrew's direction. Andrew stood up and looked directly at Paul ... who within seconds, fell fast asleep. Most in the room gasped in concern, thinking Paul had passed out, and a few started to move toward him.

"It's not necessary to give Paul aid; he is quite safe and he's only sleeping," said Dan, raising his arms to calm the guests. "Please rest assured that we would never harm him or anyone in our group." He carried on. "You have just seen that a simple gesture from Andrew has induced Paul into a deep sleep. With another gesture ..." again he nodded to Andrew, who waved his arm again, and immediately woke Paul up, "You can see our friend has become fully alert without any recollection of what just happened."

Dan placed a caring hand on Paul's shoulder. Paul, after glancing around the room, understood that once again Andrew had used his ability. He appeared a bit bemused and said, "So you did it again!"

There were gasps from the surprised audience and they demanded an explanation. Jack said, "This was a simple demonstration of what is inside each of you. This is the key to understanding who you really are. You see, we are all able to do extraordinary things using philosophy and techniques learned over time by each one of us." Confused glances met Jack's statement.

"The next moments will help answer any questions you may have," said Dan. Then he raised his hands and caught everyone in a trance. "Please listen carefully to my voice and only my voice ... your thoughts are completely free to wander where they will. I ask that you feel the release of a hidden door opening within the depth of your mind."

He paused, giving time for his subjects to feel the synaptic channels unfolding in the deep recesses of their minds, revealing hidden memories of past lives and old, familiar places. "The recollections you might have may be uncomfortable ... they may even be painful," he warned, "But most likely, a strange feeling will simply flood your mind with memories that initially don't seem real and have the appearance of dreams."

He paused again, letting each person's thoughts fill their individual universe, waiting for changes within their brains to begin. He thought about the unused capacity within each human's brain and telepathically instructed certain closed doors inside their brain to allow synaptic transmission. Dan was able to control signaling molecules, called neurotransmitters, and to ensure they reached appropriate receptors. In doing so, the memories of the past lives of all the people in this room could be accessed by their human 'free will' brain. Once these hidden memories were rediscovered and 'hooked up' to real time, what would be regarded as 'super human' functions, currently lying dormant, could be brought to the fore. The abilities each of the team members had were learned over many lifetimes and, at the moment of re-birth, were imprinted into their individual brains, just waiting to be awakened. In most cases, as each human lived his or her life, these memories and abilities were never recovered unless circumstances jolted the neurotransmitters into action ... or unless Dan nudged the neurotransmitters into action.

"As you feel the overwhelming flood of information coming into your mind, I ask you to allow yourselves to slowly—very slowly—open your eyes as if you've been sleeping for a long time and are trying to avoid being blinded by the flow of light bouncing off your retinas. *Slowly* ... Please focus on my voice and as your eyes open I'll give you a subliminal message that only your awareness can interpret. It is not a word, but more of a thought."

At that moment everyone became aware of being back in the room and in the company of friends. But none of them were clear about what had just happened. However, they all felt an expansive knowledge they couldn't explain.

"You'll all feel a little strange, as if a thousand university courses have been crushed into a few hours of study—but without the exhaustive effects such studying would cause on the physical body and brain. Relax, my travelling companions, and as the day unfolds you'll notice new and old memories merge as your being completes its metaphysical reincarnation. Everyone will be returned to their true origin and place in time. You will still be the person that entered *this* life, and your character will not change, yet you will be different because you've inherited your right to be aware once again," Dan delivered this message while knowing it would not be fully understood.

"Please rest now," added Jack, "And feel free to sleep or do anything that will allow you to relax and absorb the flood of information that has been shared with you. We will meet again at dinner. We will have a celebratory meal, for this is a special occasion for us all!"

Gladly, each one left, quietly drifting away to find solitude so they could grasp what had invaded their thoughts. When they were gone, Jack said to Dan, "Some will come around quicker than others, but all will be essential to the tasks ahead."

"We might as well have a rest ourselves, especially as we are still free of any approaching danger," announced Dan, stretching his senses far beyond the confines of the castle grounds to double check for threats. Then he followed Jack as he wandered into his library to retrieve the package that had caused them both such turmoil.

"We've both wondered about the contents of this ... but what can we make of the numbers 10, 04, 1941?" asked Jack.

"I used to think they were geographical coordinates," said Jack. "Those longitude and latitude coordinates matches a location in the centre of Africa. The coordinate of 10:04 north and 19:41 east takes us to a desolate area in Chad, in Africa. Reversing the 10 the 04 only moves us a little south, into Democratic Republic of Congo in the middle of a forest," Jack said. "But I doubt the coordinates are the answer. Of course, we both know that's the date, in British order, of my birthday

... but as you and I know, it was in your uncle's possession before I was born."

"Yes," agreed Dan. "I was made aware of this package in my early childhood by my uncle Frazer. He's 95 now ... and he still resides at his home is Scotland." Jack nodded. He'd met the man a few times. "He gave it to me in the strangest of situations," Dan continued. "I must have been seven or eight years old and he would have been in his mid-twenties at the time. I visited his family in Prestwick, as my family was taking a short holiday in Troon, just a few miles north on the Scottish coast. I remember the lovely sand dunes beside the sea— hills of pure white sand—and how much fun we had playing hide and seek in the long grass. What a wonderful area and a beautiful country!"

Jack nodded agreement. "Yes, I've been there," he said.

Dan continued, "After a brisk, windy day on the beach, we joined my uncle and his family at a large house facing Prestwick beach. We felt it was a mansion, as it had over 10 rooms. My cousins and I played games throughout the house and Frazer never once stopped our noisy squawking."

Dan paused to sip his brandy, which had just arrived, thanks to the perfect timing of Jack's butler who. Dan realized they hadn't been introduced.

"Hey there, good fellow. What is your name?" asked Dan.

"I'm sorry sir, please call me Arthur, Mr. Flynn."

"You're very kind Arthur and your timing is impeccable, thank you," responded Dan with sincere appreciation.

"What do you mean by 'strangest of situations'?' reminded Jack.

"Well it was clear Frazer wasn't short of money. He was living in luxury and never suffered the shortages that affected most of the nation as we entered World War II. His wife was what one would today describe as a 'super model' beautiful. She had a perfectly proportionate body and beautiful, Scandinavian features and she was charismatic to boot. And she didn't suffer the perfectionist paranoia that many beautiful people today seem to suffer from. She was a loving wife, but they did not have children. However, they welcomed us into their world without conditions."

"They sound like a lovely couple," said Jack.

"This place we were staying was only his *weekend* home. The family estate where they lived with his father and mother was in the Highlands. His duties were to look after the estate and ensure it was kept in the expected manner of aristocracy. The family had lineage going back to Clan Bruce, but Frazer never talked about his heritage."

He stopped and took another sip.

"The strange situation I was going to tell you about was the quiet, secret way in which Frazer brought me into his library and told me he had a very important package to be held in safe-keeping until needed. I thought it was very strange and as he continued, he began whispering and looking around him to ensure no one was in the room or close by. 'Daniel,' he said, 'You have to be prepared to protect this with your life. You are the true successor of this package and one day you will know your gifts are extraordinary compared to those of your friends.' Then we held a small ceremony."

"Do you remember the ceremony?" asked Jack

"Only that it caused a little pain. Then he told me, 'You are now its custodian.' He also said my 'talents', as he put it, must be kept private and only should be used when absolutely necessary. And he gave me money. He said, 'You will never want for anything, as I have provided a stipend for you, my only nephew. It may be used for whatever purpose you desire. I only ask that you use it wisely.'"

Dan continued, "Strangely, here I am, 75 years of age, and I've drawn on the stipend every month of my life, yet it continues to accumulate at a daily rate. I doubt I'll ever exhaust the funds." Dan smiled thankfully and glanced around the room, as if looking for his loving uncle Frazer. "I was set for the rest of my life and was not even ten years of age yet. I'd been entrusted with an important package, and my only instructions were to keep it safe and use the funds he'd given me wisely. Then Frazer continued with his soft whispering and explained that the package had travelled far, and all its owners had never died while it was in their possession. As you know, it's a heavy responsibility. 'Do not open in the event of my death' is motive to stay alive, don't you think?"

They both looked at the package, which was similar in size to a shoebox, as it lay on the table, still wrapped neatly in the strongest of brown paper and, after all this time, without even a hint of a dent or tear. The seal, a large, circular, waxed stamp, was prominent over the folded paper and the package was further secured by twine, double-wound around the box. The stamp embossed into the wax seal was like a crest but was worn beyond recognition due to the changing temperatures it had been exposed to over the years. The handwriting declaring the message was written clearly but in an older, cursive style, immaculately penned. Strangely, it hadn't diminished in clarity.

"Back when my uncle gave it to me, he ensured I was provided with a safe hiding place to protect the package by arranging for a private lockbox at the Prestwick post office," Dan went on. "In those days, that post office emulated a Swiss Bank security vault!"

Jack laughed at this. "I kid you not," said Dan. "It was a high security place."

"Go on," said Jack.

"I was given the only key and Frazer showed me how to place the box in the vault and what security was required to gain access. At that time, we used old-fashioned padlocks. The back room where we stored it was accessible only to me and I had the only key. I went regularly over the next 15 years to check it, but eventually I decided to move it to a proper Swiss bank security vault, as the new manager of the post office looked suspiciously at me every time I visited. In place, I left behind a small fund I can access in case of emergency. I have examined this package every which way, looking for hints about what's inside, but I have never figured it out. I even researched the history of owners, which goes back over generations. But that's another story."

Jack picked up the package and weighed it in his hand; it was not overly heavy, nor did it feel light enough to be empty. The careful packaging of the contents ensured no movement, no rattling whatsoever. He carried it nearer the warmth of the open fire, turning it gently while exposing every side to the heat. Then, looking carefully at each surface as it turned in his hands, slowly but distinctly some further writing appeared. It was at that moment that Paul returned from his afternoon nap and so Jack gently rested the package on his side table as he glanced at an excited Dan.

"Paul, my son, finally you're up ... and hopefully you're more enlightened and rested." Jack carefully examined Paul to see if he had truly awakened or was simply drifting through the memories."

"Hi, dad. I'm fine and if you are wondering, I'm here now ... but I also know who I am, past and present and I'm ready to help with our next steps." Then Paul asked with a smile, "I never thought I had travelled through so many lives and now, strangely, I feel even younger than my age. What did you do to me, Dan? And what causes people to forget their other lives? How could I live so far into this life and be unaware of all the things I am?"

"It's not unusual, son," Jack said. "Sometimes we never find our way, as the circumstances in each life aren't always conducive to recollection. When that happens to a soul, we drift through our memories as dreams, never understanding what they are telling us. Sometimes we even meet individuals who were our soul partners in previous lives and we hardly give each other a passing glance. Déjà vu can cause freak seconds of recognition, but human conditioning tends to dismiss these occurrences as tricks of the intellect. Within moments these tiny reminders are gone. Ultimately, we struggle to understand simple hints and fail to connect the dots. It can take many lifetimes just to understand that there's something else going on behind the scenes of the material plane."

Paul nodded, so glad to be whole for the first time in this life.

"Come, sit down and join us," offered Dan. Paul nodded his thanks and sat down. Then he said, "I know all of you ... we've bounded between many lives and keep touching each other's paths. It seems that every time we're together, it's a roller coaster ride. So, are you telling me all humanity is like this, that we all carry our souls through multiple lives?" Paul delivered his question in earnest, but his serious concerns were met only with lighthearted laughter from Jack and Dan.

"Everyone is at different stages of evolution," answered Dan. "We repeat and repeat, a bit like Groundhog Day, but without the 24-hour sequence. So many billions of souls, each contributing to reality, each hoping to grow and build a better human race. One ocean, many drops. We all arrive at the same place in the end."

Dan paused to ensure Paul understood.

"Where is the divine in this? Is God active or passive?" asked Paul.

"That's a good question; however, the answer is neither. The divine source is an observer who holds the universe stable. He, she or it is surprised and sometimes delighted by our meanderings, heroic deeds and unfortunate stumbles. We all play the roles we were sent here to play and we all return home when our tasks are done. It's the great mystery of being ... 'Let it be,' as the Fab Four declared."

"But I see you, Dad, as if you have been by my side in different guises, yet always there," Paul exclaimed.

"And you, by mine," responded Jack with compassion. "Ours is not to reason why, only to do our part when called upon and never doubt our purpose. It's our place in time. We are here together, and in this time, facing a challenge like never before."

Dan added, "We need everyone to be aware of what's around the corner. We need to plan and decide what we will do about the situation ahead. We don't question why; we must just do what we are meant to do."

"I feel real danger," Paul said gravely. "I can't see what it is, but I suspect it's got everything to do with that package." Paul pointed directly to the table on which the package sat, the heat-activated writing Jack and Dan had discovered earlier now faded.

"Just so," answered Jack. "Even with all our collective abilities, we don't know its content and are not free to open it and discover what's inside. Our agenda is not to interfere, but to protect. That's our duty for the moment. I've had the package scanned by X-ray machines and ultrasound equipment ... but it's as if the box is lined with lead and nothing is visible. We are not to know its contents until the time is appointed."

Where once Paul would have been confounded by this statement, now he knew exactly what his father meant.

"Tonight, we'll confer everyone at dinner," continued Jack. "Then we'll prepare our next steps before the dark energies gathering around us get too close. We must be prepared in case they try to force our hand. A stable, silent mind is essential. Every strong reaction has a way of telling the enemy who and where we are. We need to maintain calmness and hold friendship and love high. The softness of love and friendship is the greatest strength we have. Division and negativity attract and expose weak links, however small."

Paul nodded his understanding and gave his father a hug, which Jack returned with a warm embrace of his own. Then Jack said, "Dinner will be in the garden this evening. We'll meet everyone out there around five o'clock. We're fortunate the weather is unusually mild for this time of year."

Later, the group gathered for dinner on the front lawn, which had been converted into an outdoor restaurant. The tables featured delicacies to meet all appetites and tastes and the group had a feast, the way armies do before a battle. Although most hadn't yet a clue, this was the beginning of preparation for war, and the gathered group would soon be the last barrier between Earth as they knew it and a force last seen before the Earth existed.

As they enjoyed the feast, all marveled at the way they were re-engaging and regenerating. Their energy was gathering power and those who had an eye to see noticed the glow surrounding their assembly, an indestructible force field ... at least for now. Until they met the darkness emerging from the depths, which as yet was still unnoticed by any of them despite their heightened senses, they were untested. How can you foresee what's never been experienced?

The entity was growing stronger by the minute, even though it was not aware of its own existence. Having never formulated a thought, it had not yet considered what to do with its new life. Soon it would be born.

Chapter 10

The Challenge

We all face challenges in life, some simple and solvable, others avoidable, but certain trials cannot be ignored and must be faced. The more difficult challenges define us and allow us to shine—or demonstrate to us that we are not ready when we fail.

Naomi hadn't opened her eyes yet, but she was already thinking about the challenges that lay ahead. She wondered what her role would be, what part she would play to help curb the situation the world was un-knowingly facing.

Upon receiving the gift of realizing who she truly was, and what her past lives had taught her, she felt reborn. The sudden return of vast memories was like remembering movies she'd been in, sometimes as a star and sometimes an observer. Conversely, she also felt a loss of innocence; she'd liked the simple life she'd led as Naomi, Paul's sister and co-owner of their successful filtration business. She'd enjoyed the luxurious lifestyle she'd led, and, at 29 years of age, felt lucky to be young, single and financially secure. Now that life was gone and her innocence with it; yet without her new awareness she would have no appreciation of that in the first place. It was a mixed blessing, this new power. She'd lost something, but she also had a greater understanding of the beauty of the world.

Naomi was a beautiful, raven-haired Irish woman. Born in the Emerald Isle during her parents' many years there, she and Paul had a close connection to the land of leprechauns. They had moved there after her parents tired of living in Nepal. Naomi was fluent in Gaelic, having been taught it in school and she continued, on occasion, to converse with Paul in that singing language, as he also spoke it.

While she loved living in America, she missed the sense of humor and relaxed attitude of the Irish, a people so friendly and yet historically so badly treated. The Irish were strong and astute. They could see through human falseness much more quickly than other people.

As Naomi lay on the bed in her parent's house, she allowed her thoughts to travel and soon could see and feel the experiences of millennia as if they had happened yesterday. She smiled as she realized that in one past life she had been princess in a different land; not of earth, but from a similar planet. She could see oceans and mountains, grass and trees ... but the animals were different, unicorns were grazing, and much larger beasts that she couldn't identify roamed the land, all living together in the way that sheep and cattle share the pastures of England. In this world she was married to a prince who was handsome and strong but had slightly different features than humans, such as wider-set eyes and elvish ears—which she suddenly realized were her features as well, at least in that life. She was also taller and stronger and somehow moved more easily than she did on earth. She drew from her memories and understood that it was due to her former home having one-quarter the gravity of Earth. People could float or even fly short distances in that land. Now Naomi understood why humans often dream of flying; it is because we have memories of places and times in our soul's incarnations when we could do it.

It was so easy to drift from memory to memory, with the clearest pictures in such colorful detail in her mind. But suddenly she realized she felt strange, that something had changed. Eyes still closed, she felt around for her bed-covers and the mattress ... and to her absolute shock, discovered she was floating above the bed! As soon as she was aware of it, with a sudden bounce she crashed back to the mattress.

She looked around the room, wishing someone was there to witness what had happened. Of course, no one shared the moment she thought maybe she had fallen back asleep ...but when she moved to get out of bed, the sheets lifted of their own accord. Then, when she swung her legs over the side of the bed to stand up, she noticed her feet were not on the floor but instead were a little above it.

This is weird, she thought. Then she discovered she could move without any restrictions, in any direction—so she did. Immediately she lost control and crashed into the bedside table. She hit hard, but it was strangely painless. She reached down to right herself, expecting to fall over, but found that instead she balanced instinctively and without effort. Then she went to the sink and splashed cold water on her face to make sure she wasn't dreaming. She wasn't. She spent a few pleasant minutes floating around the room before a knock on her door, and the call of the maid to come in to clean her room, startled her and she crashed to the floor. She quickly stood up, back to normal and called out to the maid, "Come in. I'm just about to have a shower."

As Naomi prepared to join the late lunch in the garden, in another room just down the hall Andrew and Elena were getting ready for lunch as well after spending the last night passionately reconnecting. Andrew had recently become fully aware of his long and loving relationship with Elena. They had been together across many solar systems and had lived in both luxury and squalor and every circumstance in between over many lifetimes and on many planets. Unlike Andrew, Elena needed no reminder. She had been able to recall her past almost since birth due to a fast transition from her previous life. She knew, for example, that she had skills in telepathy and was able to move objects by thought. She was also able to stop a person's movement within a certain range.

Andrew had the same talents as Elena, but he also had an added ability to hypnotize those nearby, as he'd demonstrated on the plane. Andrew—until Dan unlocked his memory—did not have detailed knowledge of his previous lives, but he knew he had lived many times and now realized he was related in some way to the lovely Elena. But until Dan came along, he'd thought his skills to be a freak accident of nature. Now that everything from the past was clear in his mind, he was happy to see that many of the previous lives he'd had were shared with Elena. The love he felt for her was overwhelming. He quietly thanked God for his awakening and for being blessed enough to be with such a beautiful and kind human being.

"You're so beautiful, my handsome man," smiled Elena, embarrassed at catching Andrew's thoughts. It did not bother Andrew at all, since he had nothing to hide from her, the one who had loved and cared for him in many lifetimes and just as many worlds.

Down in the garden, James and Anthony relaxed while enjoying a fine buffet and an excellent pint of Guinness, straight from a barrel in Jack's beer and wine cellar. Jack always made sure it was stocked appropriately for the company that was expected. He'd had some special-order beer flown in just a week ago and the bottles were still fresh and chilled. They both were glowing—not from the fresh air or that first pint—but from the knowledge that they were not just 'rally driver' and 'engineer'. Instead, they had discovered that they were an accomplished pilot and aircraft engineer respectively ... and not only of human-designed craft, but also of craft of alien origin. They also had discovered they had aeronautic abilities that were advanced far beyond human technology. In comparison to the other members of their group, neither James nor Anthony had what could be described as super-human abilities, but their skills in relation to the aeronautic fleet were unique in this world. Only a few others knew as much as they, and they were working undercover as part of Jack's security team.

Jack met with James and Anthony just before lunch to let them know he had a fleet of fully operational aircraft stored underground only a few miles from their location and a direct hyper-loop connection to the airfield and subterranean facility. This hoard of passenger and powerful combat airliners was hidden so deep underground that even the best satellite imagery could not detect its existence.

"We finally understand why we are here, my friend," said Anthony. "I no longer feel like a useless prick being tolerated by our super-powered friends."

"I just want to get behind the controls of our toys and practice flying again," said James.

"Likewise," said Anthony. "And I was thinking the fleet might need an overhaul. I'm not sure if they've been maintained in recent years ... or potentially for a few centuries.

"Yes, and I want to be sure they're ready for takeoff!" piped in Anthony.

Ian and April stood close together. They had found out they were companions, not lovers, in previous existences and that their contribution to the company in this day and time was largely strategic—Ian's political and April's technical.

Ian had been a high-ranking leader connected to a planetary leader, on a planet where wars were no longer a cancer to society. In his previous incarnation, his responsibility was to manage and guide the expansion of his race to nearby stars, many light years away. In this life, his duty was to use his keen abilities to show why the global leaders of Earth, including the United Nations, needed to become aware of, and deal with, the catastrophe about to hit the earth.

April had an ability with artificial intelligence that was far beyond anything known on Earth. She didn't need a keyboard or a computer; she could read into any database by thought alone ... she simply expanded her awareness and could see through any camera in the world that was connected to the Internet. There were very few corners of the earth she could not connect with; only the places that had little or no technology. And even more importantly that her ability to connect was her ability to influence algorithms simply by using her thoughts to change a few digits or alter a few words. Through this, she could direct the future.

"I'm a little overwhelmed by my seriously powerful talent," she told Ian. "It scares me to know I can alter the future just by swapping a few letters or numbers! I could easily add digits to the poorest bank account and I can subtract even more from the accounts of billionaires."

Ian nodded. Everything she said was true. She was dangerous, in her own way.

She continued, "I could change the wording of the next presidential speech ... or switch the newspaper reports every morning ... or have fun texting a few misguided teenagers, bouncing their social media in any direction. It would be easy, as most people's minds are so weak they are unable to discern fact from fiction."

"But you're not going to do such things, are you?" Ian rested a hand affectionately on her shoulder and leaned in with a caring smile.

"Certainly not," beamed April. "But it would be fun," she added with a mischievous grin.

Jack walked into the garden as the group was at lunch, ready to update them on the task at hand. He had a heavy heart; the message he was about to deliver was not easy to present. His family and friends were, in this world, mortal—but the challenge ahead would affect not only this planet, but potentially the whole galaxy. Would the situation expand to galaxies and billions of earth-like planets too? He had no answer; he was concerned with how the incoming forces were going to alter *this* galaxy—and that had everything to do with his team.

Earth is 4.5 billion years old; our universe, according to latest findings, is 13.5 billion years old. According to the theory of evolution, man's ancestors have been around for about six million years, but modern man only evolved about 200,000 years ago. And only in the last 50 years has man has expanded technical knowledge ... a knowledge he seemed unprepared for, given the way it was being abused. *We are not yet ready for what is at our door—or on the doorstep of the Milky Way galaxy,* thought Jack.

Jack understood that the Milky Way galaxy was so vast it would take man four lightyears to reach the nearest star. To get to the outer regions it would take 100,000. At the speed of today's fastest vehicle, it would take 3,425,000 years to reach the outer limits of our galaxy. The fastest rocket humans have launched to date was the 'New Horizons' which reached almost 37,000 miles per hour—a snail's pace in the bigger picture. *We humans have a lot to learn*, thought Jack. Thankfully he was addressing some very aware humans today, but the burden was just as heavy.

"Thank you all for coming, willingly or not," laughed Jack. "As you may have realized, we are not gathered for a lawn party nor are we lucky enough to be celebrating our 'family and friends' reunion."

Pausing, Jack studied the group, then said, "We have a major undertaking to deal with in the coming weeks. Humans has no idea what's arriving on their doorstep. We've all watched many movies about alien invasions, and in those movies some clever tricks always help to defeat evil beings daring to challenge Earth's way of life."

Everyone nodded.

"There is intrinsic evil on our doorstep," Jack said seriously. "The entity that is currently awakening is attracting a massive army. Records of this entity do not exist in any of humanity's libraries, nor is it recorded as a mythical creature. But it is coming for Earth and will be here soon. Therefore, the first task before us is to educate the people of Earth—from the highest to the lowest level—without instilling fear in order to prepare them. They must protect themselves. And they must prepare for a different future."

He looked around to see if there were questions. Everyone sat in rapt attention, although they looked a little confused.

"Until yesterday, you were earthlings in many ways, but Dan opened the floodgate in your mind and now you know who and what you are. To achieve the massive task of awakening the seven billion beings inhabiting this planet would generally take many decades ... but we have only a few weeks. You are tasked with this because of your recently remembered experiences with such matters."

Jack sipped from a glass of water and then continued.

"If you look within yourself, you will be able to identify a darkness evolving from within the Earth. This darkness is not awake yet, but it will be soon, and no power on earth can arrest its development or stop it from evolving. We have the responsibility to rescue who, and what, we can before mankind disappears and all knowledge gained during billions of individual lifetimes is eradicated. If this creature wins, it will be as if mankind never existed. Then, if Earth is defeated, the evil this creature spreads will expand like cancer until this galaxy of 200 billion suns and their many, many planets and inhabitants are enslaved to its power. Trillions of lives—and every experience ever developed—will be gone. For those who believe in God, what I'm saying is that all good collected over the eons will be wiped out. In biblical terms 'let there be light' will be in reverse and darkness will reign throughout this galaxy and probably others. Souls who have previously been aware will cease to exist and, as a result, light in the form of knowledge will vanish."

Jack rested and let his comments settle in the souls of the group.

"The parcel that everyone knows is in our possession has been safely protected for generations on earth and, before arriving on earth, it travelled billions of miles from a different part of the universe, just to be here at this precise moment in time. No, I do not know what is in it—nor do I hope any of us ever will. It is likely that, if opened we will have already lost everything. The people chasing it are puppets of the being who seeks possession, and they work on his behalf. Humans understand the Lord of Darkness—the devil, by another name. But even *that* evil will lose power over mankind should the entity now evolving come into existence. Awareness will cease to exist; out of nothing it will come and into nothing it will take humanity."

Silently he looked around and waited for reaction.

"How do we know that the danger is imminent and can we do anything to halt its arrival?" asked Paul hopefully.

"Over the next few days, each one of you will develop your newly-regained skills to the level where, in past lives, you may have been regarded as gods—and only with these special abilities will we collectively have a chance to control this entity. Each one of you must use your time and energy to prepare Earth and its inhabitants for what is about to arrive.

The hard part is that you cannot fully disclose what's coming, as it will create collective fear and accelerate its strength," Jack announced, dismay apparent in his voice. "But we have faced entities capable of ending civilizations or making whole populations extinct before and survived."

Dan added, "Earth has faced incredible disasters ... the overnight disappearance of dinosaurs is one example. Luckily, all was not lost ... except, of course, the dinosaurs."

At this comment, a light chuckle rippled through the group. Of all of them, Elena was least concerned about strengthening her abilities, as her heritage was much longer than most in the group and her skills were already enhanced in this life. She had not been limited by long pauses between birth and re-birth.

"It's hard to accept sometimes that just a few days ago I was a normal man, planning a skiing trip in the Alps ... and now I share the responsibility of saving the galaxy!" Paul said to Dan, laughing. "I feel strange since my conversion, though. It's as if I can feel the Earth and everyone in it, the agonies of sadness and loss, and the elations of happiness and success. I can see and feel the heart of every human, and that burden weighs heavily. I don't know how to switch it off. I don't know if I can carry those feelings much longer—and it's not even 24 hours since you opened my mind."

"There is a part of every human mind that can hide their traumatic thoughts, allowing them to live through each day without carrying such a burden," Dan said soothingly. "In your mind you have the capacity to handle this—and more. I can show you how, but before I help you in this aspect, do you realize what your ability can do with minds and hearts that are open to your thoughts?" Dan asked.

"Will they become more aware of the upcoming evil?" asked Paul uncertainly.

"That knowledge would help them, of course ... but what if you actually changed the *minds* of humankind by connecting with them?" Dan responded.

Paul looked down and considered the implications. Did he really have such far-reaching powers? Would this not be the power of God?

"Do you mean control people's thoughts? You know what that would make me!" exclaimed Paul, fearfully.

"I don't want to burst your bubble, but you are not even close to the concept of God," laughed Dan, "Nor are you a lesser, mythical god, though some humans may regard you that way. God, without defining him in religious terminology, is much more powerful than anything he has enabled into existence. You and I are small matters to His power so don't get ahead of yourself." Then Dan smiled and placed a hand on Paul's shoulder to help him accept his place in the plan. "Remember, nothing any of us can do with our special abilities is ours to own. We are simply a conduit for His power; our role is to assist where and when needed. Many of us have lived lifetimes without knowing we have such wondrous abilities. We will meet later tonight, and I will help you shift the burden from your conscious mind to your subconscious. It will relieve you of the stress of carrying mankind's troubles."

At that, April arrived, bringing a warm glow with her, at least in Paul's mind. She smiled at him and immediately he felt better.

As the assembly began to understand who they were and what their powers entailed, the enormity of their collective task weighed heavily on them. They knew this was a crossroads of sorts, as if each of their combined lifetimes was culminating in this moment. Yet they were prepared to race into their new future with the full realization that they were not only protecting mankind and the local galaxy, but they were also protecting all the lifetimes and experiences of humankind, which were about to be extinguished. This knowledge brought an immensity and necessity to their tasks. Any army in history that had faced this moment—to do or die, to win or lose—and every war on Earth paled in insignificance of the battle about to be fought.

What was this entity that was forming? What was so powerful that it could make awareness vanish from the earth? How could it exist when no being knew it was there? What is the purpose of such a force?

"Will mankind disappear completely if evil wins?" Paul asked Jack.

"I don't know for certain," said Jack, "But I think our enemy is trying to destroy human consciousness as opposed to human bodies. But imagine what kind of army it could amass if no one was conscious enough to protest?"

The penny dropped for April. "It would be the ultimate army. If humans had no feeling or thought, this evolving creature could destroy anything that was in its way."

"Yes, humanity would be empty-shelled robots with no purpose other than evil," added Anthony thoughtfully. "If this being had the *will* to travel throughout the galaxy, with its vastly superior intelligence, it would have the power to move humans to every corner of the galaxy as well, with any form of craft it could conceive."

"I understand," said Ian, the tactical one. "Travelling through wormholes throughout the galaxy, it could overcome any resistance by eradicating cognizance and multiplying its power over all beings, until every light of memory in the galaxy was eliminated."

"Lord, what a threat!" said Paul. "What the entity will do next is only limited by the expansion of its thought."

They were beginning to realize that it had no limitation, since its control and power expanded every second. It was frightening to contemplate its power; if it managed to take over the world, darkness would reign and light (knowledge and awareness) would never have existed. Adam and Eve would have never existed!

As they pondered this, in a distant galaxy an entity remained undetected as it sped, faster than light, toward Earth. It could emerge anywhere and at any time it willed.

Chapter 11

Standing on the Edge of Chaos

When the briefing was over, Jack advised the group that it was time to act, time to begin their journeys. The team commanded by James and Anthony used the Hyperloop connection to the underground fortress, which contained military vehicles of a technology far beyond that of humans. They also had at their disposal a large team of engineers, as well as non-human aeronauts and astronauts, all waiting for instructions and ready for action.

Before the team's arrival, Jack had notified many important heads of state that a meeting should be held to discuss the evil force threatening Earth. Ian and Paul had been chosen to meet with the U.S. President, British Prime Minister, Indian Prime Minister, French President, Spanish President, Russian President and Chinese President at a secret location. Coded messages had already reached these heads of state, and they and their aides were on private jets, enroute to the meeting location.

It was simple for Jack to deliver the message; April just tapped into the various records hidden behind 'unbreakable' firewalls. To her, it was like following a highway in her mind.

All she did was maneuver down the cables and into the servers. Then she used her skill to open a channel within their protected systems and sent the messages directly to each leader's private phone. Once the leaders were notified of the crisis, consecutive messages were sent to the advanced forces of each country, which immediately raised the level of preparedness to the US equivalent of DEFCON 2, enabling armed forces to deploy within six hours.

There was no time for Ian and Paul to prepare elaborate presentations; instead they had to rely on their leadership abilities to quickly bring the six leaders up-to-speed with what was about to happen. The leaders knew Jack; before he'd been in the filtration business, he'd been in the military, in a very secret special operations unit. They knew right away that the cryptic message from him was not a hoax.

Ian and Paul boarded their transport, which was like a helicopter, after it landed on the lawn outside. Shortly after takeoff, the transporter converted to a compact jet of immense speed. It ripped through the air and arrived within 15 minutes at the designated meeting point, well ahead of the global leaders. They were greeted by more of Jack's highly organized security forces, who had established a secure perimeter of 100 miles in all directions. This secret location was designed and built by Jack and funded by the countries who were about to meet. It was created precisely for discussing war strategy; however, only the leaders and a select few of their closest advisors knew of it or were here for this hurried meeting.

Like Jack's house, this secret building was a fortified palace with all the amenities to provide both comfort and safety to those within. The complex and its surrounding grounds were camouflaged from prying eyes and ears by advanced, non-human, stealth technology. Even to the most advanced satellite and drone invasive devices, this area appeared to be nothing but a dense forest in a mountainous region. There were no access roads into or out of the fortress.

This base was certainly worthy of housing world leaders on the brink of war. Inside the multi-level facility were living quarters for a least one thousand personnel. The heads of state were surprised, on arrival, to find that teams had been assembled, ready to help them run their respective countries in the event of a cataclysmic event.

Ian and Paul expected nothing less; they knew Jack's abilities. He'd obviously been planning this for many years and with very few high level government leaders' knowledge and support he had silently and discretely created this place, only a few were aware of its location and existence. Everyone employed by Jack to help prepare for this day had been sworn to secrecy and well-rewarded for their loyalty. They knew lives depended on them and that they were responsible for ensuring this day—a day when world leaders assembled for a noble purpose—went as planned. Employees never left the facility—which was a world within a world—and never needed for anything. They did not earn a salary, as whatever they needed or wished for was provided by Jack and his management team. None married or had partners outside the city-state and the few who had families outside the facility rested easy knowing their parents, brothers and sisters had been provided for financially. In certain ways, they might as well have been living on another planet.

Looking out over the front lawn of this vast complex, Ian and Paul felt as if they had arrived at a beach resort in the Caribbean—and it may have been an island, for all they knew. As they walked in the gardens to collect their thoughts, the scent of the ocean permeated the air.

They knew they would be addressing some powerful heads of state and that they didn't have any real credentials, other than Jack's reputation. It would require Ian's power of persuasion and Paul's ability to see into their minds and hearts to encourage these leaders to understand the enormity of the challenge ahead. The message Paul and Ian would be delivering would be something no human could envisage; they fully expected resistance to what they had to say.

All arriving planes landed at the private landing strip within minutes of each other and everyone arrived within half a day of receiving the coded message. All were taken to their private quarters to freshen up and advised that a briefing would be arranged in one hour, mid-afternoon. These individuals were used to pomp and ceremony and luxurious surroundings, but the sheer enormity of this place and its salubrious surroundings took all of them by surprise. It was as if they had walked into ancient Rome; massive halls and courtyards surrounded them. The buildings were arranged and designed similar to those of Roman architecture, but all had the modern benefits of today's world, such as air-conditioned rooms which were welcome in this warm island climate.

As the leaders entered the facility, they walked down grandiose halls showcasing famous paintings in each hallway. Massive fireplaces seen only in ancient castles of Europe were in the sitting room and they were greeted by an army of servants who had been instructed to wait on every presidential whim. A light snack was provided along with fresh water, coffee or tea. No alcohol was served; Jack wanted to ensure all these leaders were fully alert at the briefing.

After waiting in a big hall, the group of leaders were guided through massive double oak doors into a cathedral-sized room that featured a large stage. Each took their designated seat and, even with their powerful positions in life, each felt they had journeyed back in time to their university days and were about to receive a lecture. The room was arranged like an amphitheater. Seating was widely spaced, allowing each guest their own lounge chair and adjacent table for drinks or snacks. A small video screen was attached to each chair with an extended flexible arm and headphones that provided the presentation in the language of their choice. Behind each seat was a collection of regular theatre seats, allowing the leaders to have their assistants close. However, on this occasion they'd been instructed to allow only one trusted support staff attend this presentation—and that person had to sign a non-disclosure statement before entering the place.

The heads of state were familiar with one another and had all met at different venues, such as UN and NATO gatherings. They engaged in friendly conversation as they waited for the meeting to begin. As the guests moved quietly into place, Ian and Paul were on stage preparing their presentation. It would be accompanied by 3D audio/video support.

A long-time resident of the facility, Susan, accompanied Ian and Paul onto the stage. She was the director of facilities for the 'resort' and was responsible for security, maintenance, supplies and general day-to-day operations. For the past 10 years she had awaited the arrival of this day. When Paul and Ian were ready, she introduced them.

"Welcome, prominent and honored guests. We sincerely appreciate your attendance and hope your stay is comfortable. Should you need anything while you are here, please contact me personally using the secure communication device provided. All phones, computers and laptops will simply not work in this facility. This is a necessary precaution to avoid leaked information. Please forgive the secrecy, but once you've heard the presentation, I'm sure you'll understand why we need the utmost confidentiality."

At this she had everyone's undivided attention. Then she stepped away from the microphone and Ian took over. "Thank you, Susan," said Ian, as Susan left the stage and vacated the room, leaving only the leaders, trusted aids and the two presenters in this private setting.

The presentation started with a three dimensional graphic video portrayal of the extinction of the dinosaurs, which occurred over 65 million years ago. As the leaders watched, a large meteor hit the Earth and created so much dust and debris that, over a period of only a few months, literally all light was blocked from the surface. The darkness and polluted air simply killed everything on the surface that could not hide under the ocean or bury itself in the dirt. Next, the video showed the bombing of Hiroshima and Nagasaki, along with the devastation caused to Japan and its people. Then it switched to horrific scenes of the holocaust, followed by images of man-made disasters caused by deforestation, mining, damming and draining of waterways. Then followed scenes of natural disasters caused by tornadoes, hurricanes, tsunamis and flooding. Human afflictions, including global diseases from the black plague to AIDS, were also displayed in gruesome detail. Ian and Paul monitored the faces of the leaders as they watched the video: they expressed dismay, sympathy and hopelessness during each visual performance.

When the video stopped, Paul said, "We apologize for opening with such difficult viewing of dark times in the Earth's history. All these things, except for the dinosaurs, display how humankind has not taken our roles as Earth's custodians as seriously as we should have. However, the things you have seen in this video pale in significance to the message we are about to deliver. Ian and I are here today to provide you with advance notification about the most difficult challenge ever to face humanity ... it is such a serious threat it is possible human beings could soon face extinction. I can tell each of you probably doubts what we're saying. Therefore, I'd like to present a simple demonstration."

At that, Paul went silent and delivered a message into the minds of everyone in the room without uttering a single word ... he simply telepathically inserted a thought into each mind, which clearly arrived as, "What would we be if we did not have awareness?" Everyone in the room gasped upon receiving the message and looked around to verify that they had all 'heard' the same thing.

"Yes, my friends, you heard me telepathically communicate to you, 'what would we be if we did not have awareness?'. The statement itself is more important than the method of delivery. To prove myself, you can ask me any question on your mind."

When no one responded, Paul said, "I will stick to a family theme. I can see, President Mitchel, that your wife was talking about having a short holiday while one of your aides was bringing coffee. The aide tripped and spilled the coffee over the floor of your lounge. And Prime Minister Thompson," he said, indicating the British leader. "Your daughter's request to have a sleepover was denied, as you have not yet met the parents of her friend."

Paul smiled sincerely as the people in the room gasped in amazement. "Please do not be concerned ... this is not a party trick, nor will anything I tell you ever leave the privacy of my own thoughts. I can also advise you, Prime Minister, that your daughter is currently wondering if you are okay and regrets the request. She knows you have bigger matters to attend to. If you wait a moment, Prime Minister, I will show you where she is at this time."

The man looked shocked. Paul continued, "You will see in your mind's eye a view of your house ... and then *inside* you can see your daughter looking at her phone. On that phone is a text saying she is unable to join the sleepover."

Pausing, Paul looked at the Prime Minister and saw shock and obvious concern at the invasion of his and his daughter's privacy. "Don't worry, sir, I am unable to pass these messages on to anyone else. This is simply a way to introduce you all to the next part of the presentation." At that, Paul continued relaying further messages to each of the leaders. One by one, similar reactions were displayed. Finally, he returned to the stage started to talk.

"What I have shown you is an ability I learned over a long time which you all can also learn with training. This power, however, is *nothing* compared to the power we are facing that is against us." Then once again Paul stated, "What would we be if we did not have awareness? Imagine a world where we all live and die without experiencing anything." Then he stopped and Ian moved to centre stage and looked at the audience.

"What Paul has done is to let you know that some of us have higher abilities than others. There are few with such powers but we, Paul and I, and a few others, have such abilities and they are at humanity's disposal. To be clear, you are safe from us and we seek only to do good. Due to cosmic law, we are unable to ever use any of our gifts to harm a single being on earth."

Everyone looked concerned; they hadn't thought of that, but now they realized how powerful Paul's gift was and were concerned about the gifts of the rest of the team.

Ian continued, "We have each lived as normal men until now, and it was only recently that our abilities were 'awakened' ... the last few days in fact." He reviewed the faces of each guest and saw that although they had delivered an honest message, there was still doubt in the leaders' eyes. "I know you did not come here for parlor tricks, but I assure you these demonstrations were necessary to open your minds to what is coming."

The leaders looked at each other in doubt.

"Humanity is full of mythological stories. In recent times, movie theatres have presented dramas such as *Wonder Woman*, *Thor* or, more appropriate to mythology, *Hercules*. While these stories are widely regarded as myths or fantasy, certain facts and fiction *are* based on *some* truth—it's just that we have gaps in our stories, especially the ones that talk of incidents that happened before written text."

"Go on," said the British Prime Minister, warming to Ian's words.

"Research can uncover some interesting historical facts ... such as the story of the Dogon, a tribe in Northern Africa, that had knowledge of the 'Dog star'—Sirius—4,000 years ago ... yet modern man only discovered this binary star and its two planets in 1984. How did they know this so long ago? We needed powerful telescopes and astronomical instruments to find it! I am telling you this to demonstrate how our past contains hints of extra terrestrial visitors. We have to understand our past and use it to guide our future ... and we need to introduce humanity to the idea that we are not alone in the universe."

President Mitchel was the first speak. "Clearly you are speculating on life beyond this planet. And evidently you have telepathic abilities. But what are you trying to say? And what is it you want us to understand with the repeated statement about awareness. Why should that concern us? Is the loss of our awareness the demise of humanity?"

"We are trying to demonstrate that mythology is rooted in reality but that no myth can describe what is coming into existence as we speak, a force so dark and powerful it threatens us all. The extraordinary team assembled by Jack, who have been trained to defend us, is at your service. Paul will provide a quick update on who we are and why we are here at this moment in time."

Paul immediately connected with the leaders telepathically, by-passing the aides who were left to wonder what was going on. He provided them with the unbelievable history of how humans live many lives and how he and the rest of the team had each learned special abilities over millennia. He further explained that some of his team were not human in their past lives and that it was their background that caused them to have special abilities.

None of the audience was so surprised about the admission of non-human connections, as each had at one point or another had direct experience with secret communication from alien life forms. It was aliens who had allowed humans to excel in technology in recent years. What was new to these world leaders, and a little off-putting, was to have this history lesson delivered without sound and with such clarity that there was no need to overcome language barriers. Paul concluded his introduction with the repeated message that his compatriots were all-powerful in their skills but that they were unable to harm others unless they were defending Earth. He also explained that for humans to reach their full potential, opening their minds was like upgrading software in a computer to enhance its speed and capabilities; the equipment was already built in, it just needed a password, so to speak.

The Chinese president was intrigued about the potential for humans to take a leap into a new, and hopefully peaceful, era. "There is a lot for us to understand and consider," he said. "I'm hopeful chances for humanity will improve, given your insight and preparation. I fear however, this meeting was not to bring us good news, but to show us who and what we can become. You are saying that losing awareness would snuff out everything we have achieved in our history on earth, along with the consciousness of every sentient being on the planet. What do we know of this entity? How are you aware that it is coming into existence? And most importantly, how do we stop it?"

That brought a round of questions that Ian and Paul were pleased to answer as they were relieved they had gotten to this point without delay and further explanation.

"Indeed, that is the reason for this forum. We have *some* answers ... but not all can be revealed yet. But we *will* figure out how we can stop the beast."

"Where is it and what forces do we have that can help destroy or stop it from evolving?" asked the Indian prime minister.

"Once it comes into existence, there will be no stopping it. As far as we can determine, its location is in the southern regions of Nepal."

"That's a little vague," uttered the French president.

"We recognize this, sir, but please understand it has not even become a physical form. At this stage, it's only energy finding itself," explained Ian.

"Gentlemen," interjected Paul, "We plan to address these matters as best we can. Currently we only have a vague understanding of its location, but we're able to monitor the energy more effectively each day. Our biggest concern, however, it that its power will be unlimited when it wills itself into being. 'What to expect' is what we really need to work on. And we need you to help us plan."

Ian added, "You know now that we are all eternal beings—not just our team, but *all* humans—so I can tell you that our knowledge of this evil being comes from a distant galaxy that, unfortunately, suffered the loss of awareness of billions of souls. Some individuals escaped before the entity's power evolved by fortuitously dying, allowing them to incarnate in other galaxies. Those who did not became little more than what we may call 'sleepwalkers'. The souls gave up their bodies and happy, wholesome beings literally became zombies ... and still are."

Paul picked up where Ian left off. "Imagine that everyone you have ever known or met in your entire life disengaged from their brains. Imagine going home to find your wife or husband sitting on the couch unable to communicate, their eyes pure black, never to shine again."

Ian added, "Only after millennia did the escapees begin to remember the catastrophic loss ... and only then did they begin to piece the puzzle together from their memories. It took many lifetimes; it was, for them, a bit like trying to recall every aspect of a dream—though you write it down, you have to go to sleep and revisit the dream to put together a full picture."

"I'm guessing one of your team was this escapee?" asked the British prime minister.

"It's likely you're correct, but if so, we have never confirmed it. To do so might establish hierarchy within our group which would be counterproductive to our combined effort to avoid a chaotic future. We may all have been escapees, for that matter!" said Ian, without a hint of concern,

The feeling within the amphitheater was understandably solemn. All understood that humans had never met this force and that the only possible defense was to avoid its birth. The French president said, "There is nothing in all of humanity that can deal with this situation! We are grateful for the help of the two of you and your team of extraordinary ladies and gentlemen." Then he looked at the other leaders and asked, "Do we know and trust their motives? How do we know that they are not the individuals that have this power?"

"We fully understand your concerns and you are justified in doubting our motives. We would, in your position, have similar fears," Paul advised the audience, who forgot that thoughts were not secret. "Ask us any question you want to, and we will try to explain that everything we are doing is for the human race, not against it. We have no ambition to 'rule the world' ... we are transients and have all that we have ever wanted, past or present."

Calmness entered the room, but doubt remained. It was human nature not to trust.

"What would we be able to do alone about the influence facing us? I, for one, *trust*," said the Chinese President. "You have my support, for what it's worth."

"And mine," confirmed the French leader.

At that point, all the leaders indicated trust, much to Paul and Ian's relief.

"I felt that," said President Mitchel, as he realized the relief was genuine. "I trust you and I promise full support.

"Thank you," responded Paul and Ian jointly. "Now we need an action plan."

As negotiations and planning proceeded, Jack received a message from Ian that agreement had been achieved and now the world, its forces united, was ready, if not quite able, to resist the darkness that was growing.

Meanwhile, the darkness gathered strength. *Let there be darkness,* was the thought that began to emerge in human minds as positive energy lessened across the planet. It was imperceptible at first, only felt by those with empathetic souls. Suddenly it seemed that the more sensitive were less happy and they did not know why. As night descended, over half the Earth's population locked their doors, closed their shutters and retired early to bed ... not tired, just needing to move into a safer place. The other half, in sunnier parts of the world, felt drained and gloomy, attributing their feelings to work-related stress or simple fatigue. And as the entity became stronger, energy shifted and everything seemed a shade darker.

Chapter 12

Darkness Arrives

While Ian and Paul met with the political leaders, Dan, in another wing of the vast complex, addressed a selection of the religious leaders of the world. Once again, April had utilized her powers, combing the vast reaches of the web to help organize a 'Faith Forum'.

This meeting was not so simple to arrange as, ironically, there was no global understanding that would bring these spiritual leaders together; yet they came together anyway. At the meeting was the Pope representing Christianity; the head Imam, representing Islam; Ramakrishna, representing Hinduism; the Dalai Lama, representing Buddhism; and the chief Rabbinate of Israel's Sephardic and Ashkenazi functions, representing Judaism. These were the base religions that could be brought together in the short time available.

April did her work by delivering each leader a message that effectively convinced them that a spiritual conclave was vital. A short video was imbedded into the message showing images of cities in countries across the globe. In each city, crowds gathered—but not a single person showed any emotion; they just stood still, expressionless. A date and time in each location indicated this strange event was during normal daylight hours when the city should have been bustling ... yet the background was devoid of motor vehicles and sound. A clock embedded in the video showed that no one moved or even blinked over a period of three minutes. At the end of each video was a short message, "This is just the beginning." Then the screen went blank and the words, "The soul, atman, ruh, incorporeal component or immortal essence of every living being is on the verge of annihilation." A final question followed: "Do you feel a change at the core of your psyche?" Never had such a chill collectively affected this level of the world's spiritual guides.

While these messages were being delivered, the aides of these spiritual leaders were advised that transportation had been arranged and that they should accompany their leaders to a council of global religious leaders. Each leader was informed accordingly and their aides prepared for departure.

Pope John IX immediately organized a videoconference with his counterparts to tell of the strange video he'd just seen and was surprised to find out that all the others had received the same communication. It was an elaborate story and chilling video effect, but they agreed it must be a deception, possibly by terrorists. They all agreed to sleep on it and not travel anywhere. However, as each drifted off to sleep in their secure and private rooms, a peculiar feeling, like a sixth sense chilled their bodies and the urge to open their eyes and look around the room was impossible to resist. Standing quietly at the foot of their beds was a ghostly figure resembling their respective religions' founders. Christ, Buddha, Mohammad, and Gadadhar Chatterji were in their presence. Nothing was said, but each understood the same message: *Pay attention to the change you are feeling, we are all in danger. What you have seen is happening now and is just the beginning.*

Moments later, transport arrived, and all left for the spiritual global council to which they'd been invited.

The leaders travelled with their private security, but by unusual means. The appearance of a helicopter seemed relatively normal, but then it transformed into a smooth, fast jet within what seemed like minutes, which left them bewildered. Then, within minutes, they landed at an unknown location, leaving each astonished at the efficiency of this operation and wondering how, on such short notice, planning was precise and almost military.

Upon their arrival, staff quickly had their belongings unloaded and their aides were immediately ushered to their rooms while they were taken to their own suites to freshen up. Each found their private chambers well-stocked with fruit and soft drinks and furnished to five-star hotel standards. Rooms were spacious and more luxurious than they anticipated. Within 20 minutes, a servant brought each a light meal which was laid out on the dining tables of each room and they were asked to be ready for a meeting in one hour.

One hour later, right on time, a guide appeared at each door and accompanied them to a beautifully decorated, comfortable, circular auditorium, which had at its centre a round oak table surrounding an empty central platform. Six chairs were arranged around it and behind each chair was seating for two assistants per attendee.

A large computer screen faced each spiritual leader. After everyone was in position, silence reigned in the room and holy men used the moment to gather their thoughts and engage in a silent prayer. Then each screen came to life with a short beep and an opening statement: 'Welcome honored guests and thank you for taking the time to join us'. The central platform opened, and a figure slowly emerged. It was Dan.

"Thank you for coming to our conclave, respected and honorable guests," Dan began. "I wish it were under better circumstances, but I hope by joining together we will be able to handle the challenge you are about to be made aware of, a challenge that we face as one human race."

As with the presentation to the political leaders, once again the audience was shown the same presentation about disasters inflicted upon the world, most often by humans to one another. Again, various cities appeared on the screen showing humans disconnected from awareness caused by the gradual awakening of the beast. The deathly faces on non-aware humans, in open spaces in cities across the globe, stood dazed and unemotional, rendering black images in everyone's mind once again.

"I know these last images are really disturbing. We are seeing the first images of the evil about to be unleashed. As the entity gets stronger, its effect on humanity will spread quickly."

"You refer to 'awareness' being lost, yet I'm sure you understand there is little relation between awareness and the soul?" questioned Pope John.

"I realize the difference, and accept your correction, but the force we face disables human awareness first, then it moves on to the soul ... which then loses its purpose, as, without eyes and ears, there is no longer any way to follow God's plan of expanding intelligence throughout the cosmos. The soul is therefore disabled on earth, so to speak—and at that point its connection is cut by the evil power now in control. With awareness removed from human capacity, the soul has no way to see or feel the coming chaos and the end of days." At their shocked expressions, Dan realized he had their attention.

"How close is the entity to formation and establishing full power?" asked the Dalai Lama.

"I wish I could put a timeline on its evolution," Dan said. "All we know is the process has started, as shown in the scenes where thousands are already affected. Those beings may be able to recover if we find a way to stop and reverse the influence. Our challenge is we cannot see, nor isolate the beast until it begins to take form. It's so powerful, it can change the face of galaxies—and has already done so—but thankfully that happened billions of lightyears from us."

Dan was exhausted; he had faced this eventuality in his mind so many times ... but the delivery to such emissaries brought everything closer to positive action.

"What can we do to help?" asked Ramakrishna.

"We can start by placing calmness in hearts across the nations, as it is fear that feeds the beast. It absorbs fear and converts it to energy. Messages of solidarity and bringing together people of faith from all religions will help ... and you can use the broadcasting capabilities of this facility."

The spiritual leaders nodded in agreement. They would do whatever they could.

"The hour is late, and we can start early tomorrow," advised Dan, humble with respect for these enlightened people.

The religious leaders were dazed by the information received at this presentation and relieved to be able to retire to solitude and prayer. They parted company carrying a burden greater than any had faced in this lifetime. Soon, silence surrounded the campus as residents drifted into slumber. However, rest did not come easily, and troubled sleep was all that any one of them could expect. Meanwhile, various populations across the globe felt uneasy, but no one was expressing their independent or collective feelings. However, a listlessness was developing, even among the darker side of humanity. There was very little crime as criminals began to feel hopelessness without understanding the source of these tendencies. Police forces enjoyed the respite from the routine chaos of city disturbances, but no one connected the peace with an underlying complacency.

Media around the globe faltered because journalists neither felt like writing stories of the day nor had anything to write about. The expressions on the faces of the newscasters showed little emotion ... but the audiences didn't even notice, as interest was declining by the moment. Even animals were lackluster in their motions; cats didn't frolic, and dogs wouldn't bark; birds weren't singing ... but again, no one even noticed. The fish and sea mammals continued to thrive and travelled their usual underwater courses, enjoying a normal existence—they didn't know that the situation above ground had changed, nor did they care.

Meanwhile, in Scotland a man named Frazer McKenzie boarded a flight to Washington D.C., heading for a meeting with NASA which had been arranged by Jack Keanon, a good friend of NASA's administrator, Rod Muir. Frazer was to brief Rod on developments regarding the imminent birth of the dark energy that Jack had told him about. Jack needed NASA's help.

The private jet Frazer was on was different than Frazer expected. It was small, delta-winged and more like an air force bomber than an executive jet. When he boarded the aircraft, he was met by a beautiful flight attendant in her late 20s, dark-skinned, slim with long, back hair. Her relaxed and natural smile made Frazer feel much less old than his 95 years on this earth.

Once inside the plane, Frazer was surprised by the luxurious interior, all oak panel, subdued lighting and soft leather lounge chairs—all the amenities of a first class 777 Dreamliner.

"Would you like a drink, Mr. McKenzie?" the lovely stewardess enquired, guiding him to one of the four empty lounge chairs.

"Only if you have a nice 20-year-old scotch malt," responded Frazer with a boyish grin.

"It's already at your table; we anticipated your request," the lady smiled as she pointed to the decanter just beside his seat.

Frazer settled in, helped himself to a crystal glass of the liquor and prepared for an expected seven-hour flight to Washington. Shortly after take-off, he drifted to sleep, helped by the soft hum of the plane's unusually quiet engines. However, having snoozed for only 20 minutes he was awakened by the pilot, who was sitting in one of the empty lounge chairs advising him that they had landed, and that his limousine waited.

Frazer was confused and at first he thought he must be dreaming. "Already?" he blurted, looking at his watch to check the time.

"Yes, it was a short flight, as the most recent design and engineering in this aircraft allowed for speedy transit. I'm still getting used to it myself," said the pilot.

After the pilot helped Frazer out of his chair and guided him to the exit, the flight attendant accompanied him into a limousine and joined him as they drove off to the meeting with NASA.

"I didn't realize you'd be joining me," said Frazer.

"May I introduce myself?" asked the woman. "I am Rod Muir's assistant and have worked closely with him for the past five years. My name is Evelyn. I'm pleased to meet you, Mr. McKenzie. Rod has often talked often about you and your exceptional intelligence ... and may I say, you are not what I expected! I was led to believe you were, if I may say so, in your mid-nineties—but honestly I would guess your age to be in the mid-fifties! There must be something in the Scottish water that keeps you so young and handsome." At that, Evelyn looked embarrassed and blushed a little.

"Dinna flush, lassie!" laughed Frazer. "If I had a few years less under my belt, I'd be asking you out to dinner." Frazer touched Evelyn softly on the hand to show he was appreciative of her compliments, thinking *little does this young lady know, I'll long outlive her* and *her children.*

The journey to NASA headquarters seemed much shorter in the welcome company of Evelyn. They exchanged stories about travelling and, most interestingly, about Evelyn's visit to a space station in her capacity as a microbiologist. Her profession was appropriate to Frazer's mission as well as the duties he had assumed under Jack's management.

When they arrived, they were met at the steps of the auspicious offices and guided to a briefing room by two Marine Corps corporals, where Rod welcomed Frazer with open arms as a long-lost friend. "Glad to see you, my old friend—and I hope your journey was not so tiring."

"I snoozed for a full 20 minutes and shortly after I woke I found myself here! And I spent the most relaxing time in the wonderful company of your assistant, Evelyn. You're a lucky man to have this beautiful lady by your side!" reported Frazer.

"Yes, and I'm also delighted to have her by my side as my wife, so don't be thinking any of your amorous thoughts," smiled Rod, gently touching his old friend's shoulder.

Frazer turned and gave Evelyn a kiss on the cheek and said, "Welcome to the madhouse, we're crazy scientists!"

Evelyn laughed, "I'm one of them also!" she said.

"Now, let's get down to business, my friend, we've much to discuss and lots to do. I hear the meetings with the political and religious leaders have taken place and that those groups are now preparing to address their respective countries and congregations about future changes. Troubling times lie ahead and we're just at the beginning," said Rod. "There are small gatherings of individuals already mesmerized by the evil force in a few pockets of nearby cities, but we are lucky to be in the early stages ... and hopefully we have a chance to stop this thing before it gets a larger grip. It's notable, however, that most of humanity has become lackadaisical, thought they haven't yet noticed a change in their awareness. Thankfully our group is protected for the time being, as there was more to your 20-year-old refreshment than you may have realized. We're dispensing a protective antidote that Jack's scientists have recently discovered. Our dispensation is covering the most populated regions. At this point, we're distributing through airdrops and ensuring it gets into the global water systems."

"That sounds like a good strategy," said Frazer.

"Bottled water is one of our biggest challenges," said Rod. "Many people have stockpiled it and it can't be treated. However, we expect the bottling companies to get on board as soon as they understand what we are doing. The measures we are taking right now are only stopgap efforts; the force that is awakening will become stronger and our ability to take preventative measures may be curtailed when it does."

Frazer listened intently to his friend's explanations while considering the extent of danger facing them. Then he asked of both Rod and Evelyn, "Have we the location of the beastie yet?"

Rod replied, "We've narrowed it down to somewhere in the northern region of Nepal. I guess that's why Jack gathered his team in that area and, as you know, he has resources underground that are unlike any on earth. But for now, we need to focus on what we should do with the package … we understand it may have some relation to the circumstances facing humanity, but we aren't sure who has the key to its purpose. What does it mean, 'not to be opened in the event of my death'? Whose death does that refer to? The opposite is that it is to be opened when the mysterious owner is *alive*. Do you know why it has not been opened already?"

Frazer contemplated his response before saying, "The package does not belong to any *single* human but has been protected over millennia by *one* person."

Stillness dominated in the briefing room while Rod and Evelyn tried to understand the statement and hoped for more information.

Frazer said, "You see, in general, humans are unable to envisage successive lives lived in a continuous sequence. Some religions touch on 'reincarnation'—and present a general understanding of the concept—but not in depth. Humans have lost the acceptance of such a possibility despite men and women of faith professing it as reality over the years. They choose not to hear it. The message has become lost in translation, so to speak."

"Yes, go on," said Rod.

"Until this moment, and without the arrival of this evil, elemental presence, it has generally been better for humanity to remain in a state of ignorance—or innocence about the true nature of good and evil in the universe. The development of the human mind has not reached the level where such knowledge could be accepted without ramifications. Most humans believe they still live as if this one, single life is all they have."

Rod and Evelyn nodded. They understood what Frazer was saying.

Frazer continued. "Religion has, and still serves, a purpose in aiding this ignorance. For example, if humans understood that we live many lives, what's to stop them from giving up at the slightest challenge and committing suicide in the hope of a better life in the next incarnation? In Christianity, suicide is regarded as a sin. This deters people from doing it. However, if people believed in multiple lives, the act of murder would be considered less horrendous. Individuals would understand that the murderer kills bodies, not souls. What I'm saying is that, in general, the current mindset of humans, and the lack of understanding of the ramifications of wrong action, would throw humanity into chaos."

Evelyn looked at Frazer. "Help us understand," she said.

"I will," said Frazer.

Then Rod suddenly said, "Frazer, I have known you most of my life and you have and my parents were peers ... yet you are alive and as young as ever. I know you are not a simple human. It's impossible. So, who are you and how are we to grasp the knowledge you are trying to share?"

"Rod, my dear fellow, and Evelyn, you already know the answer ... but memories need to be stirred. Some of us can unlock those memories for those who are ready to accept ancient truth about their souls. Are you ready for that?"

"I think so," said Evelyn.

"Not all previous lives have been good," said Frazer. "We inherit the sins of the fathers, in a way, but mostly the mistakes are of our own making, caused by ignorance. However, that's something we can address later. For now, let's focus on our task at hand and investigate what NASA can do to prepare for the coming 'la noche oscura del alma' or 'dark night of the soul'.

"Is that what it's called?" asked Rod.

"Yes, it was described most adequately by the sixteenth century poet, St. John of the Cross," said Frazer, "Who, by the way, was a good friend of mine."

Rod and Evelyn looked at each other and blinked in surprise.

"The purpose of the package will be revealed in due time," Frazer continued. "Meanwhile, we must deal with the arrival of Moloch, which is the name we've given this beastie. He's been named after the biblical Canaanite god known as 'god of child sacrifice' ... but this beast's intentions are much more widespread than sacrificing children. This beast poses a threat to the existence of humanity."

The room settled into stillness as the words resonated in everyone's thoughts. Rod and Evelyn were reeling with what Frazer had delivered, their scientific minds struggling to accept the mystical levels of the story he unfolded for them.

"You do realize what you're asking us to believe is a mixture of mysticism and religion, both of which are contrary to everything that we, as scientists, accept as reality?" asked Rod.

"I can understand the arrival of an alien force ... if it's using the power of the elements to convert energy from other sources to stimulate the chemical makeup of human metabolism," said Evelyn. "This could result in reduced human awareness."

"But we can't accept spiritual influence as the source of this conundrum without further investigation and proof," said Rod adamantly.

"If you hear what you've just professed, you've answered your own question," responded Frazer with a quirky smile. The two scientists looked confused, but Frazer didn't explain further.

"What you know for sure is that there is a force awakening as evidenced with the 'dulling' of human awareness in certain pockets of the population," mused Rod. "What's also clear is that you've been able to mitigate the effect by using your concoctions."

"We also need to isolate the source of the evil energy and take action to further counter its development and influence," Frazer said, "And that's why we need you."

Rod and Evelyn smiled at each other. "Maybe we can help you," they said.

"Do you think you can locate the being?" asked Frazer, raising his eyebrows in anticipation of Rod's response.

Evelyn stood up and stated, "We can do better than that." Then she asked them to follow her as she made her way through a high security door leading out of the briefing room.

They entered a long, dimly-lit hallway buzzing with energy and walked toward an elevator at the end of the hall. The elevator descended fast and Frazer felt his ears pop, indicating that they weren't just going just a few floors down. Then the doors slid open without a sound and Frazer found himself in a room equal in size and structure to NASA's well-known launch control rooms—yet the massive wall screen was not depicting a launch pad with a rocket ready for takeoff, but a live satellite image of Earth with Northern India, Nepal and Tibet at the centre.

"Would you please zoom into site 'A102'?" instructed Rod of one of the controllers sitting at a bank of computer terminals.

Immediately the screen zoomed into the designated area … and there, Frazer could see a darkened patch at the centre. The scale shown in the bottom right of the screen indicated that it was the approximate size of a football field.

"The size of this shaded area has doubled in the last 24 hours," said Rod. "It appears to be approximately 100 feet below the surface. You can see what looks like an entry point to the west of the site, just a few hundred meters away. That entry point is a gaping hole, approximately 15 meters in diameter. There's a crater there that indicates a strong impact from some sort of meteorite. Its seismic effect brought it to our attention. At first, we thought it was just a tremor relating to an earthquake, which are quite common in the region. But given what you say, it may be more."

Frazer was fascinated. "Tell me more," he said.

Rod continued, "The impact seems to have taken place some time ago and, since it's in an isolated area, we've no eyewitnesses. A special ops team was sent by the military and they will be arriving at the site in the next few hours."

Frazer felt himself shudder at Rod's last comment but hesitated to voice his suggestion that they be withdrawn immediately because he hated getting involved in another country's affairs.

"We have searched for other unique events of this nature around the globe but nothing out of the ordinary has been observed or recorded. Therefore, I think we can somewhat safely assume this is the source of the anomaly you call Moloch. There are no villages or population within miles of the site, so at least we do not have need for evacuation. But it's evident we have an extraterrestrial presence in that area and, as you say, currently without material form. However, much like a tornado, it would appear to have extraordinary centrifugal strength, enough to punch a hole in the earth. And it has created that shadow, which is only visible using radar. But it appears that whatever arrived underground is spilling over above."

Evelyn was visibly shaken. "There is every indication that it's like an iceberg," she said. "We only see the tip of the shadow but there's much more below ground."

Frazer shuddered strongly at the realization of what had arrived.

Meanwhile, in central Europe, a meeting of like minds was taking place, a celebration of sorts. One group was not affected by the dampening of their awareness; in fact, the reverse was happening to them. They were gathering to drink from the darkness, happy in the knowledge that finally their time had come.

Chapter 13

Evil Takes Shape

A castle in central Germany—built by a feudal king in the middle ages, held in care of the German government for centuries and maintained at great taxpayer expense for historical purposes—seemed an unlikely site for evil to freely flow … but something strange was going on at that place, though no one could feel it yet.

In recent years, political pressure to minimize government expenditure had forced the sale of the property to a dot.com company who used it as their global headquarters, with the agreement that most of the castle would remain open to the public.

The locals enjoyed the presence of a new 'productive' use of the historical building and welcomed the fact that some 300 local people were employed to maintain the grounds and improve the building. This cottage industry guaranteed the preservation of the building and local employment for many years to come.

The dot.com company conducted their business in a secluded wing of the castle. Their area had a private entrance, while the remainder of the property—including hundreds of surrounding acres—remained open to the public for families to enjoy. Many joyous events occurred there; private parties, weddings and corporate events were staged every day of the year and the income gained by the owner more than covered the operating and maintenance costs of the property.

The business entrance was reached via a secured road that only company employees could access. Each employee required both fingerprint and eye scanner authentication before they could pass through the main gate. Once inside, each employee was monitored via an implant that defined his or her identification and location at any given time.

No one working for the company considered this as an invasion of their rights; instead they felt 'chosen' to be highly respected members of a unique team. They were earning salaries four times the going rate for the work they did. All had to write an entry exam and only the best, those with special abilities, passed. It was not only high intelligence that the company required of its people; they were all also required to have a ruthless approach to winning in the corporate world.

The company had been operating only a few years before buying the castle, but it's success multiplied exponentially in the years after its purchase. However, they remained rather secretive about what they did, and the result was minimal visibility, which suited their objective to remain under the radar.

The company motto was, 'Profit Growth shall be the whole of the law' ... and only a few related this motto to the phrase by occultist Aleister Crowley, who said, "Do what thou wilt shall be the whole of the law."

As each employee joined, they were given strict rules to follow. They were prohibited from letting anyone outside the organization know anything about the company's works, including spouses and close family member. Over the years, some employees had passed away from seemingly natural causes—but it was noted that this happened when they had been indiscreet. The owners monitored every communication, private and public, to ensure no one ever stepped over the line.

Despite random disappearances of some staff members, this successful company was well-liked by people both inside and outside the organization and the small team of owners seemed to be family men and women who portrayed the attributes of decent human beings. Every one of them was an upstanding citizen of their community.

Money flowed into the company for the services they rendered, which included international trading, high technology logistics, corporate acquisitions, corporate law, aerospace technology, automotive advances in electric vehicles and space exploration, to name a few.

Many smaller companies were owned by this organization, but even the smartest stock market analyst would not be able to identify the smaller companies' relationships with the parent company. Ties were carefully disguised and most of the smaller companies operated at minimal profits to avoid prying eyes.

The managers of the smaller organizations were left to operate independently unless they violated tight guidelines set by the parent company. Those that veered outside the guidelines were affected by closure through bankruptcy or hostile takeovers orchestrated by the parent. All of this was structured to present a façade of 'business as usual' when something more sinister was going on and for a select few to maintain absolute control.

This gathering of profit-orientated individuals, who had no respect for anyone outside their corporate community, was a perfect place for Moloch to connect to the world. Here lay the weakened minds of men who would be ruthless in their thirst for profit at all costs. It was from within this group that Moloch had recruited the individuals who were chasing Jack and his team. Moloch already had full control over the individuals employed by this company, especially the two owners. He was using those two men completely for his own ends, but neither of them had an inkling of how strongly they were being influenced.

The two owners were childhood friends who had built the organization from scratch. They were very similar and had many things in common, including being single children whose parents had died young; being atheists; having no families of their own; being completely profit-driven; enjoying and owning toys from yachts to planes; abusing women through power; being connected with global players who made them appear of legitimate and good character ... in short, complete narcissists who each had a god complex and thought themselves infallible.

Another thing the two men had in common was that they had no knowledge of the presence now occupying their respective psyches. Subconsciously, they were aware of an important artifact they believed would bring their company profits to the next level. Intuition, mistaken as business acumen, convinced them to chase down this object. Through months of investigation they had identified that the item was in the hands of an individual in Scotland. Their private security team were then tasked to obtain the package for 'safekeeping' from the competition, which they believed was also after the item.

Unbeknownst to them, the package they were trying to obtain was one that Moloch had failed to obtain over millennia. For eons, he had chased it through galaxies, destroying the inhabitants of multiple planets in his efforts to pull together an army and regain control of an ever-expanding intergalactic territory. The evil forces of each planet had bowed down to his rule and so he had continued to grow stronger and stronger.

Until recently, Earth—which could be considered young with respect to intelligent life—had gone unnoticed. But Moloch's shadowy centurions were infiltrating every sector across the Milky Way galaxy and one day Moloch received a message from his earth-bound centurion. The centurion had stumbled across an unusual signal with a unique signature on Earth. Moloch detected the signal across billions of miles and commissioned his agent to investigate the source. When the centurion reported back, Moloch knew he was close to finding the powerful object that for so many years he had tried to secure for himself, without success.

Moloch chose to incarnate on Earth and, using years of knowledge and power, he now had control of Earth's global technology and a reach that could escalate the search. The forces at his command were chasing Jack's package and had come close to securing the relic—and all this had occurred without Moloch having yet established physical presence.

Moloch was strong. In his early manifestation, he had gathered knowledge of all human history, actual and mythical, and realized that the concept of 'gods' had played a role in the development of humans. He considered humans infantile because of this and laughed at how their connection to the divine waned as they began to doubt their own stories. It was then that the men and women of Earth became weak and easily influenced. *How simple this will be*, thought Moloch and the power of darkness expanded.

The two friends with financial and political reach, under Moloch's spell, were now focused on obtaining the item Moloch so desired. In their delusion, they thought they were trying to obtain possession for themselves and they were obsessed with it, thinking of it before anything else. Their day-to-day business dealings had been transferred to a board of directors, as both owners had declared they were working on a new project and would reveal all once they brought it to fruition. Without concern, their directors carried on and maintained the strong grip on profit generation.

Early one Saturday morning as the two friends were golfing in Florida, Alex, the elder one, said to his two-years-younger partner, "Do you remember where we heard about this relic?

I know we've been running our business 24 hours a day and seven days a week for the past few years and that its growing as if we've inherited the Midas touch. But I don't understand why I have such a need to possess this thing and I just can't place who told us about it, let alone what the relic represents." He swung at a golf ball and continued, "I have a feeling that it's invaluable and worth all of our time to obtain ownership, though."

Brian, the younger friend, nodded and agreed that he too had no recollection of a how they'd heard of this thing. "But I don't care," he said, as he putted on the green, "As long as we both agree that our instincts are never wrong."

"We're close to finding it, I think," said Alex, "But the individuals possessing the object have been unusually efficient at evading our guys. Maybe we should escalate the search and bring in our top guys ... you know, the ones we used to arrange connection with NASA."

Brian signaled in the affirmative as he launched a 300-yard drive down the middle of the tenth fairway.

"Beat that, Alex," he announced, certain his partner would rise to the challenge.

Later, while having drinks on the patio of the nineteenth hole, Alex confirmed he'd arranged for his top security team to fly to Kathmandu, as that was the last known site of the object. That was where their first search team had lost the trail. "Now we can sit and wait, while our guys do their job," he said, adding, "I wonder why Kathmandu, though? What's so special?"

"I don't know," said his friend. "But I can have our travel department fly us out tomorrow."

Alex sat up, feeling adventurous, and agreed to Brian's' suggestion. "Let's do this," he said.

So, without knowing why they wanted the relic or really caring about its purpose—other than to gain them power or wealth—and driven only by their egos, they decided to travel to Kathmandu, where neither had been before.

First, however, they went back to their office and arranged a meeting to brief their special ops team. This team was a select group of henchmen who they normally used to influence business owners who didn't follow their program. These men were not the type you would find around a boardroom table; they were more the type you might run into when the Mafia was planning a retaliatory hit. Black-suited, dark shades hiding even darker deep-set eyes, muscle-bound, military backgrounds ... these men thought that death was an honor and displayed unquestioning support and a desire to overcome resistance without mercy. *All are hand-picked and perfectly suited for the job,* thought Alex and Brian. However, they were oblivious to the extent of where this adventure was taking them, or the real dangers that lay ahead.

The next morning a private jet carried Alex and Brian, accompanied by their special ops team, to Kathmandu. Special landing rights had been approved by the government as they had set their journey up as a fictitious business trip with their Nepalese partners. Papers for entry were expeditiously arranged and they'd booked into the hotel Dwarika so Alex and Brian could maintain the luxuries in life they enjoyed so much. Even the six-member special ops team was given the best room selection, as the image was to be presented as a business trip.

Their Nepalese partners met them at the airport and made all the hotel transfer arrangements. They enjoyed a celebratory dinner held in their honour on the second night of their arrival.

Alex and Brian fully expected to have the package in their hands within 48 hours of arrival and instructed the ops team to spare no cost or effort in doing so. They thought it would be a piece of cake. All they had to do, they thought, was wait.

While Alex and Brian rested in their luxurious suites, the henchmen were in their vehicles, which had been shipped out from Germany along with other necessary armaments. The vehicles and arms were cleared through customs personnel, who were on the payroll of the local partner, without any hassle. The special ops team already had the coordinates of Jack's residence and were enroute to it within three hours of landing.

Jack had been advised of the unusual arrival of armaments and, considering the head of customs had been very friendly with him and his family for many years, Jack knew he could rely on him when he requested the entry to be processed without incident to not raise any red flags with the enemy. *It is always good to have far-reaching connections*, thought Jack.

While the ops team travelled in their fully armed vehicles toward the Keanon castle, Jack alerted his own security team and they dispatched a force of their own to meet the travelers before they reached Jack's residence.

It wasn't a difficult encounter, as Jack's far-advanced alien technology simply disabled the advancing ops team's vehicles by emitting highly powerful sound waves that targeted and disengaged their drive systems, bringing the trucks to an abrupt halt at a quiet cross-roads 20 miles from Jack's residence.

The occupants, assuming they had suffered a mechanical breakdown, exited the trucks and attempted to identify the cause. While outside, despite being astutely alert, they were shot by darts launched from small silent drones hovering just 50 feet above their heads. The injection of a strong numbing drug paralyzed all team members within seconds and Jack's forces, who arrived in a converted crew carrier, immediately lifted the bodies and vehicles on board and brought them back to their underground hanger. The whole incident took no longer than a few minutes and the kidnap site was cleared, leaving no trace of an incursion. The six-member team were locked in single cells and left to sleep off the drug. They would waken a few hours later and remain under guard, completely unaware of how they had been captured and with no clue to their location, nor would they receive any information in the foreseeable future.

Moloch was not focused on the ops team and cared not about their capture; he was working on the minds of Alex and Brian as they daydreamed their time away at the hotel. These two individuals would be his way to infiltrate the enemy … he wanted Alex and Brian to be contacted by Jack's team in the hope that they, too, would be taken into custody. Then he would be at the centre of the enemy's power!

He was cunning; that's exactly what happened. Concurrent with the action taken against the ops team, Jack's forces worked undercover at the hotel to drug the drinks of Alex and Brian on arrival. While they slept, they were smuggled out of the hotel and taken to the Jack's facility where they were restrained in cells like those of their henchmen. But although Moloch now had physical human presence inside the facility, his movement was restricted … but he would work on that over the next few days.

Jack, on the other hand, was not as naïve as Moloch thought. He was aware that he had invited a Trojan horse into the compound and was betting there was some other influence behind the arrival of the well-armed contingent and it's two directors, Alex and Brian. Now, at least, he had contained their movement and he hoped to learn about their objectives and affiliations. Two of his best interrogators would work on Alex and Brian as soon as the two men were conscious.

In short order, Ian, Paul and Dan were videoconferencing with Jack, recapping current events. "It appears our global political and religious leaders are resting before they address their respective nations and congregations," said Dan. "The challenge for them will be to deliver calmness and peace. The message may have the reverse effect and could escalate fear and uncertainty, which will feed the emergence of the beast."

"We have to trust in their abilities at this point, as we need to focus in our responsibilities and preparations," answered Jack.

"I'll get back to you on that," said Dan.

While waiting for further input, he briefed the team about the arrival of Alex and Brian and the events that led to having them secured within the basements cells. "So, we have the enemy within our walls?" questioned Paul, concerned.

"Don't worry, Paul," said Jack. "This is what the enemy wants, but the two individuals he's chosen are weak-minded and unaware of their roles as pawns in the game. We can use this subterfuge to our advantage. You know the walls and shields we have in place at our facility are impenetrable *physically* ... but they are also impenetrable to the powers of metaphysical beings. For the time being, this will keep the beast from using his minions to do harm within our walls. Our job is to get them to understand what is really happening and convert them ... make them into double agents, so to speak. Of course, they will be unaware of our guidance, just as they are unaware of Moloch's influence. When we release them, Moloch will start to control their actions again ... but we will be prepared."

Paul was not happy about the risks involved in this move, but he respected his father's clear mind and didn't contest the idea. Ian reiterated the need to prepare for the leaders' addresses to the public the next day.

"What if something goes wrong? What if mass fear and hysteria arise?" Ian asked. "I want to establish a backup plan should the need arise."

"We have presented both the religious and political leaders with the facts and they are now responsible for presenting the situation to the public. We are unable to directly affect the outcome about how it is perceived, but we can use our skills to minimize global panic and stabilize fear," responded Dan. Jack nodded his agreement.

"The group pursuing us is global. It is constantly growing in strength, and it is in every corner of this planet. Just like the fanaticism of certain religious groups, particularly over the past few thousand years, these people are blind to their cause, but pursue with venom anything that does not conform to their ideology," said Jack.

He added, "These present-day fanatics' belief is that a major shift in politics and religion is about to erupt on earth. They are sure that the current order of things will dissolve when their devious, warring cult moves into power. Their objective is a new world order. They hope to cultivate fear by spreading lies that 'other' countries and 'other' religions have been deceiving everyone for centuries."

"That's scary !" said Paul.

"Isn't it?" asked Jack. "They expect to control just about every aspect of human existence including health services, employment channels, market trading, financial institutions, housing, religions, taxes, energy, scientific research, government, TV networks and anything else you can name. They already have senior members in place throughout most governments who are influencing policy in crucial areas."

Jack looked closely at his companions to ensure they were grasping the danger of adversary they were facing.

"I had the feeling they were already in control in many of those areas, but do they really understand that what they are trying to build is superfluous to what is *really* about to take control?" enquired Paul, with an uncertain frown.

"I see you have inherited some of my intuitive talents, Paul," smiled Jack, patting his chest in mocking proudness. "They have no idea of Moloch's reach, but Moloch is using fear-mongering on earth to gain strength and evolve into form. It's the sect's activities that have attracted Moloch's interest, and, inadvertently, their actions and influence have bolstered the creature's plans for humanity."

He surveyed his friends with a solemn look, then said, "My friends, so far we're ahead of the game due to our various interjections into Moloch's plans. However, as we can see from our monitoring, certain areas within some cities show that some small groups have already been mesmerized. I have been following the media on these happenings and it appears the mesmerized tend to be debilitated for a relatively short time. Most people generally recover and continue their day's business without any memory of being affected. It seems the incidents occur without warning and last just under an hour. Doctors have tested a sample of those affected and there is no trace of any chemicals or drugs in their systems." Jack's expression was one of relief; he was pleased to convey to the others that the real effect had not yet reached 'holocaust' level.

"It's good to know Moloch's not yet reached full power and if the early effects are waxing and waning, there may be subliminal influences aiding us," said Dan thoughtfully. "However, we should not assume this will continue, we should anticipate Moloch's strength developing to an extreme level all too soon and continue with our plan." He looked at Jack and said, "And to that point, what are our next steps?"

"We wait for the leaders' to convey their messages to the world tomorrow and take action when we know how the message is received," said Jack. "Of course, we have taken various precautions that should help mitigate any unfortunate eventualities, but ultimately, we don't have much control over how the message is received. And remember ... our duty is to fight Moloch and his followers, not to control humanity. We can help this race to avoid extinction, but our code does not allow us to be their leaders."

As the men continued planning how to defeat Moloch, NASA was also at work. Not too far northwest of Jack's castle was an area bereft of roads and man-made structures, a few hectares of untended ground left in the hands of nature. This area was green with foliage, truly untouched and home of animals such as the Tibetan fox, Tibetan wolves, the rare Bengal tiger and a few wild rhinoceros. Man had possibly never ventured into this specific area of Chitwan, which had been converted into a National Park ... yet something strange was going on here. Where it used to be green and lush, previously strong and healthy trees almost overnight began to droop, their leaves falling listlessly to the ground. The normal, busy chirping of birds was silent and the soft winds stopped blowing through the bush. The four-legged beasts moved to other areas of the park. Strangely, the place was lifeless and dark, as if light itself had been sucked out. The only remaining sounds were of trees, now dead, creaking and crashing to the ground.

At the centre of this anomaly was a dark crater, 100 feet in diameter but without the usual smoke or fire left behind when a meteor strikes the Earth. The centre of the crater was completely clear of debris and only the high walls of impacted rocks and soft earth remained. Immediately surrounding the crater, all foliage had been flattened and nothing remained of the lush forest for hundreds of yards in all directions.

The NASA team was airlifted into the dead zone wearing HAZMAT gear and equipped with radioactivity detectors. However, they found no evidence of dangerous radiation in or around the crash zone. Six of their top scientists made the journey and each assumed they were visiting a meteor impact, but upon arrival the immediately surmised that no such activity had been experienced. Now their job was to identify the cause of the crater and report back to Washington.

On the satellite phone to Rod Muir back in Washington, the team leader described the site and expressed surprise at the lack of radioactive residue on such a clear impact crater. "To crush the rock at the center of the crater required incredible force, but the size of the impact would require an object only the size of a marble. However, the lack of 'fallout' is confusing. It's as if this impact happened many hundreds of years ago," commented the scientist.

Frazer was listening in on the exchange. He was not surprised at the conclusion drawn by the scientist. He was thinking the impact was likely not recent, as the arrival of the seed of darkness called Moloch may have happened a few hundred years ago. A journey of millions of light years was probably timed for this moment in earth's history and this stage of human development. In recent decades, the swing toward 'me first' selfishness and the influence of social media on minimizing real, personal interaction had resulted in negative influences across all areas of humanity that were more widespread than at any time in their history. It was this that attracted the beast.

Frazer sighed as he thought about how bad things had become. Governments were at opposite ends of the democratic spectrum; religious interaction was being strained by the activity of suicide bombers; government-backed and politically orchestrated wars were displacing more refugees than at any time in history; and, countries were strained as they tried to bring support to those destitute individuals. Without understanding the benefits of integrating these people, governments had no choice but to react defensively and close borders—and all these matters were generating collective fear that nurtured the seed of the evil that would become Moloch. Worse, Frazer knew that Moloch was only one of many 'bad seeds' spread throughout the Milky Way galaxy ... however, the Earth's volatile inhabitants were providing the fertile ground necessary for this one to grow. Other seeds, spread throughout the cosmos, would lie dormant until similar conditions arose and gave them the chance at life.

"Since they are on site, please ask your team to expand their search and look for underground caverns nearby," stated Frazer, and Rod, knowing his lifelong friend's intuition to usually be correct, instructed the six-man operation to use ground radar equipment to look through the core of the crash site and expand the search around the devastated area.

"That will take a few days, Mr. Muir, but we'll start setting up a base and get on it first thing tomorrow morning," said the on-site team leader.

Rod closed the communication but had an uncomfortable feeling that this was not going to turn out well. "I can't help feeling my guys are in real danger," uttered Rod, but Frazer did not respond. He already knew that sending the team to the site was a mistake.

Shortly after the phone call ended, the scientists set up camp on the fringe of the site. Each one of them prepared their respective equipment for the next day's work and all of them felt tired due to the long journey. Within a few short hours they were settled, tents were erected, and lights were extinguished in anticipation of a good night's sleep.

Deep inside a dark underground cavern, something sinister moved. Limited light from the surface glinted into corners of the vast chamber. Shuffling sounds clamored around the walls, like the rattling of giant spiders busily skittering in all directions.

There were creatures here and clicks of sound indicated they were communicating as they built a cocoon that floated in the center of the 150-foot high hollow cavern. The clicking sound bounced and echoed across the room as the army assembled the shell, an oval shield from regurgitated bile. If the scientific team had entered the cave at this time they would have died from the gaseous emissions. Their lungs would have evaporated in seconds due to the acidic molecules emitted as a side product of the structure taking shape. Soon after, their bodies would have melted like butter. Fortunately, this was not to be the scientist's fate this night. They slept soundly, unaware of the happenings just below them.

After millennia of hibernation, these cave-dwelling arachnids were awakened and, over recent months of feeding on anything that moved in or around their location, their strength was fully replenished. These were not sentient beings; they were more like automatons with one purpose ... prepare for the arrival of their master. They had been implanted on Earth shortly after Earth began to settle as a habitable planet. Every few million years they awakened, mostly without incident. More recently, however, they had been urged out of hibernation every few thousand years to keep track on the development of humanity as it rose to become the dominant species on the planet. Now, it seemed that after all this waiting, the time had come to prepare for their master's arrival. However, something inside them was different than the many previous stirrings ... they did not know this, but they felt excitement and adrenalin that made them stronger than ever before. These arachnids populated all habitable planets across the Milky Way, but it was earth's unfortunate privilege to be chosen to be the perfect location for Moloch to use as his base to take over the local group of galaxies and their billions of stars.

Back at NASA, Frazer watched a 50-foot screen that covered the far wall in Rod's main auditorium. On it, he could see the scientists settling in for the evening. He was also keeping an eye on the dark patch shown on an adjacent screen, which depicted the area directly below the scientists' encampment. His whole being felt danger and he called Jack on a separate line to advise him of his feeling of trepidation.

"It's almost certain this is Moloch's lair," stated Frazer as he described the darkening patch of a few hundred meters on all directions.

"I sense it too," said Jack viewing the same scene in the various monitors mounted on the walls of the operations centre at his home. "It is beginning. You have done your job at NASA, Frazer. I will send transport for you to join me in the morning. Meanwhile, sleep as best you can tonight. We will be busy enough soon. I need you here, my old friend."

Frazer would not rest well this evening despite the good wishes of his friend. He knew that meeting Jack was the first step to discovering what was in the package, long ago given to him for safe-keeping. He and Jack had not sat together for many, many years. He looked forward to it.

Back in the cave, the cocoon's assembly was complete. The clicking had stopped and it was quiet. Then, almost unperceptively, a soft murmur emanated from within the cocoon.

Chapter 14

A Child of Time

Frazer boarded the private jet sent by Jack to get him and settled into a comfortable lounge chair along with a crystal glass of fresh orange juice and a healthy breakfast of Weetabix, to which he added a cut-up banana and a sprinkle of sugar for extra flavor. He believed in starting the day with a healthy breakfast.

When he was done, he enjoyed a cup of coffee as he read the New York Times newspaper. The front page announced, Leaders *to Address the World!* He knew what the announcement was about, but apparently the press were still guessing. They speculated about a new scientific discovery that would impact every citizen in the world was to be revealed and that a statement by united world leaders would be held at 3:00 p.m., Eastern Standard Time. This global press conference had been arranged so that every country in the world would hear the same message in their own language at the same time. All the news feeds—CNN, BBC, NBC, FOX and international agencies from around the world—had provided a 30-minute window for the message to be broadcast. The media was on fire speculating about what was about to be revealed.

Frazer would have smiled at the feeding frenzy had it not been for the seriousness of the situation. But at least he would soon be joining his friends and be with them at the helm.

The flight was uneventful and this time he didn't doze off, but instead drifted into his private thoughts. He knew that his role in this lifetime was crucial to the success of humanity's defense against Moloch. However, this was not his first encounter with Moloch and he knew all about the almost unlimited power of this 'beastie', as he liked to call it.

It was millions of years ago in another galaxy, when he'd first met Moloch. At that time Frazer was in the early stages of his physical existence in this universe; possibly he was on his third or fourth mortal form.

Now, he had almost lost count of his incarnations. But one thing he knew for sure was that he had always been good at human life and had developed many skills in a relatively short period of time. For example, he had learned how to control climates on Earth merely by thought and so was capable of eliminating drought and reversing flooding. He was careful using this gift, however. He didn't like to interfere with divine planning unless he had a clear sign that he was appointed to do so.

His many lives had given him a special sense about the state of the Earth. Due to this, he could feel the anomaly of Moloch's influence; it was similar to how humans detect pain in their bodies. As expanded his awareness to search for the source of the disruption, he discovered a darkened dead area and was certain right away that it was where Moloch was growing. *There is no other reason, no oil or chemical spills*, he thought. *This area is dead because Moloch lives*. He wished he had detected Moloch's nursery earlier ... but in this existence, his skills were related more to assisting human development than ensuring the planet's stability.

Looking out the window of the plane, he felt a rush of affection for Earth's stunningly natural beauty and wished its inhabitants were more aware of the delicate balance that allowed them to exist. *Would they take better care if they knew how abusive their lifestyle was to the balance of nature?* Only recently had humans identified the damage they had caused—and some of Earth's inhabitants were trying to arrest their destructive ways and educate others. But governments were taking no meaningful action. Instead, seeking power and profit, they ignored long-term damage for short-term gain. *How sad*, he thought.

Returning his mind to the matter of Moloch, the last battle he'd had with the beastie was long ago lost and that galactic region had fallen under Moloch's control, the previously free and intelligent beings becoming automatons, oblivious to independent feeling or thought, just eating and working to build bigger and stronger armies to assist Moloch in expanding his dark forces.

The leaders of those planets were now under Moloch's control and he taught them well. They were never to allow any radical free thought from any of the inhabitants; that was the quickest way to bring the kingdom down. Occasionally a few independent thinkers gave themselves away, but they were quickly detected and eliminated. Frazer was born one of those free thinkers and was thankful to have flown under the radar ... for most of his life on that planet, he had managed to hide his special skill and strong mind. Eventually, after Moloch had long since left Frazer's home planet to his brainwashed minions to control, he escaped in a capsule. He was lucky; only a few of his companions managed the same feat. Most were eliminated.

He had lived many full lives on several different planets, but he felt his current life on Earth to be one of the most satisfying he'd had in recent incarnations. He realized all could be destroyed should he and his companions fail to stop Moloch.

The imminent battle against the vastly superior Moloch had been Frazer's ultimate fear for years. The idea that humans could cease to exist in their current state of evolution, their empty shells converted into an army that did not know what it felt like to be alive, was terrifying. With Moloch in control, there would be no independent thought ... the puppet masters empowered by Moloch would control every human action, trapping everyone's souls until body-death released them.

There will be no lovers dreaming over beautiful sunsets, no artists painting and music will never be heard again, thought Frazer. *Anything that lifts the spirit will be gone. Even the puppet masters will effectively be puppets, as nothing will emanate from their beings other than instructions from Moloch.*

In time, the puppet masters would learn to build an intergalactic spacecraft and qualified humans would be herded to the construction site. This site would be off-world. Construction crews would be housed on newly assembled space platforms and put to work. Like ants, they would commence manufacturing the structure. It would only take a few months to build. Other puppet masters would be preparing the crew and training personnel for war. That all were headed for an early death mattered not to Moloch ... to him, all humanity was solely for his use. And no one would fight back, no one would know they were being used, as their awareness was non-existent.

Frazer felt a chill as his thoughts arrived at the inevitable conclusion that this may be the end of days. Shaken back to reality, he looked around the cabin and this time was less surprised that, although it was a traditional take-off leaving Washington, he was landing in vertical fashion on Jack's front lawn only one hour later. He was aware of the advanced technology in Jack's formidable assortment of transportation ... however, he still preferred some of earth's rather simplistic and slower-paced methods. *At least in this lifetime anyway,* he thought.

As he stepped down from the craft, he decided to lose a few years in looks and stature and so it was a seemingly 35-year-old, fit man who emerged from the craft. At first, Jack was a little confused when he saw Frazer, as he expected his old friend to be just that, old! However, when he looked closely into Frazer's eyes he immediately recognized the old codger.

"Embarrassed to meet me in your true form, Frazer?" joked Jack as they embraced.

"I'm ready to pick a fight with the beastie and it just seemed better to take it on while I'm in my prime," smiled Frazer.

It was now early morning on the day when the announcement was to reach the eyes and ears of the people. "We have to be ready to act according to whatever the political and religious leaders divulge," said Frazer with a hint of concern. "Hopefully we are not going to face panic and chaos, which will only accelerate the beastie's arrival."

"We have delivered a clear explanation of what is happening to our spiritual and political leaders and now it's time for them to really demonstrate leadership," said Jack. "We can't control their thoughts and actions ... only point them in the right direction. Paul, Ian and Dan have done an excellent job of convincing them of the seriousness of the situation and you have helped by alerting NASA and ensuring their assistance."

Jack urged the sprightly Frazer into the lounge to continue their conversation.

"Coffee or tea, sir?" asked a maid as Frazer settled into a comfortable chair.

Frazer looked invitingly at the young beautiful lady and they exchanged a mutual appreciative smile. "Coffee would be fine and possibly a little brandy would help chase it down," he said and winked at Jack as the maid sped off, blushing.

Jack laughed and shook his head at Frazer who responded with a slight shrug of his shoulders and an expression of 'what did I do'?

"My dear friend, it's so nice to see you—young or old—still as cheeky as when we first met back in Scotland. It was up in Glencoe, in a little pub, wasn't it? I think it was called the 'Clachaig'?

Frazer nodded agreement.

"The room was full of smoke and the smell of beer. Logs roasted on the fire. It was a dark winter's night and the room was packed with climbers and hill walkers," said Frazer.

Jack added, "Our meeting was arranged by Dan, your nephew. He wanted to talk about the package and it's caretaking. You had looked after it for most of your life and Dan took over for a few years until it was decided he would gift it to my care."

A moment of silence was held while each recalled the horrendous loss Paul and Ian incurred on that fateful night in Keswick. It was interrupted when the maid arrived and flirtatiously presented Frazer with a steaming hot coffee and more than a fair helping of brandy.

"Thank you, my lady," Frazer said while engaging the young lady's eyes in a flirtatious smile as Jack shook his head in light-hearted frustration.

"Tragic night," said Frazer as he settled back into his chair, brandy in hand. It was likely the coffee would not find his lips. "Fortunately, we've never had to open the package and hopefully we'll never *have* to. Have you told Paul that he's next in line after it's your time to move on?"

Jack shook his head. "I've had no time yet. We've had more pressing matters to attend to. I have two unwanted guests in my cellar that I'd like you to meet. They were sent here to ask about the package and have almost no knowledge of why, other than a misconception that it has a value and that it could be sold. They're businessmen, you see," Jack said with a wry smile. "They're really quite harmless and are unaware of the influence Moloch has brought upon their weak minds."

Frazer stood and nodded in the direction of the door indicating 'let's get on with it' as he drained the remainder of the brandy, leaving the untouched coffee on the table.

Jack led him down a long, wood-paneled corridor to an elevator and they descended what seemed like a few floors but was really a few hundred feet into a cavern. Frazer felt his ears pop and realized he had emerged deep below the surface of the Earth.

Inside the cavern, it looked like a normal, well-furnished hotel lobby. There were no windows, but the décor and strategic lighting tricked the senses, so you didn't notice the lack of natural daylight. A well-dressed concierge escorted them to a small conference room. On the far wall was a large, two-way mirror, which allowed them to see both of the 'unwelcome guests', who sat comfortably at a desk.

Alex and Brian seemed perplexed but attempted to retain their businesslike, powerful attitudes. They had been kept apart since their arrival at Jack's residence and were still blissfully unaware of what they had stepped into.

As they watched their relaxed and confidently superior guests, Jack turned to Frazer and winked with a mischievous smile. Then he signaled to his control room to begin an introduction, telling the guests to address the screen to their left. Meanwhile Jack and Frazer moved to more comfortable seating and focused on a screen that had now replaced the two-way mirror. As far as Alex and Brian were concerned Jack and Frazer were on the other side of the earth, as the background behind Jack and Frazer was a view of the New York skyline on a brisk winter morning.

"Gentlemen, please introduce yourselves explain why you attempted to access the building in Kathmandu?" asked Jack in a dry voice.

"We are not required to answer your questions and don't appreciate being held captive," answered Alex, attempting to be authoritative.

Brian nodded in agreement with his partner then demanded to be released. "We will immediately inform the authorities about our capture," he said.

"I think you gentlemen forget you are trespassers ... and in *any* land that's against the law. We have every right to hold you and have you charged accordingly. We will certainly be returning you to your own country, which we understand is the United States. We have already advised your president of your actions and he will see to it that you'll be treated accordingly once in the hands of the FBI. However, we would like you to answer a few simple questions and clarify why you had your henchmen attempt to break into our property."

"Once again, we don't recognize your authority and expect to be released immediately," insisted Brian.

Jack smiled at Frazer and focused his thoughts on the room next to their intruders. Both watched as the door into the detainee's room opened slowly and gradually a smell drifted into the room, which made Alex and Brian gag with disgust; it smelled like skunk and it fully permeated the room.

The two men tried not to vomit as they fixed their eyes on the open door; a chill blew through along with the smell and Jack saw them shiver. Then, just as Alex thought maybe he could make a break for it, a creature lumbered forward and stood in the doorway. Instead, Alex sat back down in shock and fear.

The creature that stood before him was a massive biped with legs like those of a T-Rex and a digitigrade style of walking. Its upper body was double in size to an average human and was composed of sheer muscle. It had grey skin, thick like a rhinoceros, long arms and large head with wide, deep-set, cat-like, deep black eyes.

Alex and Brian were terrified. The creature stood over seven feet tall. It stooped to enter the room and then turned slowly, staring at the two shocked and now docile men. Slow, heavy steps on a solid wooden floor provided further evidence of solid muscle.

The beast approached menacingly, eyes staring unblinkingly into the souls of both men as fear entered their hearts. Neither had felt such terror in their worst nightmares. Standing a few feet in front of them was—by human standards— a monster, weighing at least 400 pounds. It stopped a few feet from the men and gradually opened a wide mouth to display shark-like teeth.

"Our ally in front of you understands you have been deflecting our simple questions and he has been instructed not to tolerate further delays. With one slight movement he will easily pull your arms out of their sockets. Now, we are peaceful people. We don't want that. But our friend is very obedient and will act swiftly on our instructions. We are giving you an opportunity to review your previous resistance and clarify your reason for being here," stated Jack. "Let me repeat our question, why did you come here?"

"I, I ... was ... was advised you had a ... a ... special package," stuttered Alex in fear.

"What kind of package?" asked Frazer.

"That's the strange thing ... we don't know and can't even recall how we heard of it ... and even *worse* ... we have no idea what it is," replied Brian in a quavering voice. He looked at his partner in concern, wishing he were back in Germany at the castle.

At the lack of *real* answers, the being shifted a few feet closer to the men which made them jump up and run. Now they stood pressed against the wall behind them. "Please, we are telling the truth! We thought this would be a simple acquisition and we apologize for intruding."

Jack looked at Frazer and Frazer nodded his acceptance of the response, which supported his feeling that the two individuals were rather basic, greedy businessmen, with not much common sense between them.

Frazer turned his mental attention onto the two individuals and within seconds they passed out from his strong, hypnotic influence. At that, the beast withdrew and returned to its chambers next door.

The slumbering gentlemen were taken to a small hospital unit a few meters from the holding room. "When they awaken, they'll not remember any of this incident," said Jack. "Additionally, they'll have forgotten all about the package and have been advised that their visit here was simply a short meditative trip to our spa. While they sleep we'll make a few adjustments enabling them to subconsciously resist Moloch's influence. We can have them work for us as double agents once we do that. We will also implant monitoring devices that can provide us with minute-by-minute action as they return to their daily lives."

Frazer was satisfied the two visitors would no longer be an issue.

"We have also provided all our staff with the same microscopic implant which, placed strategically within the brain, resists the influence of Moloch's telepathic thoughts. The beast attacks the human mind in the same way a hypnotist controls a subject. Our subconscious mind attends to over two million bits of sensory information every second ... and when those channels are interrupted, people are no longer in control of their actions," Jack told Frazer as they walked back to Jack's study, which was on the ground level.

Paul, Dan and Ian, who had just arrived, joined them to catch up on this morning's events. All were eagerly anticipating today's announcement.

Jack arranged a light snack for the team and brought them up to date with the rather entertaining use of his alien cohort. Dan and Ian had met the alien, who was a pilot of one of the crafts in Jack's fleet. He and many of his race had lived in the Kathmandu area for many years. Their existence, while on earth, was subterranean, as exposure to strong sun damaged their skin within moments. When they ventured topside they needed to wear protective clothing.

Paul was fascinated but felt he had been kept in the dark about the different species who were serving Jack. He was curious to meet this alien.

"Don't worry Paul, you'll get to meet our allies soon enough," his father told him. "They are one of the species that had been affected by Moloch's destruction of a planet in the Andromeda galaxy, 2.5 million light years away. Small sections of Andromeda's one trillion stars are now under Moloch's command and his armies are gaining ground in that region. Obviously, our alien friend has many reasons to assist us in the upcoming conflict ... but general knowledge of their arrival on earth is limited to our group and only one or two others. We don't want to create chaos by announcing, on top of everything else, that aliens, friendly or not, are on Earth. It's too much for people to comprehend. But in time we'll tell them that their advanced knowledge has helped our own development, especially in the high-tech sector. It has moved in leaps and bounds over recent years."

Paul was almost as excited as a little kid at this news. "I can't wait to meet them," he said. "They must have so much to teach us!"

"Yes," said Jack. "Especially regarding technology. Unfortunately, their bio make-up is so different from ours that we've not been able to benefit from their truly remarkable medical advances. Each of these beings easily live for more than a thousand years, as their DNA has been manipulated meticulously so that a few simple adjustments can regenerate organs, muscles, bones and skin on a continual basis with no use of chemical ingestion."

Paul was impressed. "It's regeneration," he commented. "Some people think that's the Holy Grail."

"Our top scientists are mirroring their procedures and we are beginning to better understand where we can make such genetic adjustments to help eradicate certain diseases," Jack said. "We are still primitive in this field, but progress is being made."

Frazer cut in, "As amazing as our friends and allies are, we need to get back to the point. The anomaly that NASA and we have been monitoring only a short distance from our current location. It is almost certainly the site where Moloch will materialize. There are NASA scientists camped at the place right now and we are preparing to further investigate underground later tomorrow."

Jack said, "By the way, our alien friends from the Andromeda galaxy are referred to as 'dromas', which is better than continually addressing them as 'aliens', don't you think?" Jack asked. "Dromas are powerful yet friendly allies. They have no intention of residing on earth but have indicated that they are keen on terraforming Mars, since it's a suitable distance from the sun."

"That would make sense," said Frazer. "Its temperature is normally below zero and in the polar regions much colder, but I would think that's attractive to dromas, as it's similar to their home world."

"Their technology will assist in minimizing the current high radiation which has been pounding the surface of Mars for a few billion years," Jack said, "And hopefully the terraforming activity will re-establish permanent protection against such radiation."

"Do you think humans and dromas can work together and potentially cohabit Mars in generations to come?" Paul asked.

"Oh, I think so," said Jack. "In return for allowing them to colonize Mars, they can offer us technical knowledge to help reverse the effects of pollution on Earth ... but we need to get past the Moloch issue if we want a chance to build a better future."

Frazer smiled. He welcomed the idea that cooperating with the dromas would help stop climate change and protect the Earth for millennia. Humans needed a chance to evolve. He again smiled to himself as he thought about why humans had not yet landed on Mars. Given the moon landing in 1969, and spacecraft launched throughout the last 50 years, people often wondered why. Frazer knew the answer was quite simple ... top-level individuals in the US government and NASA were aware of the dromas and their plan for Mars. Humans were prevented from landing there until the world was aware of the joint human/droma venture.

"We communicate telepathically with dromas, or at least *our* team can, since we've developed our skills and senses to the point where we can carry on such advanced conversation," said Frazer. "No language is required; spontaneous imagery replaces the spoken word and so misunderstanding is impossible. Dromas are not able to read minds; they only receive intentional thought. But even so, we are protected. The human brain, it seems, has a built-in defense mechanism that resists intrusive communication."

"That's a relief," said Paul. "Tell me more about dromas."

Jack smiled. "The droma ability to release a rancid smell, like a skunk, is a strong defense mechanism, but is only used in extreme situations ... as was well demonstrated in the recent encounter with our uninvited guests," Jack added with a chuckle and catching Frazer's eye.

At ground zero, as the crater was now being referred to, the NASA scientists were busily working their way underground. After a day's work, they finally reached a massive cavern. The air, although a bit stale, was breathable and clean so they didn't don oxygen masks. Slowly they looked around ... and were amazed to see a large cocoon floating in the centre.

There was nothing else in the cave, just the cocoon. They estimated the cocoon to be 30 feet high and 15 feet in diameter at its widest point. The surface was as hard and smooth as granite. The scientists estimated it to weigh about a thousand tons, but their equipment showed the shell to be no more than a millimeter thick. They looked through monitors at X-ray video of the contents and found that, other than a small, fist-sized pulsating object at the centre, it was empty.

The special forces team leader called Rod Muir, the NASA administrator, back in Washington. "The pulsating element inside is floating, gravity free, at the centre," he said. "We cannot determine if that fist-sized object is a living organism or mechanical; our equipment is not picking up anything other than size. We've tried to penetrate the outer shell but even our diamond drill bits don't make a scratch. The cave is completely free of debris. It's as if the cocoon just appeared. Temperatures in the cave are normal, about ten degrees Celsius. Humidity is nominal ... in fact, nothing is exceptional other than this giant cocoon floating in the middle of the cavern. Yes, you heard me, floating! There are no connections tethering it to the ceiling."

Rod asked the scientists to leave cameras, lighting and radiation detectors in the cave and instructed the team to withdraw to a safe distance away and to ensure their camp was safely away—a few miles—from this strange thing. Within 30 minutes the team was back at camp. Then they packed up and retreated as they had been advised to do. After setting up again, a few miles from Ground Zero, they completed the hook-up for live feed so headquarters in Washington could monitor things. This live feed was also available to Jack's team who were learning of the latest events as the team communicated with Rod. Then, communication complete, the scientists rested, unusually tired after an emotional day.

It was now early afternoon and the media were ready for the global presentation. None were given the location of the leaders, nor the opportunity to ask questions in advance. They received clear instructions: make the broadcast available at precisely 3:00 p.m. and ensure at least 30 minutes for each presentation. Both the spiritual and political leaders would be in the same room, presenting collectively.

Jack's team gathered in his private auditorium: Dan, Frazer, Ian, Paul, April, Elena, Naomi, Andrew, Anthony and James. Jack liked this auditorium. It had lavish trappings and special features for comfort. The walls were decorated with paintings by famous artists from all over the world; he favored Salvador Dali, William Blake, Gustav Klimt, Paul Gauguin, Pablo Picasso and of course Leonardo DaVinci. All Jack's art were priceless originals, and each conveyed a message. Pictures Jack owned included Blake's *The Ancient of Days*, Dali's *Christ of St. John of the Cross*, Klimt's *The Kiss* and more recently Thomas Kinkade's *The Valley of Peace.*

Jack smiled at his collection. Various museums and art galleries around the world were certain they had the originals, yet he knew otherwise ... After all, he was friends with those artists, having known them in his previous lives when their lives had crossed with his. He enjoyed the benefits that sometimes came with the ability to travel in different bodies. He particularly enjoyed that he was so evolved that he knew where he would end up in the next life and retained complete recollection of each life.

Jack said to his assembled team, "I'm so glad each of you is contributing to addressing the coming challenge. I appreciate everyone's help in this time of need for Earth and humanity. We know that whatever Moloch achieves in the days or weeks ahead, the planet will suffer little … but intelligent life will diminish. Only a few small pockets in outlying areas will survive mentally, at least for a while. I'm glad you have all reconnected with your previous life experiences and been able to regain your specific talents. To be clear, we all have different skills and in a few days, you'll find your abilities will become instinctive and stronger in their effect."

Everyone nodded at his words and Jack continued. "Paul, your ability to link with minds and communicate with humanity through telepathy will protect them as Moloch attempts to gain control. We will need your full attention around the clock."

"Naomi, your capacity to alter the effect of gravity on any object simply by visualizing it becoming heavier or weighing nothing at all will help when we're facing armies and their weapons."

"Ian, my lifelong friend and companion, without whom we wouldn't have made it this far, your powers of persuasion have already helped join leaders together and I'm certain your influence will be required if those leaders lose sight of who they are under Moloch's influence."

"April you're a sight for sore eyes, but your talents are much more than skin deep," Jack teased. Everyone was relieved that Jack at last brought some light-heartedness into his address, so they laughed. He carried on, "Your strength probably has a wider reach anyone in the room, since technology is almost everywhere on Earth. Your insight into data, your skill at avoiding complex firewalls … these things allow you to get into the most guarded secrets of nations, or personal files of anyone. We will rely on you to help change a few bytes of information when the time comes."

"James and Anthony, I'll bet you're having fun with your fleet of airships. As you know, they have originated from many different planets and have powers way beyond any craft developed on Earth. You have met your team of pilots—over 1,000 in total—in the subterranean fortress. I understand every unit is battle-ready and waiting your command."

He looked around at the rest of the team and said, "Just so you all know, the benefit of these special crafts is that they can operate autonomously if the pilot is injured or otherwise incapacitated. Each spacecraft has already been in action against this particular foe and has built-in intelligence to help defend against Moloch." He looked back at James and Anthony. "Your joint command of this force will be essential."

"Dan, also my life-long friend, how you manage to stop time has always amazed me. Still, after all these lives, I am amazed at how you do this. You can induce any person to sleep on command, and while they sleep you can direct their minds to past or future events. Amazing! You are very important to our team."

"Andrew, warping space is phenomenal, but, in addition you can reposition objects from one point in space to another *instantly.* While busily shifting material around like furniture, you can also control the minds of others! You've certainly not been slacking during your incarnations," smiled Jack as he turned to the penultimate member of the team, Elena.

"Elena, my lovely lady, the most mysterious of our team," stated Jack with a gentle smile, which brought a little laughter from the group. "You've travelled long through the galaxy and experienced more than most and we're lucky to have you alive in this incarnation at this point in time. I'm certain that's not *so* much of a coincidence, as before joining the human race, we all had knowledge that our team would be together in this life. And we all had an inclination of our mission."

There were nods all around. What Jack said rang true.

"Your abilities, are telepathy, telekinesis, the ability to stop anyone's physical movement just by looking at them and, just as important, you can heal others."

"Frazer, my confidant, mentor, lifelong friend and ally … not to mention connoisseur of whisky …" this brought hearty laughter. "Your ability to see into the future with 99 percent certainty and to shift certain aspects of the present to push mankind in a generally positive direction are special skills. And your further ability to influence weather patterns should have been used a long time ago to give Scotland a warmer climate!" At this last comment, Jack laughed to himself, as no one really understood how bad the weather could be in Scotland except he and Frazer.

When Jack was done, he looked around the room, making sure the team fully understood the roles each must play in the days and weeks ahead. Soon, they would know when they were needed and where to join the conflict.

"Hold on, dad" exclaimed Paul. "After all this, you've ignored one very important person … Jack Keanon!"

The room was quiet in anticipation of an answer, but only after a few pensive moments did Jack respond, "It is better, for the moment, that I stay in the background, behind the scenes. The skills I have I will reveal in due course and use if the time for them is right. I'm sorry, but at this moment I must remain incognito."

No one wanted to question what that might be, so the room remained silent. Elena looked innocently away in case her face revealed her knowledge of Jack's gift.

"May I ask for your understanding? At this moment my secrecy is better for us all." Without hesitation, everyone nodded in agreement.

Paul was deep in thought. He had come to this group as an innocent, both in his terms of knowing of his power and his many lifetimes. He found it hard to believe he was someone completely different than he thought himself to be. He wondered if the façade he gave of the happy-go-lucky but sensitive individual was actually just his way of hiding his weakness—grief over Jessica's death. It had been easy to take on physical challenges after Jessica died. That was adventurous. But inside, he knew he had never gotten over the loss of his wife and he still hurt every day. Oh, he still maintained aspects of his life where his attention was required, such as business and family ... but inside he was damaged goods. If anyone could see through his disguise, they would be shocked at his weakness. Before he'd come on this trip, he'd been drinking more than usual and smoking pot. No one in this room other than Naomi had an inkling of the cliff edge on which he stood ... but now he was holding a power that could change the way human minds think. Was he capable of knowing what to do with that power?

He felt like a child lost in time without anyone to help him understand how to read the clock face. He was scared about letting the team down, but he didn't have the courage to confide in his companions, as they were now reliant upon him and his skill to overcome the uncertainty facing humanity. He felt he was drifting into a dark corner and he wasn't aware that Jack noticed the shift.

Jack felt a massive burden enter his soul and Moloch grew stronger.

Chapter 15

A Global Message

The clock approached 2:45 p.m. and Jack's team was in place, ready to ensure the world would hear the address of their political and spiritual leaders on this eventful afternoon. The media scurried around testing their sound and vision equipment, making sure all was ready to receive the signal from Jack's technical experts. No media announcement had ever been attempted on such a grand scale before. Usually, news breaks and is only copied by lazier journalists who simply put a dramatic slant on the truth to make it more sensational; in this case it would be delivered live with no embellishments.

Would people care? Jack wasn't sure. The world had already become desensitized to the almost everyday catastrophes that affected 25 percent of the population. The rich sent money to the latest disaster, the middle class built charities to support the victims and the poor volunteered ... yet rape, murder, crimes against humanity, war and genocide continued to happen every day. It was sad, mused Jack, that wars were fought in poor nations and the only ones who benefited were those providing armaments and encouraging further conflict so they could line their pockets. Technology provided the average household with instant knowledge of these horrific events and so humans became more fearful every day. The perfect storm of greed, power, fear, abuse and genocide was evident to those who paid attention to the messages delivered by various media globally. And it was the perfect environment in which Moloch could grow.

Of course, atrocities have afflicted humans since Adam ate the apple ... but past disastrous events did not take place on a global scale. Beginning with the first world war, things changed. That war created the kind of energy that was a signal to Moloch. Negative vibrations got significantly stronger and reached a level where evil paid attention. Humans were rotten and ripe for the picking.

In the cocoon in the cave, the fist-sized object noted by the NASA scientists stirred. Moloch's heartbeat pulsated in anticipation of taking over this human race that was so damaged and ready to be absorbed. The monitoring equipment left behind by the scientists for this very reason somehow didn't detect this almost imperceptible change, however, Jack felt it and he stumbled a little as he poured a glass of water.

There was only 10 minutes to go until the announcement. Jack asked Paul to come for a few moments into his office.

"What's up, dad?" Paul asked. "There are only a few minutes to go until the announcement ... what's so urgent it can't wait?" When he saw his father's face, he immediately grew concerned. Then he looked at what his father held in his hand, and his face paled. It was the package.

Jack held the package out to Paul, who stared at it, a little frightened. Then Jack said ceremoniously, "It's time to pass this baton to you, Paul. Don't worry, I don't plan on dying soon, but we must make these transfers in a time of peace ... and who knows what's going to happen immediately after the announcement? When a shift in the balance between war and peace seems imminent, the long-standing agreement is that the package move to a suitable heir … and you, being my son, are that heir."

Jack pointed in the direction of a camera mounted in the corner of his office, walked over and switched on the record button. Then he said, "I am Jack Keanon, caretaker of the Scion. It is November 4, 2018, and I am in my private office in my house in Kathmandu. In the office is my son, Paul Keanon, but no other individuals. It is my sworn duty to transfer the ownership of the Scion and we offer our blood in accordance with the ancient law."

At that, Jack retrieved a ceremonial knife from his drawer and asked Paul to offer his right hand. Before Paul fully understood what was going on, he held out his arm and Jack sliced into his palm. Then he swiftly repeated the cutting stroke across his own right hand and forced his hand into Paul's, squeezing hard to ensure a bond and forcing their mingled blood to spill directly onto the seal of the package. In an instant, the package changed its appearance; the string unwound, and the wrapping was instantly replaced, though the contents were not revealed. Afterward, it was still the size of a shoebox, but all the markings disappeared and were replaced by new dates and other shapes. It was as if a shop attendant had freshly wrapped a new gift.

"Shit, that hurt!" Paul said as the procedure ended, but when he looked at his hand there was no cut, blood or further pain at all. He glanced at his dad's hand and realized it was the same.

"Now you are the caretaker, my son. I'm sorry to have done this so quickly … I certainly cut down the ceremony a little … usually it takes an hour and is witnessed by a few trusted friends. However, there is little time and we have to get back to the auditorium immediately."

Jack picked up the package and placed the package back in his safe. He instructed Paul to close it and to change the code so that only Paul had access. Like a robot, and still reeling from what had just transpired, he carefully closed the safe and within seconds it asked him to create a new password. Paul turned and looked at Jack, surprised he didn't need his father to cancel the old password.

"I know what you're thinking," Jack said. "It's quite simple, it recognizes you by DNA sample from the sweat in your hand. It's already searched its database of past, current and future caretakers to see if you are one. You can't be a caretaker twice. Now that it knows you, only you can open the safe. There is no combination required, just a sweaty palm. I'm sure you've seen movies where fingers have been cut off and the dead fingerprint is used to access secure areas. That won't work here ... only you, when you are alive and warm blood flows through your veins, will be able to open it. It is tamper-proof. If anyone else tries to access it, Elena will remove the package telekinetically to another location for temporary safekeeping and you will be advised telepathically where it is. This safety procedure has protected the package for millennia. I will give you further information once we know the direction we will be taking after the announcement."

Paul shakily nodded his understanding. Jack embraced him quickly then said, "Now, how about we watch the announcement?" Then he extended his hand to shake Paul's.

While Paul could not get over the speed at which this dramatic switch in responsibilities had happened, Jack felt worn. He had passed a massive responsibility to his son, who had very little real knowledge about what was involved with the job. But it was done.

There were now only a few moments until the world was notified about the danger they would all soon be facing. Jack's team was apprehensive about how the message would be received. They settled into their seats, coffee, tea and soft drinks at hand, and waited. In a minute, the room lights dimmed and the screen in front of them came live with an expanded view of all the leaders. It was Jack's communication director who first spoke.

"Good morning, afternoon and evening to the world. We welcome all nations, religions and cultures on this momentous day. It is with great honor that I introduce some of the world's most respected government and religious leaders. I request each one stand when your name is called.

U.S. President – John Mitchel
British Prime Minister – Eric Thompson
Chinese President – Xi Tung
Indian President – Ram Bhavan
French President – Brigette Macron
Russian President - Marina Severinovskaya
Spanish Prime Minister – Pedro Gonzalez
Pope John IX – Representing Christianity
Imam Hassan ibn ali – Representing the Muslim community
Swami Prabhupaba Ji – Representing Hinduism
Dalai Lama Gendun Gyatso – representing Buddhism
Rabbi Israel Cantoni – representing the Jewish community

We acknowledge that not every country nor religious leader is represented in this forum. Please understand that we have assembled this conference at short notice. In due time, all heads of state and faith will have an opportunity to voice their opinions. Rest assured that they have been contacted and will be kept apprised of developments. Now that the formal introductions have been made, you will hear the voice of a selected spokesman from each of the two groups. By mutual agreement, the British prime minister will speak for global governments and the Dalai Lama will speak for our leaders in faith.

At that, the British Prime Minister took to the podium.

"On behalf of leaders of nations, I have the duty and honor of speaking to the world on this momentous but precarious occasion. Together, humanity has faced horrific conditions, sometimes caused by the cruelty of man and sometimes through the power of nature. These calamities have made us stronger and we have grown as a species though adversity. Today, however, we address a different foe, one not of human origin, and for the first time in our existence we must truly come together if we are to successfully face this presence. This 'elemental', as we will refer to it, has the power to attack all of us without raising a finger. It can and will attack our very *consciousness* and, in doing so, remove our feelings, effectively eliminating the human awareness that is part of our being. We are only beginning to understand its capabilities but know that its objective is to reduce humans to billions of puppets who will unquestioningly do its will. Under the spell of this evil, we will never experience love, sunsets, music, happiness, touch or the sound of the waves breaking on a beach. Even the pleasant smells of nature won't register in our minds. Under the spell of this evil, our only purpose will be to blindly follow the elemental's instruction. We'll have no ability to resist it. My understanding is that this evil entity intends to build an army of humans who will go to war without caring about what happens to the planet or our species as a whole. It may be argued that this is similar to our known history of war with one exception, our leaders and warriors were aware of their actions. Eventually, every man, woman and child will be used up in the elemental's fight to eradicate free will in *any* being, human or alien.

There was a pause as the prime minister took a sip of water. Clearly, he was upset. Then he said:

"The war this elemental would draft us into would be against peaceful beings, not against an enemy that we understand. In a war of this creature's making, we would kill without conscience and when every person on earth is expended, humanity would cease to exist. To gain power, this creature feeds on fear. We realize our message today might escalate global fear and inadvertently help the creature to grow, but that's a risk we need to take, since without a warning, you might drift into the automaton state that the creature's presence induces. Our nations must unite to fight this. The group of leaders assembled today will provide as much support as possible and we are working every minute to eliminate this foe before it gains strength on Earth. We don't know how it got here, nor exactly when it arrived; what we do know is that it is in a fetal stage and is growing in an area of the world far from large population bases. We realize you will have many questions and have set up a website to answer them. We will continually update it with instructions on how to protect yourself and your families while we construct plans to attack its location. Thank you for your attention. I will now pass you to His Holiness the Dalai Lama … and may your God be with you."

"Thank you, Mr. Prime Minister and esteemed leaders," said the Dalai Lama. "I have been chosen by my peers and your spiritual leaders to address the world in this difficult time and be the voice of our concerns. Whatever you believe in, one God or many—or no gods at all—we have one thing in common … we are human. We are therefore collectively addressing *all* humanity, without segregation. We are challenged today to look to a future that will be different than any of us have ever imagined. It holds major changes for us. In blunt terms, we will either be extinct as an intelligent race or we unite. If we want to survive, we need to quickly evolve into a unified humanity, one without borders of country or divisions based on color, race or religion. At this crucial moment in time, we need to realize we are *one* species and we must create a new horizon in which we are completely unified. It is time to acknowledge that our DNA joins us all. One race. The *human* race. This elemental that has arrived in our midst is the most evil and dangerous enemy the world has ever faced. Never has anything threatened our very existence in this way! However, we are fortunate to have the awareness and understanding to resist its influence, at least for now. You may not have noticed anything affecting you yet, but consider this ... have you recently lost interest in what normally drives you? Do you care, for example whether your sports team will win? Are you looking forward to your family holiday? Do you feel love for your partner or children? Or is life beginning to lose importance? When did you last smile? If you have noticed your own apathy, then understand that this elemental is beginning to have an effect. The way you feel is what happens in the early stages of its influence. Shortly after, you will lose awareness of your feelings. Consider this, if this evil takes hold, your partner, friend, brother, sister, mother, father, daughter or son will have no significance anymore; you will just exist. The elemental, after removing your awareness, will control every thought and action you take ... but sadly, you will not care. You will simply be a pawn in his game. Free will as we know it will vanish."

The Dalai Lama looked upset as he continued.

"You have the right to ask how we know this. We are fortunate to have been notified by individuals with special abilities who have come to help us fight against this enemy. They have travelled far to be with us. They have experienced this evil entity before, many years ago, and are providing guidance and help so we can resist and hopefully conquer the beast. Nothing in our books of wisdom has recorded such evil. Yes, we're aware of the devil and his works—but even the dark lord has no power to remove awareness. He may twist your thoughts and pull you in a negative direction, but at least your consciousness and some reasoning remained intact. We understand that you may think this is a major hoax, but please feel what is happening inside and look around you. Do you hear the children play?"

He paused again. Then he said, "We are distributing an antidote that will help mitigate the effects this evil may have already had. It will reach you through your water systems and will also be distributed by mist delivered from airplanes in some areas. The antidote will restore emotion for some and help resist the evil influence for some time. However, as the elemental gets stronger, our remedy will become less effective. At that time, we will be fighting at a different level. Our allies are currently preparing for this battle. Our best line of defense is to remain peaceful and to help neighbors, family and friends by being strong. This is the first time in our history that all political and religious leaders are working together, without conditions—that's how big this threat is. Let's resolve to defeat this monster *together.* During our meetings in the last 24 hours we have made major advances in global cooperation and this will help us grow as one species. It is important that we are *all* together as leaders and as people. More than anything, we recognize the damage caused by segregation in our past and we must now move past our differences and tackle our future together. Thank you sincerely for listening to this important message. We will be with you all the way during this time of crisis. Namaste, my brothers and sisters in life."

The screen went blank.

"So now we have it, panic and confusion, fear and uncertainty, lack of trust and doubt about the future. A nice place to start, might I say," said Paul to the team.

"At least everyone has been alerted ... or should I say, everyone who has some way of viewing the message or hearing it on radio," said Jack. "Irrespective of how extensive our audience was during this live event, likely only half of the world's population will have seen or heard it. The media have been instructed to repeat it once an hour over the next 24 hours to capture more people. At the end of that period, we estimate we'll have reached 90 percent of the population."

"Yes," said Dan, who'd been silent for a while. "After the first 24 hours the message will repeat twice daily for a month. Yet it's probable that still some percentage will miss the communication. And the distribution of the antidote will only protect the population in more populated areas; it will be missed by those who live far in the countryside. Those individuals may have no protection, either physically or emotionally, and will be lost souls."

"Now we need to prepare against those attempting to create anarchy whilst awaiting the emergence of their lord and master," said Frazer. "We know there are millions of these individuals across the globe. They have weak minds but powerful ambition ... and an armory that any terrorist nation would be proud of. They will be difficult to recognize, as they will not be distinguishable from the average citizen. They could appear anywhere and at any time. They want to influence those who have power—such as politicians, executives and government officials—in short, anyone who controls money, society, the military and so on. Lives will be taken as they move into those positions of power, and chaos will reign."

"The effect will inevitably expand the fear frenzy desired by Moloch," said Ian, who now clearly understood how much his 'power of persuasion' over the minds of mankind was going to be needed.

As the team planned their next moves, an unusual disruption of the New York Subway system started causing major delays, leaving millions of commuters stranded on trains that had suddenly stopped mid-tunnel. Communication was cut and cell signals stopped working. The air in the tunnels got stagnant because the ventilation system shut down. In the short 15 minutes of this event, panic ensued. Emergency services commenced evacuating the underground tunnels, but bedlam reigned.

At the same time, a call was placed to the New York mayor's office. A heavily disguised voice told the mayor, "You will be aware your subway system is at a standstill. Your emergency services will be unable to remove sufficient numbers of people before phase one of our destruction falls into place. In a few short moments, poison gas will reach the lungs of all who remain trapped. We estimate we will eliminate over a million people today and this is just the start of our global operation. There is nothing you can do, as the gas has started pumping. Your citizens will be dead before 60 seconds have passed."

The phone went dead, and the mayor briefly stared at the blank wall facing his mahogany desk. After a few seconds he placed a call to the New York state senator. "I have no idea who is behind this action," he said, worried. "They did not demand anything, nor did we have any warning before this call. I notified emergency services, including the police tactical force, but it's too late ... that is, if the threat is real."

CNN were showing Central Park North on the news. Thousands of people were pouring out of the station, with some passing out within a few moments of reaching the exit. Then the stream of people stopped abruptly. The chief fire officer was first to venture to the head of the subway stairwell, fully suited with a gas mask. He was horrified to see that the stairwell—and as far as he could see beyond—was covered with lifeless bodies.

He checked the pulses of the few within his reach and confirmed their death. It was likely, therefore, that all in his view had suffered the same fate. He immediately announced to his crew that all nearby hospitals had to be alerted. They would receive those who had just made it through the exit. Then he sent immediate instruction to cordon off the area and informed all emergency crews to do the same at every entrance of the Metro network. He knew however, that it was too late.

At a local bar, televisions were all turned onto one channel. On it, a masked man sat in front of the camera and announced, "By now your protection agencies will have realized that your subway system has been compromised and all those who were using the underground in the past 30 minutes are dead!"

At that, everyone in the bar stopped talking and stared at the screen.

"We are not holding anyone ransom. This is just one example of what is about to happen in major cities throughout the world. Do not look for terrorist factions as being responsible; we are an unknown entity who have been lying in secret, waiting for this momentous occasion, the arrival of the 'elemental' as your leaders call him. We will undertake more strikes at random. No city is safe, and your security services will be proved useless in the days to come. Your so-called leaders are helpless to stop us, as we are unknown. To your eyes, we would appear exemplary citizens, your smiling next-door neighbor or your best friend at work ... you will never know. You cannot join us, and it would be futile for you to try to identify us. Just know that you cannot trust anyone. Maybe even your brother or sister is a member of our league! Yes, you should fear ... don't listen to your leaders! Fear will help us *all* ... and to resist is pointless. You will become our army!"

Then the screen went blank. There was no return of any channels for the next few minutes. Panic and fear began to grow as Moloch took form on the other side of the earth.

Similar situations were happening in all major cities. Almost instantaneously, the world population dropped by 50 million. Each city was in chaos. Emergency crews were stretched to the limit. Bodies would soon start rotting, rats would multiply, disease would spread fast and hospitals would be unable to cope. The Dark Ages returned in an instant. Any positive message the global leaders could conceive was now nullified. Nothing they could say would be helpful; almost everyone on earth had lost a friend or relative in a period of 10 minutes. Sadness, helplessness, anger and fear entered the heart of much of humanity; normal life would never resume.

Moloch laughed.

Back in Jack's fortress, he and his team watched in horror at the developments. Although they had expected an attack, this had taken them by surprise and they had drastically underestimated Moloch's advance team. They were saddened by the massive blow inflicted on humanity and knew the battle ahead was going to be long and widespread. The enemy was not completely invisible; April tracked the communication and shut down their computers with a virus that infiltrated their infrastructure and, at least for now, restricted further communications, externally or internally. She also provided Jack's special forces with precise locations of the enemies involved in this catastrophic event.

Within a few hours, Jack's far-reaching secret service had apprehended over 100 enemies from various global locations and, using Elena's ability to teleport each one into a secure cell, brought them to a secure site in the central United States. Paul was transported to the secure site as well and within minutes he had connected with each of the enemy telepathically. He gathered sufficient information from them to alert authorities about a few remaining target sites. Within a few hours, special forces had disabled the poison gas containers and removed them to secure facilities.

"Your powers are impressive and not unexpected, but we have initiated a global event that cannot be erased from history and will create enough pain and fear to help our master arrive," said the unimpressed terrorist spokesman to Paul. At that moment Dan entered the room and induced sleep on all the terrorists.

"Let's look deeper into their memories and establish the identity of the terrorist leaders who remain at large," said Dan. Then he started reviewing the leader's most recent memories and identified numerous co-leaders of the global terrorist gang. Paul telepathically provided the information to April, who located all the individuals through Internet connections and concocted a general message to each that would seem to have originated from their human leader, who was now sitting in front of Paul fast asleep.

The message read, 'Now that we have initiated plan 'airborne' and have inflicted a massive blow to humanity on behalf of our master, we can withdraw into hiding and await further orders'.

"At least this will put a hold on further global terrorist activities," said Paul to Dan, "But the damage has been done. Now Moloch will arrive in full force." He started wondering if the package might now be vulnerable, and ordered Elena to move it from his father's safe to another location that only she and he would know.

Meanwhile, unbeknownst to the group and to Moloch, moving swiftly through the ether, a universal being continued its journey, undetected, toward earth. It sensed changes and knew that its presence was urgently needed.

Chapter 16

Emergence

The butterfly effect grants the power to cause a hurricane in China to a butterfly flapping its wings in New Mexico. It may take a long time but the connection is real, if the butterfly had not flapped its wings at a precise space and time the hurricane would never have happened. In a similar understanding scientists are investigating 'entanglement' where at the quantum level a minute particle that is simply being observed would instantly change the properties of another particle light years away. Albert Einstein called this 'a spooky action at a distance'.

Jack was explaining this to the political and spiritual leaders. After the horrific events that had happened across the globe, he advised his audience that Paul, April and Dan were stopping further damage by the terrorists. All had been appalled to hear that the death toll was estimated to be at least 50 million, and, considering over 150 major metros worldwide were hit, Jack thought the estimate may be low.

The mood was somber; the light had gone from the eyes of the world leaders. They felt helpless and people were asking for their guidance. It was agreed that they would each return to their respective countries and make it known they were putting plans in place to help. Jack arranged for their immediate transfer and urged utmost caution once they arrived back home. Once they left the compound, he could no longer protect them against further action by the terrorists. They all agreed to ensure they were guarded by their security teams and promised to join teleconferences every day to keep each other advised.

"We will continue the widespread delivery of the antidote," Jack said. "It will help mitigate Moloch's power. However, at some point his power will be too strong for humans to resist and the antidote will be ineffective. Therefore, our focus must be on ways to fight the beast directly. Its earthbound army's influence has been reduced by our capture and control of their leaders. However there remain millions of radical individuals and factions who may create a revived force under new leaders. We will monitor this as best we can, but most of our effort must be put toward preventing the arrival of the beast." Then Jack wished his audience a safe journey.

Frazer and Jack retired to Jack's comfortable lounge for a brief respite from the strains of the past few horrific hours. Ian, Elena and Andrew were called to join them. While waiting on their arrival, Jack issued orders to his flight coordinators, Anthony and James. He wanted to ensure his air combat force was ready to launch at a moment's notice. Both assured Jack that they were ready and on standby. Jack nodded to Frazer, confirming everything was in place. It was time to mobilize the rest of the team. The air team was at the ready; now they had to make some serious decisions.

Andrew started with his impression of the situation so far. "We have lost the first stage of this battle, at massive human cost, and it's not clear where they will strike next. Do they plan further population annihilation? Why would they do that? I thought they wanted to create an army! We've searched the globe, but it's difficult to see through the veil produced by

Moloch's developing powers. Even *our* considerable resources will be strained as his evil influence takes hold."

He continued, "I've constructed a large titanium dome at the crater site, enclosing the cocoon. If cracks appear in the defensive dome, they will be reinforced automatically. However, there is a limit to the strength of the outer casing and at some point, as Moloch evolves, it will simply push through, like a dinosaur cracking its egg. The titanium dome will only buy us a few days."

Ian said, "I have been in contact with global leaders who were not part of our earlier forum and they are ready and supportive, though apprehensive about our venture."

Elena added, "Jack and Frazer, you are our last line of defense. We must protect you both if we hope for a positive outcome, so for the next few days you have to be removed from the direct conflict to a place where you can oversee the global movements of the terrorists."

"I agree we need to have a backup plan, but this is in Paul's hands," Jack said. "The package is his to apply when necessary. I passed the Scion to him for safekeeping. You, Elena, know what that means—especially since you've already have had it transported to a location only you and Paul know. Therefore, Paul and Frazer will be the final line of defense. Paul will return here shortly. Dan has the support of my military and can command it when necessary."

Jack looked around the room to ensure he had full agreement about his plans and all nodded their compliance. The team retired for short recess as they waited for Paul's arrival. When he got there, everyone regrouped in Jack's private lounge.

"Paul, right on cue," Jack said. "We are agreed as to the next phase of our battle plans and I'm happy to bring you up to speed. You and I and Frazer will adjourn to my study while our guys here rest."

Paul felt nervous about this meeting. He'd decided to come clean about his mental state.

"Dad," he said when they were alone. "I have no idea what's in the package and I've been thinking ... I'm not ready to take this responsibility. You know me, I'm the playboy of the group. I have no real responsibilities other than running my small business and I have no experience in global matters ... yet you're entrusting me with 'the last line of defense'? To put it simply, I'm scared!" said Paul, after receiving the briefing from Jack.

Jack looked at this son with compassion and said, "You may need to activate the package and we need to discuss how and when. You may not believe me, but none of us know what's in it. There is only the one simple rule regarding its use that we are all aware of, which is, 'do not open in the event of our death'. But there are some further conditions attached to that rule that you need to know now."

Paul listened, his eyes and mouth open in anticipation.

"Frazer and I have carried this burden for many lifetimes. We've been fortunate to die and reincarnate without incident. Our predecessors have also been as fortunate. Now, all that we've learned from them will be passed down and revealed to you," Jack said, raising a glass of brandy Frazer had poured for him and sipping. "I ask your patience as I give you the knowledge of the ancients. We know the Scion originated long before the earth was born. We also know it was guarded by the earliest beings, in galaxies further away than we can imagine. It's been guarded for billions of years and many different civilizations have had it in their care. This is not too hard to imagine, since our universe is estimated at 13.5 billion years, our galaxy and sun half that. It only appeared on earth in the last hundred years—relatively speaking, a mere few minutes in time—but for all we know it came from a different universe! Clearly, at no time has it been opened ... which we imagine to be a good thing."

Jack smiled. Then, when he saw his son's expression, he recognized this was not helping Paul in the least.

"Let's put it this way," he said, "The group of friends currently with us have all been together before, most recently millions of lightyears from the Milky Way. We are escapees of another of Moloch's actions, which destroyed many civilizations in the part of the universe in which we lived. At that time, the package was transported off our world and sent to an emerging star formation called the Pleiades, a star cluster around 400 lightyears from earth. The Pleiades is only 100 million years in formation and is a rocky planet with limited resources and no breathable air."

Paul nodded his understanding.

"One of our team, a 'custodian', was sent to that planet to locate the package. It was encased in a metal box within a large rock. This custodian sent it to earth. Its arrival was recorded in recent history as the Tunguska event, which occurred in June of 1908. During this event, a 2,000 square kilometer area of forest in Russia was flattened. The name of the event was derived from the name of the region, Tunguska Yeniseysk Governorate."

Paul was fascinated.

"Interestingly, many civilizations on earth have noted things about the Pleiades; these have been significant throughout history. The Celts, Maori, several traditions of Aboriginal Australians, Persians, Arabs, Chinese, Japanese, Maya, Aztec, Sioux, Cherokee—all have references to this group of stars. They are commonly known as the seven sisters. In Hinduism, they are associated with the war god, Kartikeya, and they are also mentioned three times in the bible. Homer mentioned them in the Iliad and Odyssey ... not bad recognition for a small group of stars only 100 million years old!"

Paul sighed at the astronomy lesson, but knew his father had good reason to explain the background.

"Several thousand of us survived Moloch's attack, which occurred almost a million years ago in earth time. When we escaped, we dispersed throughout various galaxies to prepare civilizations against further attacks. I guess our current group drew the short straw; we evolved as humans on earth," Jack chuckled. "Not that earth is an inhospitable planet … much the reverse. But we're now the front line in the universe's defense against Moloch. The most recent changes in human global awareness, made possible by the Internet, and the easy access to immediate news—fake or real—has allowed uncertainty to reach into the psyche of mankind. This has subliminally developed into fear. Fear is a magnet to Moloch. It's the source of his power. Even the past century's two world wars did not induce the level of fear and uncertainty of today. The world is more global and informed and the human race has doubled in size since the first world war. The energy from fear our global culture has been cultivating is like a light switch for Moloch. Now, getting back to the package ..." Jack smiled and nodded for the rest of the crew to join them. They did.

"If the package is opened it will be the first time in the history of this universe. As mentioned, until it came to earth it was safely stored it on a young, unformed planet, near the star Maia. The guardians of this package lived with it and it wasn't fun; they lived like hermits for many months within a shielded environment in that inhospitable place. Finally, the transport of the package to earth was arranged by survivors who lived on the mothership in orbit around the planet. The ship's enormous and advanced power produced the energy needed to direct the rock toward Tunguska. It landed in an unpopulated area, planned to minimize collateral damage. And the hermit who guarded it all those years on Maia, by the way, was an earlier incarnation of our friend, Elena."

Everyone except Jack and Frazer were surprised by this information and Paul's jaw dropped at the announcement. *More surprises*, he thought.

Jack said, "Each of us in this room are survivors of Moloch's last attempt to wipe out a civilization that was once ours and so it is our universal duty to stop the beast. You, Paul, are now the leader of our group, since you are the custodian of the package."

The frown on Paul's face showed his anxiousness at inheriting such responsibility.

"Don't worry, Paul. Your father is correct, no one knows what's in the package," Elena said as she reached over and touched Paul's arm. She noticed his hands were trembling.

"You will be unable to open the package without understanding the process by which it is done," advised Dan. "Only the carriers have information about that process and each one of us in this room, except you Paul, has been a carrier. We hold the information to protect you until you need to know."

"But I think we need to discuss it now," said Jack. "Paul needs to know what he might have to do. Elena would you do us the honor of bringing the package here?"

At this request, Elena asked Paul's approval to bring the package to Jack's study. Paul nodded, and the item appeared on Jack's desk a few feet away courtesy of Elena's telekinetic ability. Paul carried it over to the small table in front of the group, noticing the differences it had taken on when his father had changed ownership to him. Not only was it no longer wrapped in brown paper secured by string, but all the markings had changed ... and the date on it was now *Paul's* birthday. The covering seemed plastic to the touch and it was much more rigid than the brown paper. Further, the seal incorporating Jack and Paul's DNA covered a metal band that encircled the box.

"Don't worry, Paul," Jack said, "Only the peripheral packaging looks different, as it has been modified to blend in with today's expectations of package wrapping. The brown paper was a bit out of date. Now, don't be nervous. All you need to do is hold the box in both hands and imagine it opening. You have to be alone when this happens, as any interference from others could have catastrophic effects on them, including all of us."

"Since no one has ever opened the package, how do you know this?" Paul asked the group. "A scion, as you call it, is a young shoot of a plant, if my memory from gardening days with Mum is correct."

"It also means descendant from a notable family. I believe either understanding is suitable," said Ian.

Paul studied the box and its new design and inscriptions.

"Bring it over here, near the fire," advised Frazer inviting Paul to join him.

As Paul held it closer to the heat, he noticed some inscriptions appearing. This time the words were in plain English. In addition to the already well-known opening line 'Do not open in the event of my death', other words became visible.

> *Do not open in the event of my death, but if intrinsic evil is at my door, stand still in silence, alone in darkness, and silently call my name, 'Melchizedek'. This will unveil the Scion. Beware that such an event will unbalance time and reset the future. Many will die but those who survive will begin again. Evil will be curtailed; knowledge will be changed.*

"What in hell, or heaven, is this?" asked Paul, shaken.

"Now you see why it has never been opened—at least, not in this universe," explained Jack. "We believe there is an essence in this scion that somehow will change destiny. Moloch's aim is to erase awareness, to take over our souls and your essence of being. Under his rule we will no longer be self-determining. Our free will as we know it will be gone and we will never have an independent thought again. However, if you must release the scion, time will shift. We have no idea what is implied by 'reset the future'."

"I get it, we start all over again ... but what does that really mean for humanity?" Paul, asked, thinking aloud.

"It means a new beginning. Humans would be reduced somewhat if we are to believe that 'many will die'. However, I have never speculated on what the message really means ... my focus was simple; don't open the package," explained Jack.

Andrew added, "Moloch will be affected if it's opened. It stands to reason that it may be a weapon against his influence. That may be the reason it's here."

Silence descended in the room; only a crackling fire could be heard. The weight on the shoulders of the team suddenly became heavier. Paul struggled with the enormity of the situation. Would it not have been better to leave the scion on Maia, the star it had been stored on so long under Elena's care?

"Can we not send the scion back to Maia?" he asked loudly, surprising his crew.

"That would not stop Moloch," said Elena. "He is here because of humanity's fear and uncertainty, and that will remain even if the scion does not. It is possible the scion is chasing Moloch and not the other way around."

Paul looked at the box in front of him and wondered at such power now in his hands. *Terrible*, he thought, and wished it was not his responsibility. Yet something inside him understood this was his destiny. He felt sick at the thought of ever having to open the box, which he'd silently nicknamed 'Pandora'—even though he knew Pandora's box was really a jar—but he knew he had to do this.

"Okay, my friends, now that Paul has a better understanding of his responsibilities we need to return the package to a safe place. Elena, would you do the honors?" Jack asked. Promptly, the package vanished, transported telepathically to its hiding place. "And now we need to move ahead with our plan to thwart Moloch's arrival," said Jack. Then, using the in-house communication system, he asked for an update on the prisoners from Dan.

Dan responded, "They are secured in single cells which, as you know, block every signal including those from telepaths. They will also not be able to receive instructions from Moloch or his worldly associates," Dan said.

"What about the two entrepreneurial guys you have in custody?" Jack enquired.

"Both are in similar holding cells in the basement; they will not do any damage either."

On that note, Jack returned to the group and reported that all was well so far.

"What's next, Jack?" asked Ian. "What action will we take to destroy Moloch's nest? I know Andrew has constructed a shell around the cocoon, but that provides only limited protection against the beast. Is there anything more radical that we can do to prevent Moloch evolving?"

"Possibly," Jack said. "This is why Naomi hasn't joined us today. She's been working with Rod from NASA to move the cocoon and its protective shell to a safer location and they have placed it in the Arctic. I'm amazed at how well her power over gravity has developed in such a short time. It's also surprising that no one noticed such a large object travelling. Every day we get reports of UFOs and yet this massive structure floated through the darkness over a great distance without any media picking up on it. It indicates that Moloch may have greater control over people's minds than we think."

"Can't we just nuke it?" announced Andrew in a mischievous manner.

"We don't fully understand its structure and can't chance fallout affecting the world's climate," replied Jack. "It would also alert everyone to its location ... and if we failed to destroy the nest, we would have other, worse challenges to deal with."

Pensively the group began discussing battle plans, while Paul stood to one side, still struggling to grasp his inherited responsibilities. He thought about when he'd first received the call from his father while he was back at home in Minneapolis. He wished he was still back there, planning on going skiing. When Jack first called, he had no idea what he was getting into. The subsequent opening of his memories and unveiling of his abilities had changed that significantly. The innocent person he was just days ago was gone and he had now become a global leader who carried an unbelievable burden. He, Naomi, Ian and the rest of his newly acquired friends and partners had come a long way in the past few weeks, facing changes that were almost impossible to handle that were thrust upon them without warning. Paul especially felt his role was too much; but he understood that his predecessors had suffered the same feelings. However, they did not have Moloch the monster to deal with. Then he thought, *if Moloch was around and overcame the planet on which the previous incarnations of Frazer or Jack held the Scion, then why did Jack not open it then? Why me? Why now?*

"Dad, here's a good question ... why did you not open the package when Moloch attacked the planet from which your incarnation escaped? Weren't you responsible to act in the same way as I am today?"

It was a few moments before Jack responded.

"I was not the holder of the package on that planet; someone else held it but they did not survive and so the package out-lived that individual. They had not passed it to anyone in their lifetime, unlike our situation. This meant it passed to caretakers to be passed to a new incarnation of the keeper in a later life. I was part of a team, like the group now gathered. The custodian of that time did not prepare the transfer in time as she was facing insurmountable odds. When she was in the process of enacting the ceremony to activate the Scion, her life was taken ... and Elena, who was part of our team, transported the package to safety."

"And that's meant to make me feel good?" asked Paul rhetorically.

"There's no question you have a heavy burden, but this time, at least, we are forewarned about Moloch's arrival. We have the advantage of a strong team and better intel as to Moloch's intent and powers."

Paul drifted further into dismay. He hadn't the experience of his father, and, although he now had significant powers, he couldn't see how they would be helpful in the days to come.

"Don't worry, son, you have a strength yet unchallenged and I know you will be able to make the right decision if you have to. The rest of us will do our best to make sure you won't have to make that decision."

The direct line from NASA buzzed, interrupting them. Jack answered and within a few seconds Rod appeared before the group on the 60-inch screen. "Good day, my friends, my apologies for taking so long to get in touch, but I've spent the past few hours briefing the president and his generals on the current state of affairs. There are some doubting Thomases in the group and they are asking why we are entrusting the fate of mankind to a group of strangers. Obviously, President Mitchel doesn't have the persuasive abilities of Dan or Paul. The result is that at this moment they're about to launch a nuclear attack on the cocoon. They know where it is, and the submarine USS Virginia is under the ice only five miles away. Virginia has the nuclear capacity to do the job. I've been tracking the Russians and they are of a similar mindset." Rod was obviously stressed.

"Okay, Rod, we'll take over from here. Please keep in touch—and if you need anything else, the line is always open."

Jack called the airbase and spoke with Martin. "I'm sending Ian and Andrew over to you, with coordinates. Please transport them as close as you can to where they need to go. Once you get close, Elena will look after the rest."

Paul was happy but surprised to see Martin. He looked at Jack and asked, "When did Martin get here?"

"Martin was the pilot who brought Frazer here from Washington. We need his skills to work with James, Anthony and the dromas. Sorry, so many things are happening that I forgot to brief you guys," said Jack with a shrug.

"Ian and Andrew, we'll get you on the Virginia and you can deal with the captain directly. If he won't be persuaded by Ian, we'll need Andrew to use his abilities to ensure he stops. Ladies and gentlemen, we expected this mission would not be plain sailing, excuse the pun, but now we need to stop a missile launch."

He turned to Ian and Andrew, "I anticipate you'll also be able to deal with the Russians? They'll be near. Elena will communicate with you as you need."

Inside the cocoon, heat was building and the pressure of the air between the cocoon and the outer titanium structure was becoming intense. The source of the heat was unclear, but scientists stationed at a laboratory in Resolute Bay in Canada were monitoring it.

"We're noticing a major spike of heat building up within the structure surrounding the cocoon," one scientist told Jack. "This is causing the air captured within the space between the outer and inner ovoid to expand. We have no idea how much pressure the outer casing can take; would Andrew be able to assist in the calculation?" enquired the chief scientist who had now been patched through from the British link directly to Jack's conference room.

"I'm not a scientist and we don't know the construction of the cocoon. It's possible the outer structure may force the cocoon to implode, but who knows?" Andrew said.

"We're in unknown territory here," Jack advised the Canadian science lead. "We can only monitor for cracks in the outer structure that might cause leaks. I'm afraid we can't offer much help at this stage. Please be careful. May I suggest you evacuate the lab immediately?"

At that moment, an alarm sounded within the science lab. The alarm was located only 1,000 meters from the cocoon. The scientist quickly said, "I think we've just received the answer. A crack is appearing around the centre and it looks like a breach is close. We're signing off now and ..."

The signal was lost, and the screen went black.

"The air steaming out must be so powerful it destroyed the lab!" exclaimed Paul.

"I fear it has begun," said Jack solemnly. "Take care Ian, Andrew and Martin. God speed."

Although the pressure was tremendous within the walls of the ovoid, the strength of the outer layer stopped a complete explosion from happening; however, the air steamed out with hurricane force. The titanium structure maintained its general integrity and, due to Andrew's unique design, it started repairing itself as the pressure equalized. However, Andrew knew it would not be long before the automatic restoring of his construction would reach its limits and cracks would form and weaken the formation. Eventually it would collapse.

The embryo inside the cocoon lurched, as if Moloch was laughing ... its first emotion in a million years. It felt good.

Chapter 17

Earth in Danger

The cold war was a thing of the past, and in recent years the Russians and Americans had grown to respect each other, at least in the scientific community. Otherwise, the governments were competitive with each other. Each used the Internet to clandestinely toy with elections, causing ripples in democratic stability. Fake news and interference in propaganda reached the front page of the average person's cell phone. It was a game that confused everyone. Because of this, there was no way to predict how individuals would react to the stories being peddled by the meddlers worming their way around the web; however, most of the orchestrators of the fake news didn't care about the effect. They enjoyed the confusion that reigned. Such turmoil attracted negative aspects of humanity to emerge, which fed Moloch's power.

Martin's skilled piloting of the advanced alien technology he was controlling enabled arrival at the lab within minutes. As the aircraft reached the site, they looked down on the titanium structure and it seemed stable; however, the lab was blown to smithereens.

From the White House, President Mitchel was in direct contact with the submarine near the site of the lab and he approved both Ian and Andrew to come aboard. To the surprise of the captain, both materialized in the control room. The officers and crew were shocked into silence.

"Don't worry captain, we've made some advancements in transportation. I'm sure you'll get used to it in the future," said Ian nonchalantly. "Meanwhile, we must not use nuclear force on this object. There is no way of telling what will happen, as the target will likely absorb the energy of the bomb and use it against us in retaliation," advised Ian.

"Our orders are to attack and I'm afraid I only take orders from the president directly. We are 10 seconds from launch." The captain nodded at the clock counting down.

The remaining few seconds flashed in front of their eyes and Andrew tried to use his power to stop time, but nothing happened. *Three, two, one* ... then suddenly the clock stopped at one—however, Andrew hadn't caused the halt. The captain asked his lieutenant to check the instruments, which were fine. Then the captain turned to Ian and Andrew and accused them of interference, but the expression on both their faces was enough for the captain to know some other influence had disabled the launch.

The captain opened a channel to the Russian vessel. He enquired if they had success in launching, but they reported the same result; their launch sequence stopped at one.

Ian and Andrew were confused. They communicated with Martin, who was waiting topside, approximately 1,000 feet above the US submarine.

"There's no point on us staying aboard. We should now leave the area, please advise Elena to handle it and let's return to base," said Ian to Martin. Within moments they were back with Martin, returning to Jack's location.

While Ian and Andrew were in transit, Jack confirmed to them that he had arranged for April to intervene. She obtained the launch codes and intercepted the launch sequence.

"We cut it a little close, don't you think?" asked Jack, winking at April who sat with him in his study.

April smiled. She'd had fun watching Jack's face uncharacteristically show a little stress as they observed the count down from their base. "Sorry!" she said with a chuckle. "I couldn't help having a little fun ... you should have seen your face, Jack."

"Okay, you got me. I guess I'd have done the same. I can see you've complete control and that's the main thing."

"Yes, but I can't do anything about the beast's actions and that's our main concern," said April.

"We'll handle it!" said Jack with thumbs-up sign.

The two submarines maintained their position and launched drones to maintain a visual on the object and all that remained of the science lab. The feed from the drones was open to NASA, the White House, the Kremlin and Jack's operations room, which, unknown to the other parties, was capable of monitoring the most secretive actions on a global basis, thanks to April's ability to track anything that used digital technology.

Jack thought, *at least we have two superpowers working together!*

Meanwhile, situations in major cities worldwide continued to be overwhelming. The catastrophic subway attacks that took millions of lives had crippled emergency services everywhere. Hospitals were packed with those who had survived, and fire, police and ambulance services were strained with the horrific task of removing the bodies from the subway stations which had now turned into caverns of the dead and rat-infested hellholes. Army units were working with other emergency personnel, but nothing had prepared them for the sheer scale of the recovery effort needed. The terrorist group's leaders may have been captured, and further activities restricted, but the world had been dealt a major blow and the energy required to recover was limiting every aspect of normal daily lives.

Almost every human being on earth had lost someone. The grief spilling out of homes and churches was overwhelming. Cremation was mandatory as there was simply nowhere to bury the dead. Industry come to a halt; trading stopped; only essential services were operating. Martial law, for what it was worth, was being applied everywhere. Looting became the norm—businesses had guards at their doors to protect what was left of the world's goods and services because the global supply chain had ground to a halt. Transportation of food and medical products were given priority over that of luxury goods and all production workers had been diverted to produce only things crucial to existence. Farms were of paramount importance and were guarded by armies under government control. Commuting into downtown cores of cities was restricted to those providing essential services only. Borders were closed, and flights were approved on an emergency basis only. It would be a long time before services returned to normal and the world would never be the same again.

Food rationing was reintroduced for the first time since WW II. Vouchers were issued to households on a per capita basis, with special bonus coupons issued to families with children under 12 years of age. Schools were closed, and students were educated online in their homes. Those in the suburbs had life a bit easier than those in inner cities; some public transport was available when fuel could be obtained. Children were shipped from city centers to family or friends living in the suburbs or the country. Buying or selling property was forbidden.

The daily news that reached households held little hope for the already devastated public. Most understood the cause of the catastrophe as a terrorist attack but couldn't understand why government or special police services hadn't done anything to prevent it. Trust and uncertainty were rampant; fear of what would come next populated conversations and permeated the air. Moloch, still without form, sensed the hopelessness threatening the planet. The malevolent force gathered strength by the minute.

Paul sat quietly alone in his father's study; it was now 1:00 a.m., two days after the metro attacks. He could feel the burden of the world and the strain was something he didn't think he could take much more of. The fact that the last time Moloch successfully devastated a planet ended in the death of the Scion's custodian left him uneasy. He doubted his death to be a certainty, but world events and lack of a clear battle plan didn't fill him with confidence.

As he sat in despair, and for the first time since the loss of his wife Jessica he didn't know what to do next. Everyone close to him was tangled in a web that left them with unprecedented duties. It is just as well they had lived their various lives in blissful ignorance of their abilities and destiny. No one would choose such a weight.

As he wandered through quiet thoughts, reminiscing and partly just feeling sorry for himself, there was an interruption in his consciousness. At first, he thought he heard someone speak, but there was no one in the room. He looked around, thinking he was imagining things. Then he heard it. '*Yes*' a soft voice said distinctly, but where did it come from? '*Yes*' the voice in his head repeated. It sounded familiar, but confused Paul so much that he wondered if he was hearing things now that his special powers were becoming so strong. *'It's alright Paul, it's just me'*, he heard next.

Startled this time, he stood up and searched the room for the source of the voice. He could see no one. What was happening? *'You have the strength, don't despair, you are not alone.'* Paul was scared to answer. Wide-eyed, he began to doubt his sanity. If he responded, it would surely mean he had lost it. *'Help is on its way.'*

Paul screwed up his face in concern, still resisting a conversation. *'Be still and look deep inside, you will know the answer. Expand your senses and you'll feel us.'* Still disbelieving his senses, Paul didn't answer.

'Soon' continued the voice. *'Do NOT open the scion, it has more power than anyone has told you.'* Paul started to shake his head to rid himself of the voice. *'We'll be with you when you need us.'*

"Are you alright, Paul?" Jack was holding Paul by the shoulders, staring into his eyes. Paul blinked awake, wondering if he had been dreaming. "This room is under video surveillance and one of my security guys told me to check on you. You've been walking around the room looking for something or someone ... are you okay?"

"Would you believe me if I said I was hearing voices?" Paul shook himself to ensure he was now truly awake.

"What voices, who?" asked Jack with concern.

"It seemed I knew the voice ... soft female intonations, pleasant, peaceful and reassuring. If I didn't know better, I'd say it sounded like Jessica."

"You've been working hard and are extremely tired; go and rest and we'll talk again later this morning." Jack took Paul by the arm, guided him toward the door and asked a maid to take him upstairs to ensure he took some rest.

After a while, Martin returned with Ian and Andrew and the team met in the breakfast room. Paul was refreshed. Everyone had some time to recover from the desperate issues the world had faced during the past 48 hours.

Naomi, Paul, Ian, Dan, Frazer, April, Andrew, Elena and Jack all enjoyed a little lighthearted conversation over another succulent British breakfast. They truly enjoyed the luxuries and felt pampered at every moment while living with Jack and Harriet. However, access to news or newspapers was restricted to give everyone a period of recess. They would need all their energy channeled into clear and objective thought and action soon enough.

"Paul's been hearing voices," laughed Jack

"That's not funny dad, it bothers me."

"But you must admit, it's still funny," Jack teased, laughing along with the whole table.

Paul also saw the funny side. "But I didn't answer," he said, adding further hilarity to the moment.

"Good, my son. You'll benefit from a sense of humor, we all will."

"Did you see the light?" sniggered Naomi.

Paul threw a breakfast roll at Naomi, which started a bun fight, along with a few spillages, but the atmosphere was happy, and the team became stronger.

"We'll all meet in my conference room around 10:00 a.m. and schedule our day. No outside news until that point. We'll start by briefing the global leaders and after that we'll discuss our next action."

To which Frazer interrupted "To tackle the beastie!"

"That's the spirit!" Jack shouted as he left the breakfast room.

Naomi consoled Paul, asking if he was all right after hearing the 'voices'. Paul smiled and nodded. "We're going to be fine," he said.

The group disbanded and moved to their private quarters for a little solitude before the day's battles. They all knew what was ahead would be worse than what had already occurred; however, it was important to carry on with the right spirit.

A meeting was underway on the other side of the earth in Caracas, Venezuela. The room was dark and filled with smoke. The attendees were a rough-looking bunch, a mixed group of Europeans, Latin Americans and North Americans. There didn't seem to be a significant leader and there was no order to the conversation. They were having a debate was about global power. Some of those in the room already managed to get the leaders of their countries under their control and influence. In many cases, democratic leaders were being removed by this evil group and puppet leaders put in their place.

Suddenly the door to the room blew open and everyone looked at what had caused the sudden noise. Standing in the doorway was a tall, dark-cloaked, hooded stranger. The room fell silent, all eyes were fixed on the newcomer. It seemed like the man drifted, rather than walked, into the room, his long cloak flowing around him with each movement. How did this man get past their security?

Each person in the room felt a chill deep inside, they were not used to this feeling ... fear, the type of fear that brings an urge to vomit. Though the room was dimly lit, the stranger's eyes glowed red against a dark face, which had no expression. The stranger moved silently to the end of the large conference table. No words were spoken; everyone was riveted to their seat. The sunken, red eyes shifted, slowly but deliberately, from person to person as he surveyed the room. Each person felt that he had looked directly into their soul and, without exception, everyone felt a cold sweat as the red eyes drilled into their very being.

The being lifted his left hand, which was more like a claw than a hand, and before anyone could blink he slammed it down onto the large wooden table, rocking the room with vibration, leaving a dark, smoking, burned impression of his claw smoldering on the wood of the table as if he had branded it. Gasps were heard from various members of the group, yet they stayed riveted to their seats.

The being rasped, an attempt at speaking, its voice harsh. It spoke as if each breath was taken in pain.

'It was my breath that provided the poison which killed the millions of humans travelling in their underground transit structures. Nothing could have been easier. However, I am

being thwarted. A force of above-normal human intelligence and capability, has captured your leaders. I need to find out more about this group. They have technology beyond your knowledge and abilities that would seem superhuman to any of you. I am your guide for the next phase of our preparation for the arrival of our true leader. Our true leader will provide the human race with peace and tranquility never experienced before. You will not want for anything and the struggles you face daily will subside. There will be no governments or countries warring and you will not fight among yourselves ever again. It will be the utopia I know you dream of. Yes, I hear your thoughts and feel your needs. Don't worry, everything will be given to you in time. Listen very carefully ... go home to your people and tell them of our need to prepare. Our next attack will be on all telecommunications as well as a sudden increase in radiation levels. It will become unbearably hot in certain regions of the world and many more will perish. I am cleansing this race in anticipation of the next coming. Our leader will not tolerate resistance. With a simple thought from me, you will die.'

At that moment, three of the meeting attendees rose to their feet grasping their throats, as they suddenly were unable to breathe. Within a few seconds, they were dead.

'You may wonder what happened to these conspirators; I received their thoughts and each intended resistance. There's no need to worry about them anymore. Now go and spread the word without hesitation. You will all be saved, if you follow my instructions—and you have seen what happens if you doubt. Each of your families and friends will survive the coming radiation buildup if they move underground at precisely twelve noon, Greenwich Mean Time, seven days from now as you humans define time on this planet. The exposure will last for a few hours. Anyone outside and not undercover will perish within a few days due to radiation exposure.'

Then the being drifted silently away into the dark hallway and vanished.

The group looked at each other in astonishment. Then the bodies on the floor were taken away and the remaining twelve departed for the airport to travel home as instructed, while the stranger laughed at the irony. He enjoyed leaving just twelve to spread the word.

Inside the cocoon, Moloch was beginning to emerge into form, comforted by the knowledge that his commander had prepared the way for the next phase of his operation. Moloch needed a last boost of energy, which it would receive as humanity developed more pain and fear when the earth heated up. Then, with his new strength, he would eliminate all doubters of his plan.

Walking together, Paul and Elena felt a sudden rush of anxiety. They had been monitoring anyone connected to the captured leaders and sensed something had developed. Elena asked Paul to join her in the library.

"Did you feel that?" asked Paul.

"Yes, and I know the source. It's Moloch's commander, he—or should I say, it—prepares the way for Moloch and brings chaos. I can sense him and will try to link."

At that, Elena sat, eyes closed. In a few moments she said, "I can feel him, Paul. It was this creature that caused the underground attack and he's planning another scheme ... oh my God, it's worse than the recent metro disaster! We need to get the group together, right now."

Paul contacted all the team and within a few moments they joined him and Elena in the library. "Moloch's commander is here," Paul said. "He caused the first disaster in the subways and now he's planning another disaster on a much wider scale. You are all familiar that earth is spinning at 25,000 miles per hour? I'm sure you also know that the Sun and solar system are travelling along a plane within our galaxy, the Milky Way. The

Milky Way spins like a cartwheel and moves through cosmic dust, or harmful radiation waves, as it rotates through space. We are normally protected from these harmful rays by earth's magnetic field and the ozone layer."

Everyone nodded at Paul's explanation.

"The sun emits solar flares, massive bursts of solar plasma, on a regular basis. These are usually harmlessly deflected by our magnetic field, but if that field is weakened and those emissions enter through gaps in our ozone layer, we will be exposed to direct sunlight on a massive scale. Mars lost its atmosphere three or four billion years ago and scientists expect that solar flares were a factor in its demise. The thought is that they punched through Mars' weakened gravity, scorched the land and surface water evaporated into space, weakening the planet's natural cooling system. It seems this beast has the power to attract a major solar flare to Earth. This could wipe out satellites and disrupt all telecommunication. Are you with me so far?"

All of them nodded.

"His plan is to direct a major flare toward Earth while we are passing through a turbulent sector of the galaxy. There is residue of a gamma ray burst caused by two stars colliding a few thousand years ago and we're moving through that emission of intense energy seven days from now. Moloch's commander will use that electromagnetic effect, combined with a massive solar flare, to augment it. He will direct this energy at Earth's northern hemisphere for a long enough period to have a devastating effect. During that exposure, radiation will pass through holes in the ozone and reach the earth's surface. This will have short and long-term effects on every living being. Anyone exposed to this direct radiation will die within a few hours."

Paul looked at his friends to be sure they understood the seriousness of the situation. "We need to act fast. Ian, please contact Martin and ask him to prepare a strike on this 'commander'. Elena, can you locate him?"

"Yes, he's in Venezuela. I can see a major waterfall nearby."

"Ah-ha," said Paul. "He's at Angel Falls in southeastern Venezuela. I hiked there once after my wife died. Coincidentally, the falls cascade from atop Devils Mountain. Okay, Ian, please ask Martin to have the dromas prepare for action, as we will need their technology and stealth capability. I would ask you to be the one to go."

Martin and Ian met with the droma leader at the subterranean air base. Ian was astonished at the size of the cavern, which seemed to go on into the distance for some miles. The droma leader stood a few feet above Ian, who was tall for a human. Ian could see that a large force of dromas had been assembled and were ready for action. It seemed there were thousands. Ian thought, *how is it possible for such a large population to go unnoticed*?

"Elena, please provide the coordinates of Moloch's commander to the dromas," Ian requested. Soon the data was uploaded into the flight plan for all five aircraft undertaking the mission. Ian boarded the lead craft and was joined by Martin and Anthony as well as the droma leader and his crew. The oval-shaped craft could accommodate up to 20 personnel. The other four crafts were smaller fighter jets. They would lead the attack. Within moments, they were in the air. Ian felt a little motion sickness due to the incredible speed they were traveling and Martin laughed at Ian's pale color and said,

"Don't worry Ian," said Martin. "It will pass soon. We'll be on site within minutes."

Jack linked in through droma conferencing technology and said, "While we are targeting Moloch's creature, we need to examine Earth's path through this section of the galaxy and establish if our friends the dromas, with their advanced knowledge, have a way to deflect the energy being unleashed on Earth should the attack fail in Venezuela."

He called the droma lieutenant to his conference room and said, "Elena and Andrew, would you please join me for this discussion? Frazer, please work with Rod at NASA and keep him advised of our actions."

Recess was over, and the team was in full action mode. As the team sprang into gear, Paul paused briefly, feeling the human pulse which, despite the current threat, was surprisingly peaceful. *How resilient we humans are,* he thought. He felt there was hope.

In most major cities however, the aftermath of the subway disaster had required the authorities to dispose most of the bodies without any attempt to reconcile identities in order to avoid major disease and resume some form of order. Some objections to the process were voiced, but common sense prevailed and families and neighbors consoled each other that it was a necessary evil and mourned their lost ones within their hearts rather than at a gravestone. Everyone knew that treating human corpses like cattle, without burial rituals, would have ramifications in years to come, but the certainty of infection and the sheer magnitude of the tragedy was so overwhelming that there was no choice but to deal with the cleanup in the most expedient way. The process was faster than expected, but the smell of burning flesh lingered in the atmosphere.

At Jack's headquarters, Paul and Naomi worked on disrupting the twelve evil minions who were on their various journeys home from Venezuela. April had already cancelled their flights, which had been privately arranged at great expense. The twelve would only realize this predicament at the time of check-in. Also, in accordance with global restrictions on non-essential flying, aircraft were grounded worldwide. It would take some time for the twelve to make alternative arrangements. April was happy with her work, which effectively held the twelve at Caracas airport indefinitely.

The dark force that was Moloch's representative on earth, his commander—an old being with many names—waited to make his next move. He was an orchestrator extraordinaire, usually appearing when there was an opportunity to disrupt mankind's development. When good leaders emerged and helped human development rise another level, he prevented their good intentions from becoming reality. He usually did it by simply killing the leader; a sudden illness was most discrete, or an assassination if he felt like being dramatic. Everything he did appeared to be accidental ... giving birth to one conspiracy theory after another.

Alternatively, when a less scrupulous person came to power, he helped them rise in popularity. In recent decades it had become easier since technology could globally circulate information in an instant. He liked developing 'fake news' ... a little invention of his. *Humans are gullible,* he thought, *and I like that ... their minds are easy to mold.* A devil by any other name! He'd been on Earth for millennia and he liked it. It was mostly his very own kingdom.

He had many names, but he particularly liked Satan, as it had biblical connotations.

As he waited for Moloch's arrival, however, Satan was perplexed. Despite his sworn allegiance to Moloch he felt uncertain about his master's emergence, as it would diminish his own power on Earth. Yet if he did not attend to his duties, he would simply cease to exist! And so, he carried on with his evil intent. And he knew he had to find out who was thwarting his master.

That team was hard at work. Jack, Elena and Andrew were meeting with the droma second in command as well as the American President and the British Prime Minister, both of whom had just finished their daily calls with the other global leaders. Jack disabled video to ensure no one could see his droma collaborator.

"Thank you for joining us, Mr. President and Mr. Prime Minister. In the room with me is my vice-chief security, Mr. Droma. You already know Elena and Andrew, both of whom are invaluable team members." Jack smiled to himself at referring to a species as 'Mister'.

"I understand you've located a splinter group and they're being delayed at Caracas. Good move on your part," said the American president. "What do you know about this group and the creature that seems to be guiding them?"

"We don't have full information on the creature managing the splinter group," Jack said, "But we do know he manufactured the poison that was pumped into the metros ... and we have knowledge of the next initiative being planned."

At Jack's request, Elena provided an explanation to the two leaders.

The president was shocked. He said, "We'll issue a global alert and tell everyone to stay indoors and, where possible, we'll open school gyms and stadiums for people to take cover. At least we have some notice of *this* event and can try to mitigate its effect. Our progress on the subways is moving well. We've cleared all the remains and now the stations look like ghost towns. However, we are now able use the subways again and this time have backup systems in place to provide venting. Do you think this creature will try the same attack again?"

"I don't know," said Jack. "But we studied the chemical compound involved and have manufactured an antidote. However, we don't know if we can produce enough to handle the millions affected. We're sending the formula to all pharmaceutical companies in the next few hours," he advised.

"We'll instruct our people to support the distribution and we'll inform all world leaders accordingly," advised the British Primc Minister.

"Thanks to everyone for their help ... and our prayers are with you all," added the president. "We shall now end this session."

When the world leaders were gone, Jack said, "Mr. Droma, do you like your new name?" and laughed. "Little do they know we are indebted to you and your race. Please look at the earth's trajectory and identify this energy cloud that we will pass through. I hope you are able to deflect the flare should it get to that point."

Because the droma method of speaking was impossible to comprehend, the droma leader's thoughts were transferred to a computer screen for all in the room to see.

"On our home planet, we currently use loop technology, which is basically a large loop of conductive wire that acts like a magnetic field, placed at a distance from our planet. Constructing such a process usually takes a few months, however we have already erected a large structure strategically placed to reduce future harmful rays reaching Mars as part of our terraforming initiative on that planet. We're happy to have helped your technological advances over the last few decades as you've hosted us underground. We are willing to continue cooperating and we plan to drag the magnetic deflector to the appropriate geo-coordinates to repel harmful particles from reaching earth. I will dispatch our cruisers immediately."

Jack acknowledged the support by clapping, and the rest of the crew joined him. Then the dromas departed. "I guess we'll need to inform the political and religious leaders of the Mars plan soon, since it will have major ramifications on the human desire to have Mars as our next home. I presume we'll all have to learn to share," remarked Jack with a grin.

"Do we have all the bases covered?" asked Jack of Elena and Andrew.

"Yes, I think so," said Elena.

Meanwhile, in northern Canada, something inside the cocoon began to stir. Now almost fully formed, Moloch noticed energy sources were not at the level required to boost his material body to full maturity. It sensed his commander was having issues and this needed attention.

In a deep cavern far behind the waterfall under which he lived, the commander sat in complete darkness. He was aware his twelve minions were ineffective and there was a task force on its way to him. However, the puny powers of earthlings had no effect on him; for millions of years he had roamed where and when he willed, doing what he wanted, feeding the sadness of mankind from the beginning of time. And so, it was not the arrival of the task force that concerned him, nor the ineffectiveness of his disciples. He was worried about the timing of his influence on the solar flare ... should he fail, his master would be unable to evolve. Yet Moloch's strength was already more powerful than anything he had experienced before, and this produced an uneasy feeling. He was not sure what would happen to him once Moloch had complete control of humanity; what would be his role?

'You have such doubts and I sense mistrust.' Moloch's easily entered his thoughts, shaking him. *'Even now you try to question, has it been so long that you do not realize?'*

Don't realize what, thought the commander?

'Do not fail me, we have so much to do'.

The intrusion ended, but the disconcerting feeling remained. He knew what he must do.

Meanwhile, the political and spiritual leaders of Earth informed their subjects and flocks of the impending solar flare, letting them know it would likely cause massive disruption to electrical grids and telecommunications, along with an increase in radioactivity. Instructions as to where everyone should find shelter were issued. Though they realized this news would build more uncertainty and fear, especially after the recent underground attacks, they had to let everyone know. Chaos ensued; once again, major panic and anxiety peaked. The commander was pleased at this turn of events. Without having to raise a finger, fear had returned.

Moloch felt the rush filtering through his frame; it would not be long now until he was free to move around once more. After a few million years travelling aimlessly through the cosmos, once again he was about to experience what humans take for granted ... the use of five senses. Jumping from galaxy to galaxy was only possible in the most basic form, that of non-material energy. While wandering through the ether without form, Moloch's only sensual ability was awareness. This enabled him to observe, but not to physically act. He could not see or touch from the void; he lived in hell ... but he was now close to having form. He would soon be able to build an army again. However, there was a residual doubt at the back of Moloch's mind. He did not remember what caused the loss of his form all those years ago; all that he knew was he was about to be reborn ... and that his memories would return shortly after. Then he hoped he would understand.

Those intent on stopping him continued to work against him. Ian, Martin, Anthony and the droma commander approached the site where Moloch's commander was hiding. The four fighter aircraft located the target and awaited authorization to open fire. The droma leader instructed his crew to prepare to transfer the subject on board. Their tracking system locked on and instructions were given to bring the target into a holding cell.

"Now locked on and transmission complete," advised the flight engineer.

The droma commander and his human companions moved down to the holding chamber to consult with their captive. To their surprise, the object transferred into the chamber was not a living being but a small crate. Within seconds it began to release a gas and the three humans were immediately overtaken by fumes and fell unconscious. However, the vapor did not affect dromas and so the droma commander quickly got his human companions out of the cell and to safety.

At the same time, a message was received from the four attack ships saying that the target had vanished. They had completed an extensive search of the surrounding area, but nothing resembling the target's heat signature was detected. The droma leader ordered an immediate return to base, but first he placed Ian, Martin and Anthony in a quarantined area and instructed his medical staff to monitor their status and do anything to help. Jack was immediately informed about the situation and he, in turn, instructed his hospital staff to prepare for three casualties.

Moloch's commander monitored the activity on board the ship and was confused. He expected the gas to knock out all the crew on board, but it was still operational. This was strange; how could the gas not work? Then, unaware of the dromas on board, he got busy trying to create the radioactive flare that would bring chaos to humanity and make his master strong.

He'd recently felt a change in Moloch; his master was becoming stronger thanks to the recent panic that ensued at the latest warning issued by the global leaders. *A nice twist* thought the commander. He always enjoyed the frailty of humans. They were so easy to control.

He smiled when the attack ships lost him, their target. To get away, he simply transported himself to an area near Moloch. This not only protected him but ensured he would be in attendance when his master arrived. However, he'd learned by this point to control his subliminal thoughts, especially when he was this close to Moloch. He didn't want complications to arise should the master read his mistrustful thoughts again.

The dromas, on the instruction of Jack's medical officer, placed Ian, Martin and Anthony in comas. At Jack's fortress, they were immediately taken to the hospital wing where doctors tended them. Jack consulted with the doctors. They said it was clear the same gas that was used in the subway had been used on his colleagues, but that the quick action of the droma commander—and the fact that each had been given the antidote earlier—prevented major damage. The doctors inoculated them with more of the antidote and advised Jack that they'd be taken out of their comas in a few hours.

Jack had the crate of gas secured in one of the containment cells and asked his scientists to examine it. He hoped to use it to produce a better, more reliable antidote, and to hopefully make it useless against humans. He asked the dromas to work with the scientists, as it was clear the fumes had no effect on them.

Jack was worried he'd placed his friends in harm's way. He knew there were more challenges ahead and hoped and prayed they would all be able to survive the coming days.

In the quietness of the lounge next door, Paul and April met as they were both searching for coffee. The struggles of the past few days had taken precedence over their mutual attraction and this meeting was one of the few times they'd been alone since being in Ian's house. Paul's stomach tightened when he saw her and his heart raced as the beautiful lady stood close while they gathered their cups. He felt like a teenager on a first date. April inadvertently touched Paul's hand as she brushed past him. She, too, felt the nervousness of a teenager on a first date. Gently, Paul took her hand and looked in her eyes ... and in that short moment, they re-connected.

They'd both known this moment would come and they gave into it. For a short time, they forgot everything happening in the world and kissed as if neither of them had been kissed before. It was the deep kind of kiss that brings two souls together. They knew they had found each other, without knowing they had ever met before ... but as their embrace continued, something in the depth of their memories emerged and within a few moments they knew they were lovers in past lives—not just once, but several times. Tears flowed from both at this realization, leaving them gasping with joy.

"My lady, you have been there all along, and I with you," said Paul.

April nodded in agreement, tears in her eyes and a smile on her lips. This knowledge brought such happiness to them both. Then, in true teenager fashion they secretly left the lounge, sneaked up to Paul's room, locked the door and spent the next few hours getting to know each for the first time in this life.

They say the devil never sleeps and the commander was living up to his reputation. He had detected the source of where the Sun's coronal mass ejection would erupt. All he needed to do was urge the timing to coincide with the remaining energy from the two colliding stars. *The force of such concurrence will be wonderful, the master will be proud …*

Chapter 18

Moloch is Born

Ian, Martin and Anthony stirred from their induced comas and woke feeling surprisingly strong and healthy. Jack was standing there when they opened their eyes.

"That feeling of elation you are experiencing is due to the induced sleep, which restored every cell in your body. The extra antidote we pumped into you also has an energizing effect," Jack told them, relieved that his friends had survived their ordeal.

"It felt as if someone had squeezed our lungs, we couldn't draw breath!" Ian exclaimed.

"We've examined the gas," Jack said. "It's the same as the one that killed millions in the subways and it is new to every pharmacist and scientist who has studied its complex signature. However, it does not affect our friends the dromas ... and with their help we've perfected a stronger antidote that has been distributed globally. Again, the antidote is delivered through air and water and within a few hours the gas will not be able to affect anyone on earth who has ingested it.

"Have you told people to drink the tap water?" asked Ian.

"Yes," said Jack. "No more bottles. Admittedly, isolated areas of the world that have limited water resources were more difficult to reach and treat ... but it's amazing what happens when humanity removes borders, religions and government differences. Humanity is finally acting as one, without concern about race and color. No longer are there any forms of discrimination." Jack was pleased at the turn of events.

He added, "Once you guys are ready, we'll meet in my library, our full team plus the droma leader. I will try to find Paul and April so they can join us."

Suddenly they were in the doorway. "Did I hear my name?" Paul said as he joined them in the medical recovery ward. April followed meekly behind, a slight blush on her cheeks offering a hint as to the cause of their absence. Everyone looked at each other and laughed.

"What?" asked Paul, now also blushing.

"Nothing," smiled Jack, who turned to wink at the rest of the team. "We'll see you all in the library in half an hour. Bring clear minds, we've lots to discuss."

Soon all were settled in the library. As usual, the library was comfortably arranged to accommodate the whole team including the droma leader and a few of his aides.

"Thanks to our friends the dromas, we have both an immunization and an antidote for the gas produced by the entity we'll call 'the commander'. That entity has been on earth since time began. As humans developed, this creature was there, watching and meddling. He may also be known as Satan. Yes, the Lord of Darkness is a reality. He has danced in shadows and has been the subject of belief, speculation and superstition. Whatever we wish to call him, he is the main source of evil on earth and is the creature is in charge of preparing for the arrival of Moloch," Dan told them.

"My human friends, take a close look at your companions, the dromas. It may surprise you to know that you are looking at one of your incarnations. Yes, we all lived before, in different guises, human or alien. You have benefited from the opening of memories and the expansion of your abilities and it is important for you to know that all of us survived the last attack by Moloch while on the planet Droma in the Galaxy, Andromeda. Only a few hundred dromas, survived, including us. The majority perished or were taken under Moloch's control and now fight in his armies. We need to stop this from happening here on earth. We failed on Droma and the caretaker of the package was killed before activating the scion. We want to destroy Moloch before considering the use of the scion. We don't want to fail. We believe the power within the box could cause ramifications throughout the universe. We're prepared to take that chance, but we would prefer to avoid it."

Everyone in the room looked at Dan in disbelief. How could such power be contained in such a small box?

As if reading their thoughts, Jack said, "It is possible this package holds the key to connecting multiple universes. And where better to hide this key such than among humans who are innocent of knowledge about its absolute power?" He added, "This innocence has been the best protection against prying eyes, like those of Moloch's. Never in all human history or mythology had humanity come across such a major form of evil as he. If humans had faced Moloch before, all awareness would be gone and the only way we would know would be if it was recorded somehow. The fact that we are contemplating him right now is proof we are facing Moloch for the first time."

Dan added, "The dromas failed to stop Moloch and, except for the few hundred sharing Earth with us in secret, their history is gone. The dromas have given us advanced technology that, under normal circumstances, would have taken humans centuries to develop in exchange for protecting them and allowing them to live under Earth's surface. Only a select few humans know that the dromas are here."

"How did the dromas provide us with this advanced knowledge?" asked Paul.

"Dreams," answered Dan. "While the brain is in a subconscious state, it has the ability to receive subliminal messages. Humans who properly understood their dreams converted those communications into reality. "Humans only use ten percent of their brains. Each of us in this room uses more of our brains than most people do, and we have special abilities we've refined over thousands of lives. The power within the human brain, combined with the driving force of the soul, can engage divine energy, which, as Jack has mentioned, can only be used for good or it will be removed—with disastrous consequences."

Back in remote northern Canada, Moloch's commander watched the ovoid float in front of him. The blustering cold winds of the Arctic had no effect on him. While he was generally used to extreme heat, cold was of no consequence to him either. He examined the outer casing of structure that contained his master and found it to be unusually resilient. It was titanium, but it seemed stronger than that.

He was curious about his adversaries. First, the crew of the aircraft had not been affected by the poison gas and now this overly strong titanium shell was surrounding his master. He realized quickly that some alien force was at work here ... although he was confident that once his master was fully formed, the outer casing would collapse.

He could feel his master's energy emanating from within the cocoon; the time was almost at hand for him to be set free. The heat and pressure building up within the structure had reached maximum limits and the commander waited for cracks in the outer casing. He did not have to wait long; along the circumference, he could see a red glow, a fire from within. The shell was beginning to give way. As he watched, a release of gaseous pressure began easing through the fractures. Then suddenly a massive explosion occurred, and the frame began to show gaps. However, it retained its overall structure and—oddly, he thought—it managed to repair itself after the pressure normalized.

Meanwhile, he had other important work to do. The day was approaching when he had to engage the solar glare. This would take all his skills and focus and was of paramount importance to his master's arrival. Leaving the cocoon, he retired to a suitable underground location where he would perform this masterpiece of planning. Still, he wondered about his role in the new world and was concerned about losing control over Earth. But he proceeded to do his duty.

Back at NASA, Rod noticed the second eruption and the regeneration of the outer structure. *Impressive work, Andrew*, he thought and messaged Jack accordingly.

"Seems like we've had some activity at Moloch's lair," Jack told the others. "Rod has been monitoring another release of pressure and was pleased to see Andrew's construction has once again repaired and delayed Moloch's arrival. Now it's time to focus on our options. We already ruled out nuclear action. We considered using Naomi's ability to move the cocoon out into space but decided that would not stop Moloch from returning ... after all, he traveled millions of miles without form already. And Elena's telekinesis won't work on such a massive scale."

Ian nodded his understanding and said, "The United Nations forces have moved weaponry into position to attack the beast when he emerges. Our own advanced forces will work alongside the UN while the dromas will use stealth technology and be active but not visible."

"The rest of us will have to prepare as best we can and use whatever skills we have to divert his actions," Jack said. "Dan, Frazer, Elena and Paul, your abilities are now front line in this battle. Other than this team and avoiding the solar flare, which I'm confident we can do, we are in the hands of God."

Out in deep space, the dromas had re-positioned the magnetic field. Meticulous calculations had been checked and rechecked to ensure the location was precise. There was no room for error but predicting the exact trajectory of the flare had elements of uncertainty. The speed, power and volume were complete unknowns.

On Earth, the people in the northern hemisphere were preparing for trouble. Many took refuge in their basements; others moved to underground car parks, subways, and enclosed stadiums. Warehouses had been cleared of products to create temporary accommodation. Ships had been converted to passenger vessels and millions had sailed south, leaving their properties boarded up. Any vessel capable of making the long journey was now moored at ports and marinas across the southern hemisphere.

Thankfully it was winter in the north and farmer's fields had already been plowed, the produce harvested and stored in temperature-controlled warehouses. Containers of perishables were sealed and stored under water. Domestic animals were taken to warehousing complexes. All nuclear armaments had been taken miles underground. Places of work had been closed for days and boarded up. The global village had never been so cooperative with its neighbors and the milk of human kindness flowed in abundance. Only while the wild beasts of Earth and those who had not received the message were left to rely on their own resources.

Nevertheless, though all humans were working together as one, the logistics of the evacuation process were extensive, and they strained available resources to the limit. Dismay, despondency and stress reached high levels which fed Moloch. He continued to feel energy enter his being and grew strong as suicides reached the highest point in human history. Before long, despite humanity's best efforts, people started falling prey to Moloch, showing up in public parks worldwide where they stood motionless like automatons, awaiting instructions from Moloch or the Dark Lord.

Those who had gathered in groups in warehouses or underground facilities were more able to fend off Moloch's mesmerizing influence, mainly because of the positive energy generated by working together. Families at home in basements also avoided his hypnotic impact as they, too, were together as one unit, communicating, playing games and generally being distracted. Animals, who were not of interest to Moloch, were left untouched and their human helpers were too preoccupied with caring for them to be caught in the wave of mindlessness.

It was now only a few days before the solar flare would reach earth. The damage inflicted would result in a second wave of disaster in as many weeks. The defense in place might work, but only time would tell.

Frazer and Paul met in the library. Frazer had been trying to see into the future as best he could. "I can see certain events that may come about in the days to come," stated Frazer, looking Paul in the eye to get Paul's attention. "However, the outcome I foresee is not a certainty, only a probability. In this case the magnetic shield set by the dromas is not certain to have the desired effect and I see traumatic events unfolding. The radiation will reach earth and may cause millions of deaths over the coming months. The satellite systems will be disabled by the impact and our satellite navigation will cease to exist. The charged particles from a coronal mass ejection, or CME, will create a sufficient magnetic effect to blow out transformers and power grids. It's just as well aircraft are grounded, as they would lose their navigation systems. The resulting chaos could throw us into the dark ages."

"I can feel the hearts of people and read their minds and at this moment they are unaware of the effect of the CMEs," Paul said. They only understand that exposure to radiation must be avoided." Paul was gravely concerned about Frazer's predictions. "The question is, what can we do about it?" asked Paul.

"Our duty is to focus on Moloch. We need to get out there. I've asked Jack to have transport available to take us to the site where he is growing. Maybe with a closer look at this thing we will get a better understanding of what we are up against."

Paul nodded, accepting Frazer's plan. Soon, a team of dromas and humans assembled to accompany Paul and Frazer to the site, which was surrounded by UN forces. The dromas were working in stealth mode and so were invisible to their human companions. Only those equipped with special lenses, like Jack's group, could see them.

The aircraft on site was an assembly of human and droma technology, the armaments too. Paul and Frazer boarded the lead aircraft, which was piloted by Martin and James.

"Well here we are, together again ... except this time we're not sitting by a comfortable fire back at the pub in the Lakes; this time we're walking straight into the fire," joked Martin, trying to lighten the moment.

"Yeah, and I wish we were back in the Lakes right now ... and this time I wouldn't be objecting to another pint," responded Paul.

"Don't worry Paul, I'll buy the first pint after we deal with this beastie," said Frazer.

Even while engaging in easy-going banter, Paul felt the blood drain from his face at the thought of the enormity of the enemy they were facing. The fact that they were going to be right there, in the front line, filled him with apprehension. He wondered about the first wave soldiers during both world wars who had walked into battle, facing almost certain death. The fear of walking onto a battlefield, directly facing bullets, was something he had never considered until this very moment. How did those soldiers of yesterday find the bravery to do what they did? He now had a greater respect for their courage in the face of war and would never take lightly how many millions had lost their lives, hoping to give others the luxuries today's world offered. He wanted to vomit at the sheer horror of it all.

Within moments they were at the site and communicating with the UN leader, who had been advised of their arrival. The wind and cold had not subsided; it was still around minus 40 degrees Celsius and enduring the cold was only possible with appropriate clothing, which of course had been supplied.

"Nothing has changed since we arrived," advised the lieutenant in charge. "We're monitoring the buildup of pressure, as the outer casing releases gases on a regular basis now."

Frazer and Paul were now witnessing Andrew's work first-hand. However, it appeared the walls were weakening, and he expected their imminent collapse any moment. Judging the delicate state of the outer casing, Paul announced, "I would advise everyone to move back, as this structure will collapse soon. Let's get everyone to a safe distance." At that, the lieutenant instructed his people to withdraw.

They retreated to a safe distance a mile from the object, but left floodlights and cameras focused on the structure. Now they watched as the outer casing seemed to expand. Gases were seeping out all around the ovoid and the red glow became brighter as the walls thinned.

Suddenly, as Paul had warned, the shell dismantled. It was like a nuclear explosion without the mushroom cloud; a temporary vacuum was created as air circling the object was forced out of the area and all structures within 1,000 meters were flattened. Fortunately, the force dissipated as it reached the armies assembled further from ground zero; yet the effect of the blast, even at that distance, was sufficient to throw heavy machinery located at the blast site all the way to where the soldiers cowered. The creaking and straining of metal screamed in the air and fragments buzzed like bullets as metal whizzed past them.

After a few moments, the dust began to settle. Gradually they could see the outline of the exposed cocoon. Glowing red, it floated like a massive pulsating heart, but it was now possible to make out a dark shape in the centre. Paul could sense the intrinsic evil emanating from within. He could also feel that it was not fully formed and even though it exuded power, there was a child-like innocence to it. For a moment, he almost felt pity.

Frazer paid attention to Paul's reaction. "Don't get caught in its disguise of frailty, Paul ... it's the most malevolent force in this part of the universe and although it does not have *physical* destructive abilities, it has power over the minds of men and in an instant can wipe everything from a soul that ever made it human. He does not want to kill men, just use them; but in my way of thinking, they'd be better off dead."

Now that the cocoon was visible and possibly weakened, the lieutenant called for orders. Paul was monitoring the conversation between the lieutenant and his command structure. At this moment, they had no plans to use force, but there were many guns and missiles pointed at the thing and any one of the soldiers was capable of launching an attack at any moment. Tension filled the cold air as the soldiers waited silently and the light of day began to drift into night. Paul couldn't believe that, even in this tense moment, he smiled when he saw the breath of the invisible dromas. He noticed that some soldiers also saw the mist from their exhalations appearing in midair. Their expression at this phenomenon lightened the moment for Paul, helping release the stiffness in his muscles.

Hovering ominously in the air, the ovoid continued to glow in the now-darkened sky. Paul could feel the moment of birth was still some time away; Moloch was simply not strong enough to break free. He communicated this to Jack and Elena, who were listening telepathically and watching live feed from the cameras, which showed a 360-degree image of the site.

"We're too early," stated Paul to Frazer and his two pilot companions. "We should go back to base and leave the UN in charge. We can be here within moments when the emergence starts, but I doubt this will take place before the solar impact. We probably still have a few hours to consider our options."

Jack signaled his agreement and the team boarded the aircraft, leaving the lieutenant to supervise the operation.

Meanwhile, Moloch's commander, Satan, continued monitoring the scene—yet still he remained unaware of the dromas. Over millennia, his awareness had grown until he could feel the heartbeat of every sentient being who had grown out of the Earth's soil, but droma DNA was not detectable to him.

He smiled as he watched the pitiful armies surround the cocoon. He knew their capabilities and that they would have no effect on the structure or his master. Feeling comfortable about his master's safety, he returned his focus to the activities on the sun. He had already initiated the CME, which was now only a moments from reaching earth. Soon the humans would detect the energy and their fear would rise to a crescendo. He would enjoy their reactions as they entered panic mode ... and his master would feed and finally be strong enough to take over the minds of men.

Back at Jack's castle, Frazer and Paul joined the rest of the team who were now secured in the underground facility with all windows and doors at ground level shuttered and closed tight.

The command centre was busy. A team of operations personnel were manning all activities above and below ground. There were large monitors covering the four walls of the room, depicting a variety of observation points: satellite images of ground zero; videos of automatons standing mesmerized at various outdoor parks across the globe; the Hubble telescope focused on the magnetic field loop positioned and ready to deflect the CMEs as they raced toward earth.

A live feed was set up, connecting to NASA, the oval office and the British prime minister's bunker on Downing Street. Various U.S. controlled drones were flying over the major cities on earth, supplying live images of the cities looking peaceful, but eerily silent, as there was no traffic on the roads and not a single human being walking the streets. Stadiums and massive warehousing facilities were all full of humans seeking shelter. The Space station was on standby and all six astronauts were suited and on board the emergency shuttle ready to detach at any moment.

Paul mentally reached across the globe and sensed global apprehension. People were quiet—even the criminals sat quietly in their cells. Churches, with windows boarded up, were full of congregations all praying silently.

Ian conversed with the global political and religious leaders one by one and ascertained they had taken all precautions possible and were themselves in secure lodging. April monitored the web and searched for any unusual activity, but even the dark web had gone silent. She realized that if the CMEs reached earth in full force, she would become blind to all electronic activities. In the midst of this uncertainty, she was glad to be sitting next to Paul and was hoping there would be a future for them.

On the other hand, Dan's ability to stop time was limited only to actions he could see in his direct line of sight; therefore, he was unable to influence anything outside of the control centre. However, Andrew's senses were searching the magnetic field and reaching out to the speeding solar energy coming toward them. He would do everything he could to help influence the course of the CME as it travelled at tremendous speed toward earth. He had never contemplated a feat as great as directing solar emissions, but was on standby, ready to try if needed.

Finally, Elena was ready to transport the package to Paul if all else failed ... that is, if the CMEs reached Earth's northern hemisphere and Moloch broke free from his lair, while Frazer's influence over climates might yet have a bearing, as cloud cover would filter some of the deadly emissions. He sat quietly, looking solemnly at his friends who were all preoccupied with their massive responsibilities.

Jack observing it all, thinking of strategy. He had watched his team come together in a very short period and he wanted more than anything to have this task taken from them. He dreaded the possible outcome of an earth devoid of love, happiness and freedom and so he watched every emotion, every sensitivity. He could feel the heavy air and felt that he was in suspended animation while awaiting the inevitable. All his team's skills were needed to defeat Moloch; most of all, those of Elena and Paul.

Everyone knew what to do and when to act. They did not need him breathing over their heavily burdened shoulders. Yet he sensed something different from the last time they'd fought Moloch on Droma, which, although it was eons ago, was still fresh in his mind. At that time, they were uncertain of Moloch's power and so they'd had less time to prepare for the fight. Their knowledge of his abilities and destructive intention was limited in those dark days. However, something was different this time, and it wasn't the team's state of readiness, nor the preparedness of the vast numbers of people spread across the northern hemisphere. It wasn't even the influence of the Moloch's commander and his scheming. *What is it*, he asked himself? He wasn't sure.

Meanwhile, Paul started hearing voices again. '*You are ready Paul,*' said the voice inside his head. '*Do not despair, I will soon be with you.*'

Paul glanced around the room and could see his father looking at him. "Is that you?" he blurted to his dad.

"What?" Jack replied.

"I heard the voice in my head again and you're looking right at me. It has to be you."

"Sorry Paul, it's not me. I'm just watching the team and happened to be looking your direction."

Paul resumed his focus, but the voice had gone.

Silence descended on the room, with the only movement emanating from the various monitors switching scenes as they recorded strategic locations across the globe and out into space. This silence was the eerie silence of trepidation and the air seemed so heavy it was hard to breath. You could almost taste the anticipation.

Andrew sensed the magnetic field was correctly placed and felt the CME waves approaching. He braced for impact. Within seconds, flashes of light sparked from the loop. The impact warped the array of wiring, thousands of miles long, like a sheet of laundry blowing in the wind. It lit up the sky with an explosion of light. The Hubble screen went blank.

"Looks like we placed the field in the right coordinates," stated Andrew, who was watching the screen depicting the loop as it contorted in the resistance again the CME. "Not sure it's going to hold ... the CME is incredibly powerful ... but so far, so good."

At that point, the loop exploded into millions of parts, its ability to absorb the powerful plasma ending almost as quickly as it began. The mangled wires splintered like a spider web breaking down under the weight of a hurricane. Everyone wondered if it had done its job. They would know in a few moments.

Before anyone had time to react, the northern hemisphere was drenched in deadly rays. Invisible to the naked eye, the level of energy pulsed as static filled the air. All screens went blank and electronic communication died. Cities were plunged into darkness, all lighting extinguished, and only those with backup generators not connected to the main grid had power.

Thankfully, the authorities had anticipated such an eventuality and public shelters had been supplied backup power, avoiding mass panic.

The Earth had received its most catastrophic impact since the dinosaurs were made extinct. This time it was not devastating physical destruction that was affecting the life there, but electronic fallout; satellites were fried, and electronics destroyed. The full extent of the impact on the ground would not be assessed for months.

Almost immediately, the shell around Moloch exploded and red hot molten liquid fell like lava onto the ground beneath as smoke billowed in all directions. The sky lit up as fire scorched the ground near the remains of the cocoon. The glow reflected upwards and settled ominously on the creature floating in mid-air, arms outstretched and eyes glowing red. A beast born in nightmares was alive.

Chapter 19

Fallout

"There is darkness everywhere," announced Paul as he turned to meet the gaze of his companions. "I feel deep uncertainty in people's hearts. Fear is everywhere."

In Jack's castle, they were safe. Backup generators supported the castle as well as all droma planes and vehicles. Because they were on their own communications channels, the group was unaffected by loss of communication. They worked on independent, non-human energy sources which had also been installed into all of Jack's military equipment. Throughout his fortress, everything operated as normal.

Some aircraft were dispatched immediately to assess the situation at ground zero. They would report back to Jack's control room in a few moments. Jack and his team were watching the only monitor that was relaying from Earth after the attack on Earth's communications systems. He quietly thanked his droma allies for their technological contribution, then all eyes were focused on the scene as their aircraft arrived at the site.

The UN military were helpless to do anything. All their heavy equipment had been disabled and only handheld automatic weapons were in working order. These would be nothing against the creature. Soldiers discharged multiple rounds directly at Moloch, but nothing had any affect; the bullets simply bounced off the thick hide of the beast. It didn't attempt to stop them, nor did it even react to the aggressive attack by the soldiers.

The droma hovered a few thousand feet away from Moloch, invisible to the surrounding army. Moloch, however, turned his gaze toward the space occupied by their plane. It appeared curious, but after a few seconds it turned away as if dismissing the ships as insignificant.

"Don't open fire," instructed Jack to the droma ship. "Let's wait to see what he is contemplating. Paul and Elena, can you get any reading from the creature's mind?"

Both focused their attention in the direction of the beast, but it was like listening for signals emanating from a stone.

"Nothing," they jointly declared.

"Andrew, can you build another shell?" asked Dan.

"I already tried, but nothing happens. It seems there's force field surrounding the beast."

Communication outside of closed circuit of droma technology was impossible. Contact with NASA, the UN or any of the political leaders was terminated.

Jack had anticipated this scenario and in preparation earlier had dispatched droma planes carrying equipment for installation at all strategic points, including the Oval Office, Downing Street, the Pentagon and every major political or religious leader's headquarters. He'd also sent a simple written messages to each leader for their eyes only: *'Connection via advanced technology will be established using this secure network.'*

Jack's control room was now the world's communication centre. Within an hour, he'd briefed the various leaders about Moloch's arrival and assured them that they were monitoring the horrific scene.

Meanwhile, Paul's outreaching senses detected millions of humans losing responsiveness by the minute, leaving a dark void in the places where their thoughts used to be. Nothing was happening in their minds; their movements were instinctive but without intention. It was as if someone with a remote control directed them to eat, sleep and rest. He wondered how they would cope when the cupboards were bare. What would they do when they become hungry? Who, or what, would supply them with sustenance? He was afraid to answer his own questions.

Jack walked with Paul to an office adjacent to the main control centre. The main house was out of bounds until an 'all clear' was given about radiation. Jack wanted to be informed about the ground level situation by the hour. His security team monitored the grounds using sensors installed throughout the property. Already, levels were dropping—a sign that the magnetic field may have reduced the solar flare's impact substantially.

"What's the mental status out there?" asked Jack as he placed a comforting hand on Paul's shoulder. Then he said, "You look drained, my son. We're now at the last phase of this thing and we all need to be fully alert."

Paul told Jack of his findings, and about his reservations. "I wish I had better news," he said.

"We knew we would get to this point and our focus still has to remain with containing or stopping Moloch, despite our concerns about the world out there," said Jack. "We need to attack the source and create situations that don't help feed the monster. Global leaders have minimized panic; their support has delayed Moloch from reaching full force. We feel his lack of substantial action so far is due to how well mankind has coped to this point."

At this, Jack felt proud to be human.

April burst into the room. "I have some good news!" she announced with a broad smile. "I know how to reconnect the communication systems until authorities handle the manual repairs."

Everyone clapped.

"In layman's terms the blast of CMEs only disabled the modern transmission capabilities of the satellites," said April. "Without being too technical, I have by-passed some of the damaged circuitry and am using dormant integrated parts that were installed to handle old technology."

Jack smiled in appreciation, as he never really understood modern technology. He hired people to do that for him.

"When advanced options became available, technicians simply left the old, redundant parts in the machine. I've reconnected receiver and transmission capabilities to older circuit boards and we should have all the satellites up and running in the next few hours!" April did a little Irish jig to celebrate her discovery. Paul's love for this Gaelic girl was growing stronger by the minute.

"Excellent, April, you're a genius! My team is at your disposal," Jack said.

"That's just as well Jack, I already engaged them," said April with a broad smile. "They're working on ground-based communication first. Only some satellites will work, but it's better than nothing. It's amazing how many discontinued parts were in the communication devices ... it won't be as efficient as what we're used to, but at least we can contact each other on a wide scale." April danced out of the room as both Jack and Paul clapped in appreciation.

Moloch's commander stood near the fallout area around his master's cocoon. He admired the majesty of the scene ... ultimate power here on his doorstep, unstoppable and much more advanced than his own talents. The surrounding air crackled with energy. He was filled with anticipation; he was witnessing the birth of a god.

'Are you ready to rule as my commander?' Moloch's request echoed in the Satan's mind.

'I am prepared, my master ... our forces are in every corner of this planet and waiting on instructions.'

'They are already under my control. There is no need for instructions. They have my intentions built into their puny minds and are preparing our global army. Soon the planet will be ours! I'll have forces ready to take over this corner of the galaxy. Soon my power will be ultimate ... each time we acquire more intelligent beings and remove their awareness, my enemy loses supremacy,' said Moloch.

Satan laughed in agreement.

'When I am done with them, they will not be aware of their God ... and without awareness of God's will, His will 'will NOT *be done'.'* Moloch laughed at his twist of wording.

'Now we need the scion,' said Moloch. *'Its power is the last remaining defense He has against my rise to supremacy. Find it and bring it to me and we will rule for eternity.'*

Satan knew who had the scion, but the location of the package was hidden from him. He did not understand how he could not see through the veil protecting it. He decided he would attack the one who was the caretaker.

Back at the castle, Jack told Paul, "You asked about my abilities. In simple terms, I can place a protective shield around us. Whether it's providing stealth coverage of this home, or to protect an object from prying senses, I can do that. I have hidden the package to protect it over the eons. However, whenever it changes hands I need to drop the protection to enable the transfer. That's why those guys were chasing you around the UK; they briefly saw it when I gave it to Ian. Now that I have passed ownership to you I'm sure they saw it again. We can expect an attack soon and we need to be on our guard. Moloch will do anything to have it in his possession."

In the basement of the castle, in Jack's cells, the two forgotten businessmen were back under Moloch's control and planning their escape. They had been watching the movement of guards and now, with Moloch's help, had the ability to control their actions. Although the castle was secure from telepathy, Moloch's power was too strong, and it was seeping into their weak minds.

At first the men practiced giving the guards simple instructions, like asking for a glass of water. Then they worked on getting a little more freedom, asking to have their ankle braces removed. The guards began to fall under their spell.

Alex and Brian enjoyed their little games ... and were ready to act when they received further instructions. Neither had a clue they were being manipulated, as their egos were too strong to accept being subordinate to anyone. Moloch instructed his commander to pay them a visit. He advised him to appear human and to disguise his red eyes. Satan was adept at disguise and smiled at his masters instruction.

Moloch had picked up the recent signal from the scion and he gave the coordinates to Satan. They knew the fortress was in the middle of a forest and well disguised. Upon arriving at the fortress, he could feel strong energy and knew that the building was heavily fortified. Satan was unable to use his powers to transfer himself inside and, once again, was surprised at facing an obstacle he could not surmount. After all, Earth was now wholly his domain.

He could feel one or two humans in the area ... but where were the rest? As he pushed harder he sensed what appeared to be an entrance, yet it was not visible to him. He used his powers to influence a security guard into unconsciousness and then walked through the front door. Then he changed his appearance to that of the guard's.

Immediately he contacted Jack via the internal communication channels.

"After checking the levels of radiation on the surface you'll be pleased to know we're already back at normal levels," he ad-libbed. This information was consistent with the hourly messages Jack had been receiving, so Jack was not suspicious.

Now that the devil had access to the property, his job was to free the two prisoners and have them cause a distraction while he searched for the package. *This is easy,* thought the commander, *now it is time to act and recover the scion.*

He made his way to the elevator without being noticed and then descended to the underground labyrinth of rooms and quietly moved to the holding cells. With a simple act of will he unlocked the doors of the two cells and telepathically instructed the two puppets to make their way to the control room where Jack's team was currently assembled. As the door of the control room opened, everyone turned to see the two men, armed with guns. They instructed everyone to back away from the computers.

Jack told his team, "Follow their instructions!" They all did and they all watched closely as the two men came into the centre of the room. Brian and Alex looked awkward as they tried to enforce authority. Alex made his way to one of the operators who was slow to move away from his station and without another thought, lifted his pistol and shot him at point blank range. Blood and tissue sprayed all over the console as the man's body crashed with a sickening thud to the floor. This indiscriminate killing action by an individual who, until that moment had never held a gun in his hands, stunned the room. Even Alex's partner Brian looked astonished at what just happened.

"There will be more of this if anyone moves a muscle. Brian, keep an eye on the group. Who is Paul?"

The team stayed silent as Alex surveyed the room and when there was no answer, he walked up to another operator and pointed his gun directly at his head … but before he could shoot him, Dan stopped time.

In this suspended state, no one could move other than Dan. Dan made his way to the gunman and removed the gun from his hand then went to the partner and acquired the other firearm. Then he emptied the bullets from both guns, placed them back into the hands of the two puppets and wrote a quick note to Paul, which he placed in Paul's hands. Then he removed the hold on time and everyone was able to move as if nothing had happened.

"I mean it, I will shoot this guy if Paul does not make himself known in the next three seconds!"

Paul glanced down at his hands and became aware of the note, which said, *'Removed the bullets – Dan'*. Paul looked over at Dan who gave a nod of confirmation and Paul realized they were safe. Immediately Paul telepathically advised the whole team. Andrew stood up and calmly said to Alex, "I doubt you'll manage to shoot anyone without any bullets." At that statement, Alex pulled the trigger only to hear a soft click. The gun was empty.

"You'll now put down the guns and our guards will take to back to your cells," Andrew said. The guards rushed both individuals and forced them to the ground. After handcuffing them, they moved Alex and Brian toward the door.

"Hold on," instructed Jack. "Do either of you know why you are here?" he asked the men. They looked at each other and shook their heads. It was as if they had suddenly awakened from sleepwalking.

"Do you know you have just killed a person?" Jack looked directly at the killer. Alex looked wide-eyed back at Jack. He looked at the dead man and realized what he'd done. Then he placed his head in his hands and burst into tears.

Jack nodded to Andrew, who understood his message and induced them both to sleep. "They will not waken up anytime soon," said Andrew as the guards carried them back to their cells. Other guards attended to the dead body, carrying him to the hospital ward.

"How did they manage to escape and where did they get the guns?" Jack asked.

April looked at camera footage of activity in the cells and noticed the cell doors had been opened without force or mechanical action from the guards. "Their release was caused by something else," said April.

Jack realized something, or someone had freed the two from *inside* his facility. Paul did too and searched the minds of everyone in Jack's fortress. He detected an unusual signal, non-human and not droma. He located the origin of the signal. It was close by and was stronger than any signal he had felt since becoming able to use his ability.

"A strong elemental has entered our fortress!" exclaimed Jack. Elena asked Paul to guide her to where the signal was coming from. Through a telepathic message, she was given the coordinates. She immediately locked onto the being and teleported him outside the castle. The power Elena had gained over many generations was comparable to the devil's earth-bound powers.

The devil couldn't believe it when he found himself outside. *What power is this? Its source isn't human! This is something unusual,* he thought to himself. He was accustomed to having ultimate power; nothing before had been able to resist or interfere with his will ... now something, or *someone*, was blocking his ability to move where and when he wanted. This made him anxious. When Moloch became the ultimate ruler of the humans, he would lose power. But now he had *another* adversary who seemed able to control his actions! Was his supremacy over the earth threatened? Never since he came into existence had he had a thought like this. He didn't like it.

Though the new situation was concerning, he had to be careful what he did next. His job was to support Moloch unconditionally and dispatch this new alien threat ... or possibly to affiliate with the new source of power and defeat Moloch to retain his dominion over earth. *Sympathy for the Devil* by the Rolling Stones played in his head. *Interesting*, he thought. It was his favorite song from the 60s.

"What was that?" asked Naomi.

"An auld demon," said Frazer in Scottish brogue. "Mephistopheles, or possibly his master, Lucifer, whatever name we may call him ... he hovers around, interfering with the best intentions of man, picking up souls at will as he twists their well-meant deeds into evil. There are many examples of his work, such as the contributions to charity winding up in the hands of evil men, or food shipped to war zones that never reached the starving and instead feeds the bellies of the people causing the war."

Jack chimed in, "This force has existed on earth since the beginning of time, but he is nothing compared to Moloch. I wondered how long it would take before showed his hand. He was not here for our captives; he's after the scion and probably acting on behalf of his new master."

The devil, Satan, Mephistopheles, Lucifer ... *what next* wondered Paul. Bad guys driving BMWs he could deal with; bombs in hotels were nasty ... but this entity was a beyond it all. How could his simple team deal with such ultimate power? He felt more and more helpless and his heart beat faster in apprehension.

'Relax Paul, you are not alone ...' the voice inside his head was back. *'All will be revealed soon.'*

Paul looked over at Jack, who he felt was the source of these messages, but Jack was talking with Frazer at that moment.

'Ask Frazer to alter the temperature around Moloch, it will delay him a little more,' said the voice.

"Freeze the beast," Paul suddenly exclaimed.

Frazer and Jack stopped talking and looked at him with interest. "An excellent idea, Paul," said Frazer in response. "Why didn't I think of that?"

Within moments, Frazer attracted the coldest elements in the area immediately surrounding Moloch's glowing habitat. As the ice surrounding the red-hot lava underneath the hovering Moloch grew, it started melting, causing steam to rise around the creature, which was still hanging mid-air like a crucified Christ. Frazer caused the air around Moloch began to dip below minus 200 degrees Celsius. Slowly it got colder until it reached absolute zero at minus 273 Celsius. At absolute zero, atoms freeze and stop moving. Frazer was sure Moloch would ultimately be able to resist this delay tactic, but it would buy some time.

Moloch was oblivious to the temperature change. He was concentrating on his main goal—removing man's ability to be aware and removing anything that resembled consciousness. For this stage of his attack on humanity, he did not need to be fully mobile. Moloch knew that already about ten percent of the population was under his control. That was a sufficient beginning for his new army; he would bring them into action soon. *It is a pity their bodies are so frail*, Moloch thought, *they won't last long, maybe a few months at most.* He knew the majority would be dead or permanently maimed once the war was underway, but by then he would have a body and be able to control all humans.

All over the world, the radiation began to dissipate. Communication had been restored and so the crowds emerged from the protection areas and services and a semblance of normality returned. However, the various gatherings of autom-atons had grown in all cities of the world and this caused concern across the globe. Husbands, wives, sons and daughters now stood motionless in crowds so closely packed together it was impossible for families to reach their loved ones.

Armies from all nations were sent to maintain order and to protect those who still had consciousness from being captivated by the strong influence of Moloch. Riots were beginning to break out across the world and peace was becoming fragile. Once again, Moloch smiled.

Dan briefed the team, "The groups of human automatons are now growing, reaching the millions. Concerned families are trying to reach their loved ones and are ignoring the danger of being caught in Moloch's net. Nothing authorities say is quieting the panic."

"Frazer's 'ice pack' attack on Moloch limited his physical movement, but his ability to get inside the brains of humans has not been restricted. Maybe our antidotes are becoming ineffective. We know a certain percentage of the population did not receive the antidote and I'm betting that the majority of those under Moloch's control are them," said Jack.

After this discussion, it was agreed to load up as many of the droma aircraft as possible with the latest version of the antidote and directly saturate the affected crowds with airborne dispensing methods. However, even with the high speed of the droma aircraft, this exercise would take hours and the limited volume of antidote meant they would be unable to reach all gatherings. Jack instructed the dromas to drop the antidote on the most highly affected areas of population—the main cities.

'You have done well Paul.' Once again Paul was startled at the voice inside his head. *'It is time to meet with the dark being of earth; his influence on the world has been growing since Moloch arrived, but Moloch does not have him entirely under his control yet'.*

"Everyone, we need to consider another option," Paul said. "What if we meet with this 'Satan' and align his thinking. I have a feeling he's not completely happy about Moloch's arrival either." Paul stood with palms open, asking for agreement.

"That's crazy! Meet with that evil face to face?" Naomi asked. "We've just ousted him and now you want to have a chat with the devil?" She was worried for the entire group and quite emotional in her response.

"There is some logic in this approach," said Jack. "Our collective powers are not really of this earth. We've gathered abilities through the millennia. Earth's incumbent devil has been focusing only on humans; we and our droma allies may be a little stronger than this one evil force. Having Satan as our ally might to useful against Moloch. He would not expect such an approach." Jack was hiding concern that such a meeting may also have dire consequences.

"I'll set it up," said Elena, "We'll have him here in a few moments. Let me find out where the 'little devil' has gone."

Jack chuckled at her joke, despite his concern. "Bring him to the holding cell area," he said. "Dan, Paul, Andrew, please join Elena and I. Frazer, would you keep a close eye on the beastie and let us know the moment anything changes?"

The group descended a few levels into the holding cells and met in the same specially structured room they had used to meet with the two prisoners. As the group gathered in the anti-room next to the main interrogation cell, Jack instructed his security team to seal the room against any access. Then Elena transported the devil into the unit.

"Let's do this!" was Jack's instruction to Elena and a second later the team was staring at a humanoid devil who looked much as renaissance paintings presented him; humanoid in shape with red, rugged skin, almost eight feet tall, feet like a lion and claws like a T-Rex and steely, black pupils surrounded by a red glow. There was no sign of a tail or horns—but this was a twentieth century version of Satan;

even he kept up with the times. He looked dazed at suddenly being transported from his post near Moloch.

There was a strong feeling of dread in the room as the team realized they were looking at intrinsic evil. Even though they knew their own powers were strong, the ability of this creature to destroy lives and capture souls was something that sat subliminally in the psyche of every human being. However, Satan showed no signs of resistance and it was clear he was aware he was being watched. Efforts to transport outside the holding cell were futile. Jack's security guards had done their job and sealed the unit, both physically and metaphysically. All four walls looked like stone but were made from a special droma-manufactured product.

The commander was surprised that he had no ability to simply vanish and reappear outside the cell and quickly understood that the protective walls were of non-human construction. He only had power over construction materials from Earth.

"You are here because we want to talk to you," stated Jack through a speaker system.

'Whatever you think, you will not hold me here for long; I will destroy this place and kill all of you with a simple thought. Do you know who I am?'

"We are aware of what you are and now we'll tell you why you are here," announced Jack firmly.

"We are aware of the arrival of Moloch, the name we have given the beast who you are subservient to. We understand you have a vested interest in helping this malevolent being's emergence on earth. We are aware of its plans to reign over humans and use them in the coming wars to control the different planets of the Milky Way galaxy. The strategy is to remove consciousness from humans, effectively reducing each to a puppet."

'You have no idea how futile your actions have been. In the end we will rule your planet and the millions of planets surrounding you. We will become stronger than you can imagine.'

"I'm sure you know that once Moloch has established his base here you will lose your dominion over the Earth. He will discard you," countered Jack.

There was a moment of silence and Jack knew he had touched on Satan's dilemma. The beast moved around the holding room, clearly contemplating his situation and deciding whether to continue this discussion.

'Moloch, as you call him, is all-powerful—more powerful than any puny earthling can deal with. I will be his commander in the new glorious epoch after the war. I have been held like a prisoner while ruling over earth. Now I will have more power as we expand our rule over vast regions of this galaxy.'

"Moloch will not allow you or anyone to have power as he stretches his reach across the region," Jack said. "We have met this beast before and know how the ultimate desire for unrestricted authority does not leave space for you."

Again, the room was quiet. The devil had learned something new … these beings had met Moloch before? How was that possible? Nothing like Moloch had come this way before; he knew this, as he was the elder statesman of the earth. The commander was immortal; no being had lived on earth as long as he had.

"We understand your confusion," Jack said. "The individuals addressing you are of human form, but we have travelled across billions of miles, over many lifetimes. Our origin is, like yours, primordial."

Satan now understood why he was unable to read the thoughts of those addressing him. It had been a long time since he'd met extraordinary beings like himself. He missed being challenged by such as these; earthlings were so easy to manipulate. Over millennia, there were a few prophets that had come to contest him, some with considerable powers ... but once they left and passed to other realms, their influence dissipated.

How could he use this situation to his advantage? They were right. Moloch would discard him when he had full power, as he would no longer need him. But why should he work with this group? They may have had previous experience with Moloch, but they didn't seem to do well last time ... what would be different now?

'Give me the scion and I will join you against Moloch!'

"You know we can't do that," said Jack. "It has been under our protection for eons and cannot be released to anyone who does not have unconditional love in their heart. I'm sure you'd be first to admit that is not one of your attributes."

'I love humanity as much as anyone. Without my care for this race they would discard their bodies for spiritual advancement and lose the ability to experience mortal matters. Why else do you think humans have free will? If they stop experiencing the material world, the Supreme Being will not be able to expand. When humans feel love for each other, He feels that love. When humans experience magical things, such as a newborn baby, He feels that joy. When you see glorious scenery and hold your breath at the sheer beauty of nature, He sees through your eyes. You see my purpose in this world is not evil, but a balance that holds everything in its place.'

"That may be, but our battle is not with you. We need to halt Moloch. This team is here on Earth at this moment in time to save humans from becoming extinct. Their bodies may live on a few decades while Moloch uses them in the physical attack on neighboring planets, but without the will to live, without consciousness, they will not survive and God, as you state, will lose his connection to them. Without humans, God won't feel the love this race is capable of."

Jack was becoming tired of this exchange, as it was not helping to fight Moloch.

'If you release me, I will confer with Moloch.'

"You know nothing any of us say will change his mind. 'Conferring', as you put it, will only tell him you are not with him," Jack said, frustrated at Satan's attempt to manipulate him. We will release you and you may do as you will. If you help us, so be it; if not, let it be known our fight is not with you." At that, Jack turned to Elena and nodded to her to let the beast leave. In an instant the cell was empty.

"Are you sure that was a good move, Dad? Won't this creature just make our fight more difficult now? Surely if he was constrained while we fight Moloch our job would be a little easier," said Paul.

"That may be so, but my gut feeling is that this creature will no longer assist Moloch, as it knows he has no future if he does," Jack responded. "If humans cease to exist, his job on earth is done and its certain Moloch won't need him as he charges through the galaxy. This is the battle of evermore. The cancer of the galaxy will become the cancer of the universe over time. There will be no stopping him."

Andrew addressed the group. "Let's take our next steps. We are now in the front line. Moloch will emerge, all powerful, very soon. At that time, as we know from previous experience, it will be the end for us and all mankind."

"Glad you jumped in and brought us back on track," Jack said. "We know there are millions under Moloch's control. Let's look to see if our droma friends have distributed the antidote serum. It's designed to enter through the skin and lasts longer than the airborne version."

They turned their attention to the monitor screen. It depicted the largest collection of souls ever to stand in New York's Central Park. The serum had been distributed over the crowd moments before. Everyone watched to see the slightest movement. Seconds passed as the camera panned over the gathering of sad, blank-faced, tired beings. As they stared without seeing, it was hard not to feel a terrible sadness. The group knew they were glancing into the future if Moloch wasn't stopped.

"Go back," said Naomi excitedly. "Just a few seconds ago, I thought I saw someone's head turn to the side ... there ... see the coloured gentleman in the blue jacket, about ten deep into the crowd? He's moving ... and there, a few to his left are also shifting."

"You're right Naomi, it's working!" cheered April and, as they watched, more people were released from the mesmerized state. Everyone cheered and hugged with relief. At least they had halted this stage of Moloch's destruction!

"Now let's face the bastard!" shouted Jack. Paul and Naomi looked at each other; they had never heard their father swear before. Breaking into a smile they both shouted, "Let's do this!"

Jack had instructed the leader of the dromas to have a suitable ship made available for flight, as they had to make a short journey. They also advised the dromas to bring their strongest forces, as they would be fighting against the ultimate enemy.

"Paul, you stay behind. Elena please bring the scion into his care."

Paul stood, shocked by the realization that the moment had come for him to act if called to do so. Even though he knew this time would come, he was still in fear.

"Don't worry, son. We will do everything we can to avoid you having to act, but you must be ready to do this. We cannot have this evil expand, it would be the end of days."

At that, everyone hugged Paul with tears in their eyes at the thought that they may never meet again as this time even their ability to reincarnate would be taken away. Just like any journey humans must take, the realization that death is at the door and they must walk through is a terrible reality. The words 'I am scared' are on everyone's lips as they pass over ...

three of the most horrific words any caring partner hears from their loved ones as they near the end.

Paul sat in the expansive living room with only the roaring fire to keep him company. He felt more alone at this moment than at any time in all his lifetimes. Sitting in front of him was the package that was now all too familiar. He held it and looked again at the marking and thought of how Christ must have felt … *let this chalice pass from me* he thought. The burden of humanity was now his; he had travelled through many lifetimes to arrive at this moment. Destiny, whatever that may be, was in his hands.

'You are not alone' announced the voice in his head.

Like a ghost, a supreme being continued its journey. Until now he had travelled hidden within the darkness of space, but after travelling billions of miles at speeds faster than light he was beginning to slow as he arrived on the outer edge of the Milky Way galaxy. He was aware that Earth and human kind were in real danger. The custodians of the scion had done well, but the force against them was reaching ultimate power. There was little time left to act. If the scion was activated, his journey would be in vain.

CHAPTER 20

The Journey Ends

Jack and his team arrived at Moloch's site and for the first time, with their own eyes, they saw the creature hanging in mid-air, arms outstretched like a crucified Christ, horrifying yet pitiful.

'I have been waiting on you.'

A voice boomed in the air but there was no movement of lips, just sound.

'You have been wasting your time and efforts to keep me constrained. I could wipe you all out with a simple gesture. I now remember you all, yes, the dromas too. You failed before and you will fail again.'

The sound permeated the air and invoked attention from the group including the leftover disarmed UN force and the Dromas who were still in stealth mode.

"You will not be successful this time," shouted Jack as he looked up at the hostile body floating above them. "Come down from your perch, we do not fear you."

'I can feel you have no fear but that will not change destiny. I am ready to bring the humans under my care."

As those words were spoken Moloch descended from the sky. When its hooves rested on the scorched leftover lava, it stood over 20 feet high. It stepped slowly toward the group as they stood in the minus 40-degree coldness of the afternoon, eyes glowing with heat and evil intent. The ground was still smoldering and hot and Jack and the crew could see lava still lighting the burned earth underneath Moloch—however the stillness surrounding them was unearthly. They felt they had entered a different dimension, one that was held in the palms of the beast's claws.

Moloch demanded absolute attention and he had the group under his hypnotizing glare. The creature still dripped with sparks of lava through the pores of its thick, rhinoceros-like skin. It stood fully erect on legs like those of the Argentinosaurus dinosaur, though its shorter arms were shaped like those of a Tyrannosaurus. It had a thick bulging neck that supported its head ... the head of a beast for which there was no comparison on earth. Scaled skin covered high cheekbones, there were no visible nasal features, its mouth was slim and lipless and its eyes wide-set, black, unblinking and without reflection. It had no ear cavities and, as if mocking Jesus, thorns protruded all around its head.

'You are powerless to stop me now. I am here and everything I see, and feel is mine to control. Would you like a demonstration?'

At that moment, every one of the UN forces turned to stone. They were not mesmerized like other humans; they had literally become hard as stone.

Jack and his team, who were still free to move and think, watched the beast's actions without reaction. They knew they had to wait for the right time to act.

'You know this was a small effort for me, to have these puny beings terminated. I can do this to any living being on earth in an instant. Yet I will spare them for now ... they may have value to me in the years ahead.'

"You are right, we do not fear you. We know you have powers beyond any one of us ... but we appeal to you ... reconsider your attack on the billions of lives now in your power. They are finite and will die under your care ... and once you have conquered all galaxies, what will you do when there's no one left to rule?" Jack challenged the creature.

'Don't you see? I will have defeated God. His contact with sentient beings will have ended and therefore he will cease to exist. It takes little imagination to see what I will become.'

"You would be a ruler of uninhabited planets. Life would not be present for you to control. It will end if you remove the will to survive. You would be alone in the universe. Your plan, if that's the word for it, is futile," Jack said.

There was a moment of silence as Moloch, who technically was still a child, albeit a monster, processed the simple logic.

'I will give them free will again and they will be mine to rule over for the rest of time.'

Jack's team realized it was now time to ask Paul to act before the exchange came to an end. Jack telepathically instructed Paul to initiate the scion.

Paul, alone in the quietness of the beautiful living room, received Jack's clear instruction. The moment had come for him to do what no one had done since the beginning of time. He was going to destroy everything that existed—or at least that is what he believed, since the result of such action was not known. He stood, shaking, and grasped the Scion in both hands. His mind drifted to the frailty of humans, their conflicts in war, differences between religions, races, ages, genders and challenges of every kind, their fruitless fights over money and power. *What a waste*, he thought sadly.

'It is not the end Paul,' the voice inside his head announced. *'You must not invoke the scion'.*

"Who are you and why should I listen?" For the first time Paul spoke back. "We are facing the end of humanity and all you can say is 'do not act'. I need more than that." Paul's voice was shaking.

'I'm coming,' was all the voice replied.

Meanwhile, Jack's team embarked on an attack against Moloch. Andrew attempted to build a protective structure to contain him; Frazer tried to stop time; Elena tried in vain to have the beast thrown from Earth ... but nothing worked, they had no power against him.

'You can try as you might, but you will not stop me, your powers will not work, I can resist anything you try,' laughed Moloch in a thundering voice.

Jack wondered why Paul hadn't acted yet and tried to communicate with him but couldn't make contact.

'I am here now,' said the voice inside Paul's head. Paul turned and into the room walked an apparition ... it was his dead wife, Jessica. He almost dropped the scion as he stared in disbelief.

'Who you see is not Jessica,' said the apparition. *'I am using this appearance to help you relate to who I am. You could say there is an essence of Jessica in me, as there is of everyone who has ever lived. I am here to help you stop Moloch. He won the first battle when the evil forces struck down the previous caretaker of the scion. This time, with the efforts of you and your team, we have a chance to finally stop the beast. While he is distracted by your team and is displaying his egoistic power over the earth, we have a chance to act.'*

Paul struggled to accept that he was talking to a ghost. It walked up to him with the same confident step of his lost wife; her smile was the same and her voice was the same soft-spoken one he remembered and cherished.

She was now up close to him now and he felt the hair at the back of his neck rise as she took him by his hand and asked him to sit with her for a moment. He felt the warm touch of her hand. She had the fragrance of her morning shower upon her. Everything was as real as it had been more than five years ago.

'Don't worry, Paul. I am as real as you would like me to be … but we need to hurry. I can't be with you for long, I just need to take over the scion, would you help me?'

"But it will only be activated by my presence and attention. What would you need it for? You have already told me not to invoke the scion … those were your words," Paul said in confusion.

'I asked that you don't activate the scion so that I can be here to help you. The last time, your predecessor failed through hesitation. I am here to take that responsibility from you and help the human race. Please pass it over to me.'

Paul rose, scion in hand, and was ready to hand it over—but just then Frazer arrived in the room, courtesy of Elena.

"Jack was worried that you had not acted as instructed. Moloch is fully formed and beginning to gather his army. April has reported that significant crowds are beginning to assemble, much bigger than before, in all the world's main cities."

"I was asked to delay the action until …" Paul looked around and noticed she had gone. "She, she was just here," stuttered Paul

"Who was here?" asked Frazer.

"It was Jessica." Paul looked around the room in wonder.

"It couldn't be Jessica, she's dead." Frazer looked at Paul with concern.

"She was right here, she held my hand. I don't mean *Jessica*, just someone who had her appearance, her smile, the sound of her voice … even her fresh morning scent!"

"You were hearing voices … now you're seeing things, Paul. Listen to yourself!"

"I'm serious, she was right here." Paul pointed to the sofa where they sat together.

"What did she want?

"She asked me to give her the scion for protection," said Paul innocently.

"What? And you actually considered handing it over?"

"Yes," responded Paul, realizing what he had just said.

"She, as you call her, was actually Moloch. Jack asked me to check on you and thank God I did. Now you must act, Paul. Initiate the Scion. I will stay here with you. You have to do it now."

"Will this truly be the end?" Paul asked.

"We may never know my friend, but you have no choice. Moloch is too strong."

At that, Paul lifted the scion and asked Frazer to leave the room. His instructions were to be alone when he induced the package to open.

Frazer retired to Jack's library and Paul was alone again, this time without voices or apparitions. He held the Scion in both hands as instructed and started to initiate the process which seemed too easy: 'Imagine the package open' was the only command.

He couldn't believe that it was so simple; surely there should be a more secure process of this scion-opening. Why entrust a human, especially one born into this new world so recently, without experience or confidence? How could this naive man be trusted with something so powerful and dangerous that could in one instant change the destiny of the universe?

But as he held it and tried to think it open, nothing happened. *Maybe I am too distracted by my thoughts,* thought Paul. He focused again on the thought that the package was open. But suddenly he heard screaming from the library. It was Frazer. "Stop!" Frazer shouted. "Stop!" he repeated and then he came franticly bursting into the room and ran straight at Paul, knocking him—and the package—over. The force of Frazer's football-style tackle sent Paul reeling across the room. He felt his bones crack as he hit the floor and slid into the wooden coffee table. The pain was extreme. He blacked out and lay unconscious.

To Frazer's relief, the package remained unopened. He studied Paul to ensure he was all right and still breathing before getting up to let Jack know he'd stopped Paul, albeit a little too forcibly.

Moments earlier, Jack and his team, while fearfully watching the giant Moloch's every movement, had noticed a distinct change in the temperature. Suddenly the previously frozen area they were in gave way to a sticky tropical heat. They searched for a cause but could find nothing. Silence permeated the warm, still air. Atmospheric pressure made everyone feel claustrophobic. The dromas, hidden within cloaked ships hovering nearby identified an anomaly that was generating massive amounts of energy. It was in orbit directly above the site where they were monitoring Moloch.

The dromas could not isolate the source of the anomaly, nor were they able to detect any physical object with their sensor equipment. Still, the emission from the field of energy was unprecedented. After travelling billions of lightyears, a supreme presence had arrived in Earth's orbit.

Moloch recognized the entity in orbit directly above and as his attention focused on the new arrival, his expression changed from confidence to uncertainty. Moloch seemed to be resisting something; his whole body began contorting, as if he was attempting to discard harnesses. Then he rose inexplicably up into the air, his head facing skyward. Something had him in an invisible grip and he was now held in mid-air ... but this time it was clear he was not under his own control.

Jack's team watched, concerned that this was the beginning of Moloch's reign, but matters turned in a different direction. Moloch's considerable frame continued to struggle but slowly his body began to disintegrate, transforming into dark particles that began moving in a unified field, like a tightly gathered flock of birds. Then the dark shapes gradually dispersed and, in a moment, vanished. There was no sound from Moloch as he transformed from material form back to invisible energy. There was just a ghostly shadow against the sky ... then nothing.

The last words Moloch heard were, '*You have deceived me. Your desire to rule cannot be permitted. You have come from darkness and into the void you will return. No longer will I allow your destructive influence to threaten this universe.*'

Moloch had spent millions of years trying to gain authority over the universe and now he was being unceremoniously returned to his previous, formless state, immersed within dark matter that was subject to the force of gravity. The atonement for his actions was to hold the universe in balance, without awareness.

Jack understood what was happening and he immediately dispatched Frazer to stop Paul. The supreme being was visible to Jack's team as an intense white and gold light. There was a vague human form floating in the sky, then with a whoosh of air it was gone. They all stared in awe as it disappeared.

When Jack and his team arrived back at the castle, they greeted by an injured Paul and a smiling Frazer. The package lay unopened and undamaged on the floor beside a broken table. Jack lifted the Scion and handed it to Elena, saying rather anticlimactically, "Please put this in a safe place, my dear."

Paul's tried to sit up from his slouched position on the chair but it was too much strain. He nodded agreement to Elena, then asked, "What just happened?"

Jack replied, "All will be revealed in the morning. It's late and for now we can finally rest, safe at last. Tomorrow we'll advise the world that we have avoided annihilation by the slimmest of margins. For the time being, we will send a short, encrypted message to the global leaders advising all is well. We will tell them more detail will follow tomorrow." With that, a cheer went up and the crew dispersed.

Frazer and Jack retired to his library, brandy bottle on the table and crystal glasses at the ready. Smoking a Cuban cigar was something Frazer had hoped to enjoy in this moment, but deep inside he'd suspected he would never again have the pleasure. He dipped the end into the brandy for deeper flavor, then proceeded to light the cigar and enjoy the aroma drifting around the room. *Pure ecstasy*, he thought as Jack rested quietly on a nearby chair.

"Cheers to a happy ending," said Frazer, tipping his glass against Jack's.

"Slainte mhath," replied Jack in recognition of Frazer's Gaelic heritage. They both felt the weight of the world lift from their shoulders. "I really thought we were doomed, my old friend," added Jack.

Then the door opened and the whole team, including the droma leader, came in. "Do you think you're the only ones who want to celebrate?" asked Dan.

The room was quickly filled with happy faces and friendly smiles. Naomi said, "By the way we've fetched a few of your best bottles of brandy up from the cellar ... and you're not the only ones who might like to partake in the occasional cigar!" She poured copious amounts of the dark nectar into the best crystal and a new box of Cuban cigars was opened and passed around.

They celebrated long into the wee hours of the next day, Andrew and Elena, Paul and April, Jack and Harriet and a younger Frazer still flirting with a beautiful maid who did not resist his courteous gestures. Gradually the party wound down and everyone quietly moved upstairs, looking forward to sleeping without concerns and fears.

As they drifted off to sleep, the house fell silent and the security guards ensured it stayed that way until late morning when everyone awakened to the welcome aroma of breakfast. Each seemed to move more slowly than the previous night, due in part to the aftereffects of too much brandy. Yet there was a relaxed atmosphere after the previous week's burdens.

"So, we had a close escape, my friends. We prepared well, held our fort and dealt with the situation as best we could. We, however, would not have been able to defeat Moloch without the arrival of a supreme ally," Jack said, after everyone had finished the breakfast.

"What was that force that dismissed Moloch with such ease?" asked Paul, still in pain from a few broken ribs.

"The scion has an ability to alert the universe in moments of danger—the last time we faced Moloch, we dispersed the scion to the nether regions of space without Moloch being able to detect it because we had supreme help," Jack said. "Thank God it showed up again. Paul was in the process of applying the scion's power just as Moloch was being called home. That's when I sent Frazer to stop Paul."

"Yeah and to break my ribs," added Paul, grimacing as he tried to move.

"If that entity had not arrived on time we would not be sitting here celebrating our success," Jack said, anticipating the next question.

"Who, or what, was that entity?" asked Naomi.

"We may never know the answer to that question," said Jack. "But there are forces for good in the universe, the same as there are forces for evil."

"The question now is, what will humanity do with the second chance that has been given to them?" asked Dan.

"Hear, hear," responded Jack, "I don't know. Time will tell."

Knowing that, job done, everyone would leave soon for their homes, Jack offered beds and rooms for a few more nights to ensure everyone's recovery and said he would organize a farewell dinner before they departed.

The news circulating the world was that the accumulated forces of many nations and the collaboration of religious leaders had contributed to the defeat of Moloch. No mention of any other influence, earthbound or not, was made. Jack and the group were happy to leave it that way and let mankind think what they would.

"Now that we have brought our adventure to an end, I have a proposition to you all," Dan announced. He stood up to speak. "When you all arrived, I opened an aspect of your mind that allowed you to see all of your lifetimes and enabled you to use your super-human abilities. If you would like I can have that circuit switched off, so to speak, and you can go back to your old lives. Jack, Frazer, Andrew and Elena will retain their skills as they have been using them for generations already ... but some of you were only awakened to deal with the arrival of Moloch."

He looked around the room at the serious expressions.

"I don't want an answer now, but please consider your choice. We can handle this any time after our final dinner in a few nights' time. It will only take a few moments and you can have back your blissful ignorance—or retain your memories and respective skills. Think carefully; if you choose to have the ability disabled, I will be unable to reconnect your memories and skills in this lifetime, since it would permanently damage your brains' cognitive abilities."

No one said a word, so Dan said, "I'm sure I'm speaking for Jack when I say let's have a few days of fun before we disperse." Dan sat down and sipped a glass of refreshing, mountain-clear water. He was still a little parched from the night before.

On that note, everyone was happy to spend their time as they pleased. April looked at Paul and they discretely left together. They went out into the garden and sat on a bench underneath a beautiful and ancient Bodhi tree. "Well, we have a decision to make," April said impulsively. "If we revert to who we were before we were awakened, would we still want to be together?"

Paul already knew the answer to that; from his perspective, he fell in love with her the moment they met ... but did April think the same?

April was thinking that when Paul first arrived at Ian's, when this whole thing started, she'd felt inexplicably connected to him ... but she wasn't sure what Paul thought. She hoped she could get to know him better.

"You've forgotten what my super-power is," Paul said with a smile, "I try not to intrude in other people's thoughts, but I cheated just now."

April blushed. "That's not fair ... I don't know what *you* think." She stood indignantly, turning away—but still smiling.

Paul took the game a step further and sent his thoughts over to April who immediately felt as if she was inside *his* mind. It was clear Paul felt the same way. A tear of joy fell down her cheek.

That afternoon and evening, without distraction or responsibilities, they wandered the extensive and beautiful gardens and walked along the river that ran through the property. The air was thin but not cold, the sky was a deep blue and the sun glistened off the water. No one was around and so they were free to enjoy their solitude.

April talked about her childhood in Ireland; about how she was brought up on a farm and loved country life. Her childhood had no Internet or Wi-Fi distractions, just walks and long nights that were filled with games and family conversation. Her dad was a farmer, her mom a farmer's wife and they were still in love many years of marriage.

The stars shone brightly and as she told Paul her story and Paul noticed her eyes glistened with the good memories. "I miss the simplicity," she said, "That's why I love being in Ian's house and why I have enjoyed looking after him all these years."

"I understand what you're missing, my lady. I often reminisce about my life as a youngster in the English Lakes. The natural beauty of that part of England is something I would very much like to revisit ... but my life as a business owner has distracted me in recent years." At that, Paul fell a little silent as he thought of his time in Keswick, Windermere, and Ambleside and the hills and lakes that created a Garden of Eden. "Maybe it's time for a change," Paul said suddenly. "How would you like to have a long holiday in the Lakes? I can leave my business for a few months. We still own a cottage not far from Grasmere, a beautiful village in the heart of the Lakes."

"I'd love to, but I would have to get time off from my job with Ian. He may need me."

"I'll talk with Ian," Paul offered, and April nodded in enthusiastic agreement. The rest of their evening was spent in a slow walk back to Paul's room, where they discovered each other as if they'd met for the first time.

The rest of the team also enjoyed a quiet day. Ian took the opportunity to take Naomi into Kathmandu for an early dinner. They had known each other for many years ... but this was different. This time they were alone together and could be themselves.

Naomi opened the conversation. "If you don't mind me asking a personal question, I've worried about you since you lost Joan. How have you coped?"

Ian was a little surprised but welcomed the opportunity to explain his pain of loss, the solitude of surviving and how he missed companionship. "I push myself deeper into work," he said, then asked, "Since we're jumping right in with personal questions, may I ask why you've never married?"

Although surprised at the frankness of his question, Naomi was happy the conversation was going this direction. "You may be a little shocked at my answer, are you sure you want me to be frank?"

"I don't want you to be Frank; I'd like you to be Naomi." Ian laughed at his own joke.

Then Naomi took Ian by the hand, captured his eyes and said. "You may not believe this, but I've always had a crush on you!"

She searched Ian's eyes for his reaction. He avoided her gaze as the shock of the statement sank in and it seemed a long time before his eyes met with hers.

"I've embarrassed you, Ian, I'm sorry," she said.

Ian lifted his hand and softly placed a finger on her lips. "You may not believe this, but the feeling is mutual. Since losing Joan, I've considered calling you. I don't really know what I would have said. Life took over, though, and I never built up the courage. I always worried what Paul would think, me asking his sister out for a date ..."

The energy between two people finding love for the first time ties stomachs in knots. It is one of the reasons life is worth living; even for if just for that moment. Ian and Naomi were happy to feel this way.

The next morning, Ian and Naomi, Paul and April sat together at the breakfast table. No one else had joined yet. The atmosphere was strange at first, peppered only with brief exchanges such as, "Did you sleep well?" as they ate a full English breakfast and drank amazing Brazilian coffee.

"I have an announcement to make," Paul started.

He was interrupted by Ian. "That's funny, I was about to say the same."

"You go first, Ian."

"No, you go, Paul," responded Ian.

"My God, you guys," said April. "You're impossible, both of you. Paul and I are going off to the Lakes for a few months," she blurted.

"That's funny, we're going to spend some time travelling Europe," responded Naomi.

"Who is 'we'?" asked Paul.

At that Naomi looked at Ian, stretched out her hand and Ian took hers. Everyone burst into laughter and, without further explanation, they each understood their worlds were about to change for the good.

"Ian, I'm sorry but I'll not be around, will you cope?" asked April.

Ian looked at Naomi and the answer was in that exchange. "I've decided to retire. I'm independently wealthy and it's time to see the world ... now that we have one to live in," said Ian.

"Naomi, would you mind if we pass the business over to our managers to look after so we can do something else with our lives?" Paul asked.

"I was going to ask the same, Paul. I guess we're going on adventures! It's time for a well-earned change in lifestyle."

The four of them sat around the breakfast table discussing their plans, the realization of happiness an unexpected gift at the end of a tumultuous journey.

James, Anthony and Martin had already signed up to help the dromas realize their dream of terraforming Mars, which in turn was helping them realize their own dreams of travel.

Andrew and Elena made plans to take time out and to live at a country residence owned by Elena in a small town in the province of Batangas, in her home country in the Philippines.

Jack and Harriet decided to stay at their home in Kathmandu.

Dan and Frazer willingly agreed to be the emissaries who would update global leaders about the existence of the dromas and their plans for Mars. They knew there would be challenges ahead, but when governments realized that without the dromas there would be no Earth, they were sure those challenges could be overcome.

Everyone dressed in formal wear for their celebratory dinner—the last evening gathering before each travelled to their next destination. It was an exciting evening as each broke the news of their different plans and how they looked forward to adventures in a brave new world, and for some, *on* a brave new world.

At the end of their dinner, Dan repeated his question, "What's your wish my friends? Would you like to return to your previous levels of awareness or would you like to continue with the new skills opened up for you?"

Everyone in the room was silent.

"Well?" questioned Dan.

The silence was broken with loud cheers, and screams of, "Never go back! We're travelers and there is much we can do with our abilities!"

"I guess that'd be a resounding 'NO'!" smiled Dan, happy to know the earth and humanity had a few more caretakers.

The prisoners were released back into society as soon as the influence from Moloch left their subconscious. Alex and Brian swore to use their entrepreneurial talents to help build a better future for mankind and to use their extensive network to make positive changes to the environment—after all, there was money in that. They had some major apologies to make and would start as soon as they arrived back in Germany. Gifts to the ladies they abused along the way was one place to start.

Moloch's commander, Satan, was relieved his dominion was again under his control and he was planning how to disrupt the utopia that had developed since the removal of Moloch. He had much work to do.

Jack was the only one who knew what had rescued them from Moloch's destruction ... but that's another story altogether.

THE END

37610046R00190

Made in the USA
Lexington, KY
29 April 2019